Praise for the Eli Marks Mystery Series

THE BULLET CATCH (#2)

"This is an instant classic, in a league with Raymond Chandler, Dashiell Hammett and Arthur Conan Doyle."
— John Lehman, *Rosebud Book Reviews*

"A wonderfully engaging, delightfully tricky bit of mystery. Fans of magic will delight in John Gaspard's artful use of the world of magicians, onstage and offstage. It's a great story and great fun!"
— Jim Steinmeyer,
Author of *Hiding the Elephant: How Magicians Invented the Impossible and Learned to disappear*

"Gaspard's latest Eli Marks mystery, *The Bullet Catch*, has as many tricks up its sleeve as its likeable magician-hero. As the body count rises, so does the reading pleasure."
— Dennis Palumbo,
Author of the Daniel Rinaldi Mystery Series

"A real winner of magical proportions. Filled with snappy, delightful dialogue and plenty of sleight-of-hand humor, Gaspard's latest mystery in the Eli Marks series does not disappoint. Head to the bookstore and get yourself a copy now!"
— Jessie Chandler,
Author of the Award-Winning Shay O'Hanlon Series

"The author does a fantastic job juggling the separate plots and keeping readers' minds thoroughly engaged...The relationships between Eli and his remarried ex are interesting, to say the least, and the pure entertainment of the industry will leave all readers hoping that there will be a 'number three' very soon."

D1296112

"*The Bullet Catch* has a quick pace and dialogue that engages the reader from the first page...Gaspard has written a great character into an original storyline...I will definitely be seeing/reading more of Eli as Gaspard expands this promising mystery series."

– Examiner.com

THE AMBITIOUS CARD (#1)

"*The Ambitious Card* is intelligently written and...entirely engrossing."

– Ellery Queen Mystery Magazine

"This is a hugely entertaining crime novel, packed full of comedy....Warm, funny and well-plotted–a book to brighten any grey day. Do read it!"

– FictionFan's Book Reviews

"Before I even finished the first chapter I had fallen in love with Eli. He is intelligent, sensitive, witty and, suddenly, the main suspect in a series of murders...well-written, fast-paced and exciting."

– The Frugal Mennonite

"The deftly-plotted mystery is enriched by Eli's relationships with his ex-wife, her new husband, his old-school stage magician Uncle Harry, and an interesting collection of people and places in and around St. Paul...This stylish novel is filled with interesting details, snappy dialogue, and appealing characters."

– More Than a Review

"This story is very well-written and fun to read. I would definitely read another Eli Marks Mystery!"

– A Simple Taste for Reading

THE BULLET CATCH

**The Eli Marks Mystery Series
by John Gaspard**

THE AMBITIOUS CARD (#1)
THE BULLET CATCH (#2)

THE BULLET CATCH

AN ELI MARKS MYSTERY

John Gaspard

HENERY PRESS

THE BULLET CATCH
An Eli Marks Mystery
Part of the Henery Press Mystery Collection

First Edition
Trade paperback edition | November 2014

Henery Press
www.henerypress.com

This is a work of fiction. Any references to historical events, real people, or real locales are used fictitiously. Other names, characters, places, and incidents are the product of the author's imagination, and any resemblance to actual events or locales or persons, living or dead, is entirely coincidental.

ISBN-13: 978-1-940976-43-3

Printed in the United States of America

For Amy,
who delights in never knowing how the trick is done.

ACKNOWLEDGMENTS

Special thanks to the folks who helped me get this story on paper and, more importantly, get most of it right: Amy Oriani, Scott Wells, Steve Carlson, David Parr, Jim Cunningham, Joe Gaspard, Matt Dunn, Tom Forliti and Thomas Rescinti.

"Nothing is foolproof,
because fools can be very determined."
Jamy Ian Swiss

CHAPTER 1

"It is terrifying. Utterly terrifying."

"That's a strong word."

I considered my word choice. "Yes. Yes it is."

"Is this a new fear?"

Another pause. "Well," I finally said, "it's new to me."

"That's what I meant. Can you name it?"

"What do you mean? Like Pete or Louise?"

This elicited a deeply felt and well-earned sigh. I sensed, not for the first time, that Dr. Bakke regretted taking me on as a patient. However, he was young and his office appeared to be new. The rent payments had to come from somewhere. And so he had—probably, he was now thinking, against his better judgment—said yes. So here I was: a first-time therapy patient in the office of a therapist who was still using metaphorical training wheels.

"Is the fear specific?"

"Yes."

"When does it manifest?"

"Well," I said, searching for the words to describe it, "I feel it mostly when I'm walking across a bridge or standing near the edge on the roof of a tall building. Or on a balcony overlooking a high atrium," I added.

"Ah," he said, at long last taking a note on his unsullied notepad. "Acrophobia."

I shook my head. "No, I've always had acrophobia. I mean, not in a debilitating way. I know what that's like. This is different. Much, much worse. Terrifying, actually."

He stopped in mid-stroke. "How so?"

I didn't answer immediately. "My knees get weak, my head gets light and I am consumed, from head to toe, with panic. Real, palpable panic." I hesitated for a moment, as I had never said this part out loud before. "I get this feeling," I said finally, "when I'm on this bridge or high ledge, there's really nothing stopping me and I should just go ahead and jump."

Dr. Bakke leaned back in his recently purchased, slightly squeaky leather chair. There was the slimmest trace of a smile at the corners of his mouth.

"Is that the first time you've said that out loud?" he asked.

I took a deep breath. "Yes," I said.

"I knew it," he nearly cried out, coming just short of pumping his fist in the air. He sat back in the chair, clearly satisfied with this diagnostic achievement. He made a note on the pad. It was the happiest I had seen him all hour.

"So, to recap, you've got uncontrolled panic, an intense physical reaction, suicidal ideation and a sense you're losing control and might harm yourself if you can't get away from the high location?"

"Bingo," I said. Hearing it read back to me made it sound much more clinical than it felt.

"You'll be relieved to know," he finally said as he finished his notes, "what you're experiencing is not really all that rare and it is certainly treatable."

"Great. What is it?"

"Well," he said, nodding as sagely as a twenty-something therapist can, "there's no clinical name for it, although some call it the Imp of the Perverse. It's when your mind suggests you should do something that really isn't in your best interest."

"Like a voice in your head?" I asked.

"Perhaps. Or just a sudden or overpowering feeling you should do something wrong. It manifests itself in many different ways. In your case, it's most likely an outgrowth of acrophobia. Many experts think it might simply be a reaction to stress." He flipped the page in his notebook, smoothing out the next page before looking up at me. "So, what's going on in your life, Eli? What might be causing you stress?"

"Okay, let's see," I said, as I sorted through where to begin in the rich tapestry which was my life. "I'm a magician, making my living doing corporate events, parties, restaurant work, that sort of thing."

"How's business?"

I shrugged. "Not too bad. It comes and goes." I struggled to generate more information that might be construed as relevant. "So, let's see, I'm thirty-four. I got divorced a year, no, almost two years ago. My wife was having an affair with a co-worker."

"Sadly, not so uncommon," Dr. Bakke commented quietly as he scribbled.

"So I've learned. She's an assistant DA. He's a homicide cop, so you can imagine the romantic possibilities of that unholy union."

Dr. Bakke shot me a glance over his glasses; the look suggested I should stick to the facts.

"Anyway, so we got divorced. I had nowhere to live, so I moved back in with my uncle Harry. My aunt Alice had recently died and they had mostly raised me, so I moved back into my old apartment above his magic store, over on Chicago and 48th street, Chicago Magic." I sensed this was more detail than he really wanted.

"And what's that been like?" he said without looking up.

"Not too bad, actually. Harry and I, we've always gotten along really well. He's a magician, too. Very old-school. He was on Ed Sullivan, that sort of thing. Basically taught me everything I know, but, as he likes to point out, not everything *he* knows. And I've always loved the store. You know, it's home." I paused, not sure what else he needed.

He finished his note taking and looked up. "Anything else going on recently? Anything that might have caused you undue stress?"

"Um, let's see," I sighed. "Oh, well, about six months ago I was suspected of killing a bunch of people, sort of a serial killer thing. Maybe you read about it—it was in all the papers. Three psychics were killed—I know what you're going to say, if they were true psychics why didn't they see it coming? Trust me, psychics don't find that funny. Plus, my ex-wife's new husband was assigned to the case, so that was a hoot and a half.

"Anyway, during the course of the whole thing, I got conked on the head and also fell down a steep incline and got cut up pretty badly. I wasn't the killer, but I gotta tell you, it looked bad there for a while. The upshot was I got a girlfriend out of it—Megan. We were almost killed together, which sort of speeds up the bonding process. But then she felt we were moving too fast, plus, she was in the midst of a divorce and you know how stressful that can be. So we're sort of 'taking a break' right now, although I'm not entirely certain what that means. But we've been on hold for a couple of months and I'm just in limbo, waiting for the 'break' to be over."

I added air quotes and immediately wished I hadn't. I looked over at Dr. Bakke. He had ceased taking notes, although I wasn't entirely certain at what point he had stopped. It might have been around "serial killer," or maybe when I got to "conked on the head." I'm not sure. He turned in his chair, set his notebook down and picked up what looked to be an old-style day planner.

"That's great, Eli," he said very slowly and a little too calmly as he paged through the planner. "Just great. I think I'm going to need to see you two or three times a week. At least to start."

CHAPTER 2

Until the sound of the bell alerted me to the arrival of a customer, I had spent the better part of the next morning fumbling with a deck of cards in my hands, trying not for the first time to unlock the secret of the Center Deal. The Center Deal is a fabled card move in which the magician deals a selected card not from the top or bottom of the deck, but from the center. It's a sleight that had always stymied me and I take only a small amount of solace in the knowledge that I am far from alone in my inability to master the move.

I set the cards down and looked up to see who had come in, expecting to recognize one of the two dozen or so customers who still frequented our brick and mortar shop as opposed to doing all their magic shopping online. Instead I was greeted with the image of a complete stranger who also, oddly enough, looked vaguely familiar.

He was somewhere in his thirties and he wore a baseball cap pulled down over his eyes, which were covered with dark, expensive-looking sunglasses. A mop of dirty blond hair jutted out from under the hat in a random and reckless fashion. He wore a faded Minnesota Twins jersey and even more faded jeans, but the footwear peeking out from beneath his pants cuffs appeared pointed, textured and rich—alligator perhaps, or maybe from a species higher up on the endangered list. If someone had made a pair of boots out of a Komodo dragon, I thought, this is what the result might look like.

"Is anyone else here?" he asked in a hoarse whisper.

"Depends," I said, calculating how much cash was in the register and which nearby magic prop might best be employed as an impromptu weapon.

"Eli, it's me. Jake. Jake North." He pulled off his cap and the dirty blond mop came with it. The glasses came off next, and it was then I was able to put the name with the face.

"Jake? What are you doing here? In disguise? I'd heard you were in town..."

He cut me off, looking around again to double check for others in the vicinity. It's a small shop and that didn't take long. "Have you got a few minutes? To talk?"

"Sure. Absolutely. What's going on?"

Even though we were clearly alone, he still leaned in close and spoke just above a whisper.

"I need your help," he said "Someone is trying to kill me."

"Okay, start at the beginning."

We had taken a corner table at the coffee shop down the street and settled in with our respective purchases—black coffee for me and a double-soy mocha latte grande for Jake. His precise and arcane instructions to the barista had slowed the process considerably, but with his order in hand he seemed less on edge. He was still in his disguise, which I was convinced was calling more attention to him than if he had just gone with his normal look. But you know actors and their innate ability to add drama to any situation.

"All right," he said, his voice a soft whisper, "So, I'm back in town making a flick."

I nodded. "Sure, I heard something about that. Some low-budget thing, right?"

"Low by Hollywood standards, sure, but it's a real movie and my agent thinks it could be my ticket out of TV and onto the big screen."

Being in films full-time had always been Jake's dream. He and I had met in high school, and although we hadn't traveled in the same circles, our circles did have points of intersection. We're both performers. His path had put him in all the plays at school, while my path put me in all the talent shows. His real break came when he was cast as the lead in a TV series called "Blindman's Bluff," a comedy about a lout who pretends to be blind to impress a girl and then must continue the ruse indefinitely. It hit new lows on the bad-taste index, even by cable standards, and was known for its equal servings of disabled jokes, ethnic slurs and crude sexual puns and peccadilloes. So of course it was a huge hit.

"Anyway," he continued, sucking some of the foam off the top of his coffee, "the movie is a biography of a guy with whom I'm guessing you're at least slightly familiar: Terry Alexander."

I nodded slowly, surprised to hear that name after all these years. I certainly knew the name of Terry Alexander. Any magician with a heartbeat was familiar with the life—and death—of Terry Alexander. "Sure," I said. "Infamously known as The Cloaked Conjurer."

"Yes. And also infamously known as one of the dozen or so magicians who have died while attempting to perform The Bullet Catch."

"In South America somewhere, wasn't it? Peru, I think?"

Jake shook his head. "Ecuador. Toward the end, he was basically doing his act in a traveling circus."

"Wow. His career certainly took a nose-dive."

"Apparently that's what happens when you go on national TV and start exposing magic's greatest secrets." He added a dramatic flourish to those last three words.

"Magic's Greatest Secrets" had been a series of television specials in which The Cloaked Conjurer revealed the inner workings of some of the best magic illusions of all time. Magicians, of course, were outraged at his flagrant disregard for the code of ethics that binds all magicians: the promise to never tell lay people how the trick works.

Terry had broken that sacred pledge and had pretty much been blackballed out of the business from that point on. In desperation he had returned to his traditional magic act and took gigs wherever he could, finally ending up doing a second-rate act in third world countries.

"He got work, though, because he was one of the only performers willing to do The Bullet Catch," Jake continued, "and that got him work in those far-flung performance venues."

"Until someone killed him."

"Yes. Until someone killed him. While he was doing The Bullet Catch."

Jake had a distant look in his eyes. I tried to pull him back. "And you play Terry?"

"Yes," he said, snapping back into the conversation. "It's a challenging role. The script is lousy, so we're diverging from it at every point possible. But I think, in the end, I will have created a fully-rounded character with layers and depth." He took a big gulp of what I was sure was still pretty hot coffee, but he showed no reaction to it. "But what's got me more concerned—much more concerned—is that I'll have to do The Bullet Catch."

"But it's a movie," I said. "I mean, you don't have to do it for real. Right? They have stunt guys and CGI and editing tricks."

"I know, I know," he said with no real conviction. "But I just have this gut feeling..." His voice trailed off. I wasn't sure what to say to help him out.

"Certainly they've got experts working with you on this?" I finally offered.

"Oh, yeah," he said quietly. "I trained with some of the top magicians in LA for six months. I can do Terry Alexander's whole act, start to finish."

"So why are you so concerned about this one part of the act?"

"Right now, this flick is just a blip on Hollywood's radar. A little Indie about a famous, unsolved crime. But," he said with a mix of anticipation and dread, "if I actually *died* while doing The Bullet Catch?"

"Yeah?" I didn't like where this was heading.

"Then it will be a hit. A monster hit."

"You've developed some real chops," I said, genuinely impressed.

Our coffee was cold and I had steered the discussion away from Jake's fear of dying and asked him how he was doing the rest of the magic in the movie.

"The producers found some guys at The Magic Castle in LA," he said, casually dropping the names of three well-regarded magicians.

Training from any one of them would have produced outstanding results and I was curious to see what he had learned from this trio of masters. I handed him the deck of cards I always carry and asked for a demonstration.

Jake took the deck tentatively at first, then executed some nearly flawless moves—a slick top change, a false shuffle I hadn't seen before, and some flashy card flourishes that skirted the sometimes thin line between magic and juggling. His work was impressive and he was clearly well-trained, but it was all done by rote. He lacked the craft to be able to deviate and improvise. However, he handled the cards well and comfortably, and for those moments I believed he might actually bring Terry Alexander to life on screen. If he didn't die trying.

"So what makes you think your life is in danger?"

"Well, it was small things at first," he said quietly. "Like when I found out they weren't working with my LA trainers on The Bullet Catch. Those guys know their stuff, but the director said he had another resource in Las Vegas. Turns out the guy the director got is just a buddy of his from college. He runs a shooting range, but has no real training in this. But the thing that really unnerved me was when I saw the shooting schedule. They had scheduled the filming of The Bullet Catch scene last. Dead last."

"Is it the last scene in the movie?"

"Yes and no—it's all told as a flashback from the moment the bullet is fired from the gun. That might change in the editing, who knows. But these things are hardly ever shot in order. And that's the very last scene I'm going to shoot. Last day, last scene, last shot."

"A coincidence?"

"Maybe. But then I was at the director's house in California, doing a read-through of the script with some of the cast, and I noticed a DVD box on the TV. He had been watching 'The Crow.'"

I shrugged. "I'm missing the connection."

"The actor Brandon Lee died while making 'The Crow.' He was shot when a prop gun misfired. It was tragic, but it didn't hurt the film one bit. Some people say it helped to make it a hit."

"And you think the same thing could happen here?"

"Hey, if your job was to sell a movie about Terry Alexander, you'd probably have a pretty tough time of it. Sure, it's an unsolved mystery: Who killed Terry Alexander? But the downside is there's no stars, no pre-sale name value to the property, it's low-budget and under the radar. But if the lead actor gets shot and killed while in the process of recreating the scene where the main character got shot and killed..."

His voice trailed off and then he added, "That's a film people are going to want to see. Hell, if I weren't dead, I'd want to see it."

We crossed the street and stood on the corner across from the coffee shop, quietly assessing each other.

"So, what can I do to help?" I finally asked.

Jake nodded, considering his words. "I'd love to bring you on as my personal magic coach on the set. There's money in the budget and Lord knows I could use the help. Particularly when we shoot The Bullet Catch."

"I can do that. Might be fun."

Jake smiled grimly. "Yeah, film sets are a non-stop riot." He took off his sunglasses and rubbed his eyes. "We finished the bulk of interiors in Vancouver, where they recreated Terry's early years and the TV specials. We're in Minneapolis mostly to do the Ecuador scenes—the traveling circus."

"Minneapolis is their choice to recreate rural Ecuador?"

Jake chuckled. "Hollywood magic. They're re-dressing the Renaissance Festival grounds outside of town to look like an Ecuadoran village. It was cheaper than going to South America, and Minnesota finally put in some tax breaks for filmmakers. It's economics. In Hollywood, it's always economics."

We were standing in front of "Chi & Things," the store on the corner of the block that includes "Chicago Magic." We stepped aside to let some customers pass and I stole a peek into the shop through the opened door, hoping to catch a glimpse of Megan. I thought I saw a hint of her curly brown hair in the back of the store, but whoever it was disappeared out of sight behind some shelves.

I hadn't been in the store—her store—since the breakup, and the few sightings I'd had of her had been way too distant and far too brief. But we both worked on the same block and the odds were at some point or another our paths would have to cross.

I wasn't sure how I would react when we finally did bump into each other, but that didn't make me want it any less. Somewhere in my brain, I was convinced that just the sight of me would be enough for her to throw back her head, give a coquettish laugh and say, "Eli, Eli, what was I thinking?" before throwing herself into my arms.

"What?" I asked, realizing that Jake had said something.

"I said, you don't have to decide right now about being my magic coach. We can talk about it at the reunion."

I turned back, not sure what he meant. "The reunion?" I repeated.

"Yeah, our fifteenth high school reunion this weekend. You're going, right? I mean, come on." He gave my arm a playful punch. "Two successful single guys like us. We'll rock the place."

"I don't know," I said slowly, shaking my head. "I went to the tenth reunion and it was really sort of a drag. And anyway, I didn't see *you* there," I added accusingly.

"Nah, I skipped the tenth. I hadn't attained my reunion goal at that point."

"Your reunion goal?"

He smiled a wicked grin. "I swore I wasn't coming back to a reunion until I knew for sure no one would have to ask what I was up to. Because I would be so famous, they would already know. And I think I hit my goal this year with 'Bluff.'"

I had to agree he was probably right. Two more customers stepped past us to get into Chi & Things. I held the door for them, using it as an excuse to once again scan the store for Megan. And that's when I realized she wasn't in the store. She was one of the two women going *into* the store and I was holding the door for her.

Megan was clearly as lost in thought as I was. She turned to thank me for holding the door, then stopped cold, realizing who I was. Her companion turned and I recognized her elderly friend, Franny, who recognized me right back.

"Eli. Good to see you," Franny said, breaking into a wide grin. "Holding the door like a polite doorman. That uncle of yours raised you well I see." She turned to Megan and then, seeing the stricken look on her face, turned back. "Oh, I forgot. You two are on a break. Well this is awkward. Very awkward."

Franny chuckled as she looked from Megan to me and then back to Megan, clearly enjoying the small drama she had stepped into. She glanced over at Jake.

"And who is this tall drink of water with the dish mop on his head?"

I had actually forgotten for a moment he was standing there. "Oh, this is Jake." I gestured to the two women. "Jake, this is Franny. And Megan."

Megan nodded at Jake and then turned to me, looking me in the eye for the first time. "Hi, Eli," Megan finally said, her voice just barely above a whisper.

"Hi. Hello." My voice didn't do much better.

"I'm surprised we didn't see this coming," Franny said with a laugh. No one else joined in.

"Franny and Megan are psychics," I said to Jake by way of explanation.

"I understand," he said without a note of skepticism. "I live in LA."

A pause. I sifted quickly through my thoughts, trying to find the most appropriate comment and coming up short.

"So, how's that Uncle Harry of yours?" Franny interjected, seemingly ignoring the tension that had formed within the small group.

Megan looked at me again. I returned her gaze, trying not to look too intense. Nonchalance was a hard nut to crack with so little warning. I turned to Franny.

"He's good. Still cranky. But good."

"Nice to hear. Tell him Franny said 'Hey!'"

"I will. I will."

Our conversation gap started to get wider and wider, moving quickly from a small fissure to Grand Canyon-style gaping hole. None of us knew how to close it. Megan finally took action.

"Well," she said to Jake, "Nice to meet you." She shook his hand and then turned to me. "Good to see you, Eli."

Megan moved in for a handshake, which I misread as an impending hug. The resultant body mash was a messy mix of both. She then disappeared into the store. I held onto the door handle, not quite ready to let it go. Franny lingered behind, clearly waiting until Megan was out of earshot.

"I'm glad I ran into you, Eli," she said with sudden seriousness. "I had a ping about you this morning. Out of the blue. I don't often get those, but when I do, I've learned to listen to them."

Franny makes her living as a phone psychic. Literally. That is, she usually only gathers insights while on the phone. No standard in-person, one-on-one live readings for her; it's on the phone or nothing. And she really runs it like a business, putting in banker's hours and turning off the phone on evenings and weekends. As she likes to say, "I leave work at work."

I nodded, waiting for her to continue.

"I saw a gun. And a bullet," she said quietly. "A man gets shot. Somehow you are involved. And, this was the weird part: the man who got shot was the man who got shot, but he wasn't. It didn't make any sense to me. I hope it makes sense to you."

She patted my arm warmly, and then disappeared into the store. I released my grip on the door handle and the door swung slowly shut.

I turned back to Jake. I have to admit I wasn't particularly surprised to see that his face had gone completely pale.

CHAPTER 3

"Terry Alexander was a cad. A bounder. A louse."

"On his best days he was a louse."

"He was so low, he'd get the bends every time he stood up, the rat bastard."

I wasn't entirely clear on what that last crack meant, but I was certain I had come to the right place. That place was Adrian's, a bar which has stood next to Chicago Magic as long as Chicago Magic has stood. When I returned to the magic shop after coffee with Jake and found that Uncle Harry wasn't in the store or in his apartment upstairs, I knew it was a pretty good bet he was next door. He spends a good portion of each week swapping stories and insults with a group of aging magicians that officially called themselves "The Minneapolis Mystics," although my late Aunt Alice had always referred to them as "The Artful Codgers." Their numbers were thinning more than their hair, but they had a fair turnout for today's bull session.

I pulled up a chair and didn't interrupt the flow of conversational insults, waiting for an opening to bring up the topic at hand. Sitting across from me was Abe Ackerman, a hypnotist of the Kreskin variety, just never as famous. It might have something to do with his looks. If Boris Karloff and Abe Vigoda had a love child, he would have grown up to look like Abe Ackerman.

On his right was Sam Esbjornson, a magician who specialized in coin work. Although one of the oldest in the group, he was still phenomenal, even at this late stage in his life. He had absently picked up two coins off the table and was rolling them up and down the back of his left hand. It was such an ingrained habit, I'm not sure he was even aware he was doing it.

And on Abe's left was my Uncle Harry, quietly stroking his grey beard. Up until this point, Harry had been silent on the topic of Terry Alexander. This had not gone unnoticed by Abe.

"So, Harry's being a bit mum on the topic of this louse, it seems to me," Abe said.

"I was raised to not speak ill of the dead," Harry said quietly. "Regardless of what we may have said about them when they were alive."

"Who's not alive? Did I miss something?" The gravelly voice came from behind me and I turned to see Max Monarch, the best card man in the group. He was struggling to take off his windbreaker as he toddled toward us. I got up and pulled another chair up to the table.

"Sorry I'm late," Max continued, carefully hanging his windbreaker on the back of the chair. "I swear I hit every red light between here and downtown. Every red light. Back in the day, the city had the stoplights timed, you drive twenty-eight miles an hour you can soar down Portland like nobody's business. But ever since that fercockta light rail train came in, I swear, every traffic light is marching to the beat of its own drummer. In my entire life, I swear I've spent thirty years sitting at red lights. And that's not an exaggeration."

Max settled himself in the chair, looking around for a reaction, but the group had listened to Max complain about red lights for so long it no longer even warranted a comment. He waved to the waitress with a hand signal for his regular, a ginger ale with no ice, and then turned to the group.

"So, who died?" he asked, trying and failing to temper his enthusiasm with an attitude that appeared more somber.

"Terry Alexander," I said.

"Yesterday's news," Max snorted. "The rat bastard louse."

"I remember when he exposed my classic envelope switch,"

Abe grumbled. "Couldn't do it for two years. Ruined it. Absolutely ruined the bit." He shook his head in disgust at the memory.

"Not me," Max countered. "When he exposed the Dancing Queens, I put them back in my act the next night. The next night," he added for emphasis.

"The Dancing Queens never left your act," Sam said. "Nothing ever left your act. You're thinking of Lance Burton—he's the one who put an illusion back in his act the night after Terry Alexander exposed it."

"Me, Lance Burton, the point is still the same," Max said as the waitress brought him his ginger ale. He smiled up at her and she returned the smile and then headed back to the bar. "Ah, to be young again," Max sighed.

"Ah, to be sixty again," Abe added.

"Sixty, hell, I'd take sixty-five," Sam said.

"My point," Max continued, "is that exposure is all in your point of view. When people would say to me, 'Hey, I know how that's done—I saw the Cloaked Conjurer do that trick,' I'd always have the same comeback. I'd say, 'Yeah, he does it the easy way. Anyone can do that. I do it the hard way.'"

"Knowing you, you did it the wrong way," Sam grumbled.

"Stick it in your ear," Max shot back.

"Ah, stick it in your act," Sam retorted. "It'll hurt more people that way."

"Guys," I said, interjecting myself into what looked to become another escalating exchange. "I need you to look at something."

They say you can find anything on the Internet and I'm beginning to believe it's true. A relatively short search had produced a grainy, poorly-shot video of Terry Alexander performing his most famous—and last—illusion: The Bullet Catch. His was the final act in what appeared to be a mangy, flea-encrusted traveling circus that was tottering on its last legs somewhere in the poorly-lit outskirts of Ecuador.

I held the iPad for the four older magicians as they strained to see the highly-pixilated images on the screen. The performance itself appeared perfunctory. Terry Alexander, dressed in his usual black t-shirt and black jeans, selected two volunteers from the audience. The sound recorded by the small camera or camera phone was muffled and completely indecipherable, but since the conversation was likely all in Spanish, it wasn't a big issue.

Terry, looking drawn and pale, handed a bullet to one volunteer and a handgun to the other. Each examined their respective item and then Terry gestured for them to switch and examine each other's article. When this was completed to their satisfaction, Terry handed a marking pen to the first volunteer, who slowly and carefully drew what appeared to be his initials on the bullet. All the while, Terry kept up a continuous and almost droning narration, in what sounded like muffled Spanish, apparently explaining each step in the process to the small crowd.

The first volunteer handed the signed bullet to the second volunteer, who loaded it into the gun. Terry directed him to a spot toward one side of the dirt patch that was acting as the stage, and then he gestured to a glass window that had been jury-rigged in the center of the impromptu stage. Terry moved past the window, tapping on the glass as he passed it to establish its authenticity, before taking his place on the other side of the stage. During all this set-up, he continued his oration, in a flat monotone, doubtless explaining to the gathered crowd the intended effect.

The gun would be aimed at him and fired.

The bullet would pass through the window, shattering the glass.

In that same instant Terry would catch the bullet.

In his mouth.

The camera work was shaky and unfocused, but we could see Terry as he centered himself on his mark and began a countdown, in Spanish, from ten. Soon the audience picked up the countdown as a chant and took over, getting louder and louder as they got closer to the end point.

"...cuatro, tres, dos...uno!"

As they hit uno, the crowd cheered and we could hear the distant "pop" of the gun, followed by the dim tinkle of breaking glass. The camera whip-panned across the stage just in time to see Terry Alexander fly back from an impact and then lay motionless on the ground.

The crowd was silent for a split second, and then the silence was shattered by a series of screams and people began to move. Some moved toward Terry's prone shape on the ground, while others pushed and shoved their way to the exit. I heard cries of "Está muerto! Está muerto!" which were followed by more jiggling camera work, chaotic commotion and screaming. And then the video ended as the screen went black and silent.

Abe was the first to speak. "The Bullet Catch," he said, shaking his head, "was always bad news."

"Only a crazy person puts that cursed trick in his act," agreed Max.

"Crazy. Stupid. Take your pick," said Sam. He had been so engrossed in the video he had actually stopped rolling the two coins across the back of his hand. "It's the only truly deadly magic trick."

"I don't know," Abe said, leaning back in his chair and gesturing toward Max, "Have you ever seen his Twisted Aces?"

"I'll twist your aces," Max grumbled.

"Of course, the answer to the key question with Terry Alexander and the Bullet Catch," Sam continued, completely ignoring the exchange, "is the one we'll never know: Was it an accident? Or murder?"

Abe clucked his tongue. "The man had made no shortage of enemies in his day. Many a magician would have loved to see him dead."

"That's what they call a true fact," Sam said. "For a while he was the world's most hated magician."

"Took the heat off you for a bit, didn't it?" Abe said, producing chuckles around the table.

"But did anyone hate him enough to kill him?" I asked. The question received shrugs from around the table. All except Harry, who was leaning back in his chair and quietly stroking his beard. "Or could it just have been an accident? You know, a trick gone wrong?" I added.

"I saw at least three spots where the bullet could have been switched out," Abe offered.

"And I saw two more where it could have been switched back in," Sam countered.

"There are plenty of opportunities within that trick for things to go wrong," Harry said quietly. "At least a dozen magicians have discovered that over the years, to their peril. But what I saw there," he said, gesturing at the iPad dismissively, "was simple ineptitude. A magician who screwed up, plain and simple. Let's look at it again."

I ran the video again and the four men watched it, even more intently than the first time. When Terry handed the spectator the bullet, there was a murmur from the group. When he had the two spectators swap their items for inspection, heads began to nod around the table. When one of the spectators loaded the bullet into the gun's chamber, one of the guys made a low whistling sound while another muttered, "Right there. It went wrong right there."

They immediately started exchanging comments, their attention turned away from the screen, not even bothering to watch as Terry was shot and fell.

"Simple mistake," Max said, sipping his ginger ale. "Human error, plain and simple."

"Ironic justice, if you ask me," Abe added. "A man who exposed so many secrets, felled by his own ineptitude. And, even I have to admit, in his day he was a solid magician. But not with that trick."

"Even more ironic," Max added, "is the fact that to reveal the secret behind this mystery you would have to do exactly what we all hated Terry Alexander for doing: You'd have to tell people how the trick was done. Which magicians will never do. Sort of fitting, when you think about it."

"Well, if you ask me, in death he at least did some good." Sam said definitively. The others turned for clarification, but Sam let them wait while he took a sip of his coffee laced with Baileys. "Any magician who even thinks of doing that trick today will at least think twice now, because of the sad fate of Terry Alexander."

I turned to Harry to see if he had anything to add, but he simply nodded in agreement with the others.

CHAPTER 4

"Let's talk about your curfew."

"Very funny," I said.

Uncle Harry continued. "I think you're old enough now we can move it up to eleven o'clock. But not one minute after."

"Do you see how I'm holding my sides here, laughing?" I had stopped by Harry's apartment, which is directly above the magic store and directly below my apartment, to say goodnight as I headed out to the reunion.

"Now who are you going with, Buster? Is it someone I know?" He was parroting the questions Aunt Alice had asked me all through high school and using the nickname he'd given me as a kid, and I wasn't enjoying it anymore now than I had then. But I played along.

"I already told you. Jake North. My old classmate. He's the one in town doing the film about Terry Alexander."

"Is he?" Harry said absently. "Do I know his parents? I think I should call his mother, just so I'm sure we're all on the same page."

"You know, you really should have billed yourself as a comedian. I think you missed your calling."

"Calling, yes, good point," he said, jumping up to grab a pad and pen by the phone. "I want you to call me when you get there and then call me when you're leaving. Do you have a number where I can reach you?"

"Yes, it's called my cell phone. You already use it to call me ten times a day and I have the phone company records to prove it. So, fear not. There is no point in the evening when you won't be able to call me. Of course, whether or not I'll answer is up for debate," I added as I started to close his apartment door.

"Well, have fun. Don't talk to strangers. And remember—just say 'No!' to drugs." The last word was cut off as I swung the door shut and headed down the stairs.

As Jake and I pulled up to the hotel in downtown Minneapolis where the reunion was being held, I had a sudden and intense memory. This hotel had been the site of a particularly memorable past performance. The show, which was in one of the main ballrooms, was for a charity function, although I couldn't remember the specific worthy cause. All I could remember about the evening was that the Chairwoman of the event had insisted on singing before my act.

To the accompaniment of karaoke track, she had stumbled her way through *I Will Survive*, but her voice made a mockery of the title and she abandoned the song in the middle of the second verse, explaining to the crowd that she had "aspirated a filbert" earlier in the evening. Ever since then, that explanation had become my go-to excuse anytime a show went less well than I might have liked.

"How was the show?"

"Oh, it could have gone better, but I aspirated a filbert earlier in the evening."

So while I correctly remembered doing a show at the hotel, I was completely surprised by the hotel's interior atrium. It rose nearly forty stories, creating a seemingly endless expanse above the main floor lobby. From my dizzying vantage point in the lobby, I could see people scurrying along the open corridors as they moved in and out of their rooms or headed toward the elevator bank.

Ah, yes, the elevator bank. I had also forgotten about the elevators, or more likely never experienced them because the main ballroom was at ground level. The elevator cars were completely transparent, and I'm not just talking about the walls. The floor and ceiling of each car was also made of some sturdy, glass-like substance, allowing a perfect view of everyone in every elevator as they made their vertiginous journey up and down.

Looking up into the endless atrium, and also seeing the elevators, had put a sizeable lump in my throat and made my pulse rate increase to the point where I could actually hear my heart pounding in my ears. The plan I had constructed with Dr. Bakke had been that I would go up a few floors—like to the second or third floor—in the next tall building I go into and look down over the edge at the lobby below. While doing that, I would practice the breathing tricks he had taught me. I took one more look at the sickening view above me and decided this could wait until later in the evening. "Hey, dude," Jake called to me. "Where are you headed?"

I gestured toward the ballroom entrance. "Main ballroom."

"We're not in the main ballroom," he said. "According to this, we're in something called The Sky Room." He pointed at a video monitor scrolling a continuous stream of hotel events. It took a while for it to cycle through that day's agenda, but finally the logo for our high school popped up on-screen, along with the location of our reunion: "The Sky Room." Under that it said, "Fortieth floor."

"Up, up and away," Jake said as he headed toward the elevators. I didn't move. I felt frozen to the spot, but after taking some healing breaths, I was able to persuade my feet to budge and I followed him reluctantly to the bank of elevators.

The doors to one elevator slid open just as we arrived and Jake stepped in, whistling softly as he turned to press the destination button on the control panel. I willed myself to follow him in and once inside I immediately turned away, pretending to look out at the lobby. In fact, my eyes were tightly shut and I held onto the handrail with something resembling a death grip. I heard the doors close and felt the elevator begin to rise, moving up much faster than my stomach would have preferred. I could sense lights moving across my shuttered eyes as we headed up, while the sweat from my clenched hands convinced me I might have gripped the railing hard enough to draw blood.

"Whoa, mama, are we flying!" Jake laughed heartily, the voice of a man who clearly lived on the other end of the acrophobia spectrum from me.

"Yes, yes we are," I said, working hard to keep any tremor from my voice. "It's quite the view, isn't it?"

We came to a stop and as I heard the door open, I turned toward the sound, opening my eyes for the first time. Ahead of me, I saw the welcome embrace of a real floor surrounded by real walls. I started to step forward and it all would have been fine if I'd had the good sense not to look down. But I didn't.

I forgot the floor was transparent as well. My gaze fell to my feet and then to the forty floors of elevator shaft beneath me and the lobby far below.

I froze, my stomach racing up to my mouth, my vision clouding and my head beginning to spin. I couldn't move. Literally, couldn't move.

The door began to slide shut, but Jake—already out of the elevator car—stuck his hand through the rapidly closing space, grabbed my arm and pulled me to safety.

"Ground control to Major Tom," he laughed. "We have arrived. Our destiny lies before us."

Perhaps his destiny lay before him, but it was all I could do to stumble forward and place a hand on the comforting solidity of the wall in front of me. I regained my balance, making sure I didn't turn toward the railing. Jake gestured to a directional sign with our school logo on it and moved jauntily down the corridor, following the route indicated.

"We're down here," he called over his shoulder, as he moved confidently along the hallway. My movements were considerably slower and lacked any of his confidence. With one hand lightly touching the wall to steady myself, I followed him at half his pace, making sure I didn't look to my left. The railing that overlooked the atrium was about four feet away and I felt its pull like a magnet. A voice, a feeling, a sense deep in my head was whispering: *Go to the rail. Look down. Jump.*

I again tried to engage in one of the breathing exercises Dr. Bakke had taught me, but even as I went through the motions, I sensed I wasn't actually breathing, just pulling air in and out and never really letting any of it settle into my lungs. At this rate, I would hyperventilate myself into unconsciousness in a matter of minutes, which at that moment struck me as a pretty solid plan B.

Ahead of me I could see Jake stop at the open double doors that looked to be my salvation. If I could make it to that portal, I'd be able to put much-needed distance between myself and the frightening, yet tempting, rail. Once through that blessed door, it would be out of sight and therefore out of mind. I shuffled along the corridor, touching the wall as I went, more for psychological than physical support.

Jake cocked his head at my progress, and so I put on a burst of speed and was able to finally get to—and through—the door. Jake slapped me on the back and propelled me further into the room, and then took a stance next to me.

A table to my right contained row after row of nametags in plastic holders. The table was being supervised by an excessively perky woman I vaguely recognized.

"Hi, guys," she said brightly as she pulled back her wildly floral scarf to reveal her nametag. "I'm Joann. I was Joann Murray, then was Joann Murray-Hill for a hellacious four years, and now I'm back to good-old Joann Murray. Single and loving it. You're with the reunion, right?"

We agreed we were and she looked at us and then at the badges and then did a double-take, looking back at Jake. "You're not going to need this," she said with a flirtatious smile as she pulled his badge from the table. "Everybody knows you. But you can keep it as a souvenir." She then turned to me. "And you are?"

I paused, momentarily forgetting my name. "Eli," I finally stuttered. "Eli Marks."

"Eli Marks, oh yes, you're here somewhere." She scanned the rows of badges until she came to mine. "There you go," she said handing it to me. "And then we just need to do this." She deftly took my right hand, while at the same time picking up a rubber stamp off the table. She daubed it on an inkpad and, with a practiced move, applied it to the back of my hand, leaving me with an oddly shaped black smudge.

"That's so we can tell you from the freeloaders in the hotel who try to sneak in and graze from our buffet," she said, gesturing for Jake to submit to the same procedure. He put his hand in hers and she took her own sweet time applying the mark, even finding a moment at the conclusion of the process to stare into his eyes.

"You're all set," she finally said breathlessly.

"Thanks Joann," Jake said with his million-dollar smile and she blushed and turned away.

Left to my own devices, I began the slow process of pinning my nametag to my coat, while Jake softly whistled as he assessed the room. I started to step forward, but he gently stopped me with a hand to my chest.

"Wait," he said quietly. "They will come to us."

He was right and they did. Although, it quickly became apparent they were actually coming to the singular *him* and not to the plural *us*. While I was the grateful recipient of a handful of halfhearted nods, the majority of the people made a beeline toward Jake. As the crowd became larger, I felt myself disappearing, like the guy in the movie *The Incredible Shrinking Man* who eventually got so small he vanished entirely. To forestall that eventually, I wandered away from the crowd.

A food buffet took up the center of the room, while cash bars were positioned in two of the room's four corners. One of the bars was right next to an open set of double doors which led to the exterior observation deck, visible through a large picture window to the left of the door. Given the steady flow of people headed that way, the deck and its amazing view turned out to be a big draw for everyone. Except me.

Having no desire to observe anything on or from the

Observation Deck, I made my way to the other bar, where a skilled but bored college girl was happy to sell me a beer and even happier all the change she gave me went right into her tip jar. Having spent years working for tips in restaurants, I over-tip from habit and it took me a second to realize the voice saying, "Hey, thanks," was hers.

"No problem," I said, taking a quick swig of beer. My mouth had been desert-dry since the elevator ride from hell. "How's the crowd tonight?"

"About typical for a fifteen-year reunion, I guess. The guys are all losing their hair and denying it and the women have finally figured out how to apply makeup, but still can't handle walking in heels," she said with a deadpan I liked immediately.

"You do a lot of these?" I asked.

"More than I'd like."

"What keeps bringing you back?"

She nodded toward the tip jar. "And, of course," she added with a smile, "the sparkling conversation."

"You get a lot of sparkling conversation?"

"Do kangaroos get hiccups?" She grabbed a small rag and began cleaning the top of her portable bar. "You want to know the secret to reunions?"

"Lay it on me," I said.

"The secret to a reunion is this: Forget it's a reunion. Everyone approaches it like they're still in high school, and when you do it that way, all the old patterns and responses come flooding back.

"But," she continued, leaning toward me across the bar, "the truth is, if you met any one of these people for the first time today, you wouldn't give them a second thought. They'd have no power over you whatsoever. So why are you giving them power just because their locker was across from yours twenty years ago?"

"Fifteen years," I corrected, "but I see your point."

"The fact is, the counter has reset to zero," she said in a dramatic whisper. "The past has no power. Today's a new day and history can go screw itself."

"Well put."

"Now get out there and knock 'em dead, tiger."

"Eli Marks, man of the hour."

I looked up from my lonely spot at one of the many empty tables to see Roger Edison, looking younger than his years and smiling ear to ear.

"Roger," I said, dropping a limpy carrot and wiping my hand on the tablecloth before extending it to him. He returned my gesture with a fist bump, the conclusion of which included the sound effect of an explosion, courtesy of his lips.

"What are you doing sitting over here all by yourself and not sucking up to our resident TV star?" He gestured toward the crowd that still surrounded Jake.

"I rode in with him," I said, "so I've already had my fill of wonderfulness. How's it going?"

Roger sat down and leaned back in his chair, looking out across the room. "Typically pathetic. These people have no small talk in them," he said. "Most of them are good for two minutes, tops, and then they start checking their phones for emails. What has happened to us as a nation in our ability to chat?"

"Well, you still have the skill," I offered.

"That I do, but I chat for a living," he said.

"Still selling insurance?"

"It sells itself, I'm just the midwife." He stole a chip off my plate, flew it over the dollop of dip and then thought better of it. "Speaking of which, did you bring a wife tonight? A girlfriend? Or," he added with a smile, "a boyfriend?"

"None of the above. I'm currently in the box marked Single."

"Perfect timing."

"It is?"

"Absolutely. From a strictly actuarial point of view, this is the ideal reunion at which to meet a potential mate."

"How do you figure?"

"Look at the stats: Fifteen years from high school graduation, most of these folks have finished an under-graduate degree, some have a graduate degree, they've moved four-point-five times, and they're on their third full-time job since college. Those who have married are getting tired of it and are ready for a change. And those who are single are getting bored with that lifestyle and are ready to settle down. It's the perfect storm, relationship-wise. And you're at the eye of the storm. Embrace it."

"I don't know," I said. "I was just in a relationship. We're on hold. Or something. I don't know."

"Ambiguity is central to the human condition. The sooner you realize that, the happier you'll be." He stood up, grabbing one more of my chips as he did. "All right, I'm going to keep working the room," he said, putting out his hand for a quick shake. After he'd gone, I opened my hand to find that he had been kind enough to leave me his business card.

Jake was holding court at a table, with a ring of people seated and two or three concentric rings of people standing and watching the action. There was a burst of laughter from the group as I approached.

"And that's what happens when you cut in front of George Clooney in the Express Lane at Ralph's," Jake said, obviously providing a kicker to a longer story and inciting another round of laughter from the group. Just as the laughter subsided, Jake reached into his pocket and pulled out a deck of cards. "So, who wants to see a card trick?" he asked.

My experience has been the fastest way to clear the room at a party is to ask "So, who wants to see a card trick?" Next to "Anyone else here have the flu?" it's a surefire method for inducing a mass exit.

However, Jake's current celebrity status was enough to keep the audience in place, so he began to go through some standard tricks he had learned for his portrayal of Terry Alexander.

His performance surprised me. For someone who has been acting since high school and who currently makes what I can only guess is an envy-inducing salary on a hit TV show, Jake's skills as a performing magician were surprisingly bad. As he had demonstrated in our coffee shop meeting, he had gained the chops to physically make the cards do what he wanted without drawing undo attention to his moves. But his performance in front of an otherwise enthusiastic audience drove home for me one of the axioms Uncle Harry has been spouting for as long as I can remember: It's not about the trick or the effect; it's about the connection the performer makes with his audience. And Jake was not connecting with this audience; in fact, he was headed full speed in the opposite direction.

His first trick was a simple ace production, where he made four aces appear at the top of an apparently completely shuffled deck. The woman who he chose to help him I first recognized as Roseann Roosevelt's mother, until I realized it was in fact Roseann Roosevelt herself. I had fond memories of Roseann. We had suffered through a particularly grueling algebra class together, but that was nothing compared to what Jake was putting her through now.

The charm and poise that was so natural to Jake in real life completely left him in this setting. Admittedly, he wasn't helped by the constant snap-snap of the reunion's photographer, who saw before him a once-in-a-lifetime opportunity: celebrity alum does a card trick. I'm not sure there was a market for such a series of photos, but that didn't seem to be slowing the photographer one iota.

As Jake, ever the trooper, plowed on, I could feel the energy draining from the group even as the trick reached a conclusion that should have been startling but in his hands was just merely perplexing.

Undeterred, he forged ahead, unwisely choosing to attempt Triumph, a stunning card trick in the hands of a master like Dai Vernon, but a train wreck in lesser hands. And tonight Jake was definitely steering his train into the side of a cliff, stumbling through the set-up and completely missing the nuance and drama of the trick.

"Someone's clearly missing that magic spark tonight," a voice whispered in my ear. I nodded in agreement and then turned to see who had taken me into their confidence. And I nearly fell over when I saw who it was.

While I certainly suffered through my fair share of high school crushes, the one that was the most fruitless (and thus resulted in the longest-lasting heartache) was Trish Henry. She was pretty, funny, smart, popular and—at least to the high school version of me—completely unattainable. If we had exchanged two sentences in four years I would be surprised.

Consequently, I was amazed she was standing next to me and even more surprised she had deigned to not only talk to me, but to actually whisper in my ear. I felt myself falling back into those high school feelings and could almost feel myself morphing into a sixteen-year old version of me on the spot. And then I remembered the bartender and her words of advice: Treat these people like you're just meeting them for the first time. Wise words, I thought. Wise words.

So I turned to Trish, planning to give her a casual smile and nod. And I was hit with a stark realization: if I were meeting her for the first time today, I would still be stunned into stupidity. She certainly had aged, like the rest of us, but somehow she had gotten prettier while getting older. Nice trick, if you can do it.

"Everyone has an off night," I finally whispered in return.

She smiled warmly and I turned back to watch poor Jake, who had gotten lost in the middle of the routine and lacked the skills to bluff his way out of it. In desperation, he flipped over the top card. "Is this your card?" he asked with forced good cheer, even though the real stunner in the trick was that all the reversed cards in the deck should have returned to their original positions. His confused participant nodded grimly and Jake thanked her and looked around feverishly, trying to come up with a closer before his audience wandered off to find some actual entertainment. And then he spotted me.

"Okay, now you're in for a treat," he said, suddenly taking on the deportment of a club emcee. "Here's the man who taught me everything I know—and then some! Put your hands together for the magical stylings of the one, the only, Magical Eli Marks." He waved his arm in my direction and everyone turned more out of curiosity than actual interest. I could see Jake's face noticeably relax as the audience shifted their attention from him to me. I wasn't sure what was expected of me, but then I heard Trish say something I never expected the girl of my dreams to utter: "Eli, do a magic trick for us!"

Even fifteen years later the crowd instinctively fell in line with her wishes, and I heard enthusiastic utterances as someone stood up and offered me their chair. I pulled my ever-ready deck of cards from my coat pocket as I sat, not at all certain what I intended to do and hoping my performance instincts would kick in. Like, right now.

Searching for an inspiration, I looked up and saw Trish smiling down at me.

"Trish, what was the name of that dog your family had when we were in high school?" I asked, looking up at her. I could tell she was surprised I even knew she had a dog, and it took her a moment to pull the name. As she worked on it, I gestured toward the chair next to me. The current occupant bounded to his feet as Trish stepped forward and sat.

"Sam," she said. "Or, Samuel J. Smithereens, which was the full name I gave him."

"Sam was a great dog," I lied, knowing nothing about the dog but glad that my gambit had paid off. I opened the blue bicycle deck and pulled out the cards. "And I think dogs and cards have a lot in common. They both travel in packs. They do tricks. And sometimes we pick a card or a dog...and sometimes they pick us." While saying this, I had given the cards a quick Hindu shuffle. I then spread the cards, face up, and held them in front of Trish. "So, like a dog, do we pick a card or do they pick us? Let's examine that idea. Trish, pick a card. Any card at all."

She ran a finger across the card spread, finally landing on the Jack of Hearts. "Is that your pick?" I asked. She nodded and pulled the card from the deck. "That's interesting," I said, squaring the remaining cards. "Because out of an entire deck of blue-backed cards, you picked the only card with a red back." I gestured to the blue-backed deck in my hands, while Trish turned her card over. It indeed had a red back. This produced the intended "ahh" from the group.

I set the cards on their box as I took the card from Trish and held it up. "Now, that's a good trick for a card to do. And that might be all the tricks this particular card knows. Unless," I said, setting the card face down on the table in front of her, "it knows how to change back to blue.

"Cover the card with your hand," I instructed and Trish did what she was told, the corners of her mouth turning up in a smile of wonder. "And tell it to change back."

She hesitated a second before saying it. "Change back."

"Take your hand away." She did and I could tell she was disappointed the card's back remained red. "Perhaps it would help if you named your card. Can you give it a name?"

I could tell I had put her on the spot and she was having trouble coming up with anything. "It's a cliché," I said, trying to help her out, "but how about Jack?"

She nodded in appreciation. I gestured toward the card and once again she covered it with her hand. "Okay, Jack," she said hopefully. "Change." She waited a beat and took her hand away, again instantly disappointed the card back steadfastly remained red.

"Not to despair," I said. "Changing from blue to red might be the only trick Jack knows and he can't change back. Or," I added, picking up the face-up deck, "it's possible Jack is in fact the leader of the pack. And, if that's the case, it would be simpler for the whole pack to change." With that, I turned the deck over and spread the cards, revealing the once blue-backed deck had magically changed to red.

This produced the awed reaction I anticipated, but I didn't stop or even slow down; I rode that momentum. "Let's see what other tricks Jack might know," I said, instructing Trish to bury the card deep in the deck. I shuffled and cut the cards and continued the routine, with Trish's card continuing to perform like a dog— jumping up to the top of the deck, coming when it was called, and finally rolling over. This last bit closed out the routine, as I fanned the cards for her, revealing that only one card in the entire deck had rolled over and was face down—the Jack of Hearts.

Trish started the applause and everyone, even Jake, joined in. But for me the best part of the crowd's reaction was Trish's smile and her subsequent request, asking shyly if she could keep the card. I gladly handed her the Jack of Hearts and her smile seemed almost demure as she took it from me.

I looked at that smile and wondered how things—like my whole life—might have been different if she had smiled at me like that fifteen years before. And, later on, I would look back at this night and wonder how things might have also ended up quite differently if Jake hadn't, at least figuratively, aspirated a filbert.

Chapter 5

"So are you allowed to tell me how you did that card trick? Or would you then have to kill me?"

I smiled and shrugged, still amazed Trish had let me buy her a drink and marveling at the fact we were having an actual conversation. "The sad thing about magic," I finally said, "is that the solution, when it finally comes, is almost always a letdown and a disappointment."

"Well, I certainly don't need more disappointments," she said dryly, and then quickly changed topics. "So, should we join everyone out on the Observation Deck?"

Trish was gesturing to the large picture window, through which we could see the majority of the party, which was taking place under the night sky. I felt a familiar sensation of rubberiness race through my legs and hollowness in my stomach at the thought of getting that close to the forty-story drop.

"No, thanks," I said, "I've got, um, seasonal allergies. Need to avoid the night, the outside, the outside tonight." Smooth, I thought. Very smooth.

"Oh, come out just for a moment. You have to say hello to Dylan, my husband. Your remember Dylan, right?"

"Dylan Ratner? Wasn't he the guidance counselor they made a guidance counselor because you can't just be the tennis coach? You married the tennis coach?" I was rambling, trying my best to stay put.

"No, silly, Dylan Lasalle. There he is."

She pointed out the window and I peered through the crowd, finally spotting Dylan Lasalle. I was surprised to see him, as I would have guessed he'd be in prison by now, or at the very least, just getting out.

He was in a very close conversation with a woman I didn't recognize. The way his hand cupped her shoulder, I would have pegged her as his wife, and not the woman currently sitting next to me. I could sense Trish was regretting pointing him out at this particular moment.

"Oh, he's such a flirt," she said, adding a hollow laugh. "You know me, I always had a soft spot for the bad boys."

If that were really true, then she had hit the Bad Boy jackpot with Dylan Lasalle. The fact he made it to graduation without going to jail I attributed more to the boys-will-be-boys attitude rampant at our school than to any innate intelligence, although he did possess a raw charm that had gotten him out of many scrapes. Our paths hadn't crossed much during high school, but that was not by chance alone. Most people with any sense had wisely stayed out of his way.

The necessity to coax me out to the Observation Deck vanished as I saw Dylan headed our way, holding two empty drink glasses in his hands. He was clearly on his way to the bar for a refill for himself and his new best friend, but he re-adjusted his course when he saw Trish waving him over.

"Just freshening up some drinks," he said to Trish with a too-wide smile. "Can I get you anything?"

Trish shook her head. "I wanted you to say hello to Eli Marks," she said. "You remember Eli, right?"

"Absolutely," he said in a tone that convinced me he had no idea who I was. He put out a hand for a handshake and then realized he didn't have a spare hand to shake. He finally settled for a quick fist bump. "How you been, man?"

"Can't complain," I said flatly. "At least, not since they instituted the No Complaining rule."

My joke, such as it was, produced a polite laugh.

"I hear ya," he said, turning his head to watch a young woman pass by. "There's a lot of that going around."

"Eli just did a great magic trick," Trish said, trying to pump some life into a conversation that had immediately flat lined. "He's quite the magician."

"Great, I've got ten extra pounds I'd love to see disappear," Dylan said, belying the fact that he was not just in good shape, but scary good shape. "Think you can help me out?"

"Here's the secret: Diet and exercise," I replied.

"Oh, you're no fun," Dylan said and at that moment I couldn't help but agree with him. There was something about his oily personality and demeanor that sucked the fun right out of me. I just wanted to get away from him and was almost willing to move out to the Observation Deck if that would have done the trick. Thankfully, he pulled the plug on the conversation and took us out of our misery.

"Well, gotta hit the bar and then the head," he said. "You know what they say, you don't buy beer, you rent it." He winked and smiled and slipped away before I could point out he wasn't drinking beer. But since that might have extended the conversation, I was glad I had kept my mouth shut.

There was an awkward moment with Trish. I broke the silence. "So, you and Dylan," I finally said.

"Yep," she said, agreeing unconvincingly. "Coming up on twelve years. To be honest, I'll be surprised if we make it to lucky thirteen," she added, her voice dropping in volume.

"Tired of bad boys?" I asked.

Trish nodded. "The trouble with bad boys," she said sadly, "is that sometimes, deep down, they're actually bad."

Before I could comment on that dark aphorism, she steered the conversation away from herself and directly at me. "So, Magic Man, I see no ring upon your hand nor girlfriend on your arm. What gives?"

"Well," I said, not sure how phrase my current situation, "I'm sort of on a break. We're on a break. The woman I'm seeing and I are on a break."

Trish leaned forward, looking interested and concerned. "And what exactly does that mean?"

Over the next twenty minutes, I did my best to explain what I thought it might mean. In the process, I detailed my divorce from the current Assistant District Attorney and her swift re-marriage to one of the lead homicide detectives on the force. I outlined how Megan and I had met, the bizarre circumstances that had brought us together, and how that had grown into what I had hoped would be a lasting relationship.

"You know how sometimes you just *fit* with someone? Like the two of you were somehow designed to be together?" I was having trouble finding the right words.

"Not from personal experience, no," she said. "But I understand the concept." She gave me a wry smile.

"But, in the end, I guess it was too much, too soon," I said. "At least, it was for her. So we're apart. For the time being. I don't know. Maybe forever. It's just bad," I added.

Trish shook her head, once again dazzling me with her smile. "Eli, if I've learned anything since leaving high school," she said confidently, "It's that nothing bad lasts forever."

I hadn't planned to close the event down, but before I knew it the two bartenders announced Last Call, before packing up their liquor bottles and rolling their portable bars out of the room. Jake and I were one-upping each other, delighting Trish with our stories of high school humiliations. It was fun to make her laugh and we were both up to the challenge, with exaggerated stories of ritualistic hazings and inopportune public nudity.

The crowd had thinned considerably and Jake was just finishing a story of a run-in with a dreaded PE teacher, when Dylan appeared at our table. He looked bleary and a little unsteady on his feet. Jake cut the story short as Trish got up and took Dylan's arm.

"Looks like it's time to go home," she said. "I think you've had enough fun for one night."

Dylan smiled widely and then suddenly jerked his arm away, stumbling a bit as he backed away from her. "The fun's over when I say it's over," he said, not quite focusing on anyone in particular. With that he turned and headed toward the door. Trish shrugged and picked up her purse.

"It's pumpkin time," she said. "But this has been really fun seeing you both." She looked at me and smiled.

"Right back at ya," Jake said before I could reply. "We'll walk you out."

As we followed her across the now near-empty room, Jake shot me a wicked smile, mouthing the words "She likes me." I playfully punched him on the arm and he struck a boxing stance as we headed toward the door. Trish, keeping one eye on her husband ahead of her, turned and laughed at our antics. The four of us stepped out of the room and into the hall.

And that's when I remembered that I was forty stories up and four feet away from an open railing. Although I couldn't see over the edge, I knew what lay below me and I felt my stomach drop— not the full forty stories, but enough to make my throat go bone dry as my heart began to race. I thought for a moment of diving back into the room, but we were on the move and I couldn't think of an excuse for breaking up our juggernaut. I looked ahead, seeing how much ground we had to cover before I could get away from the railing, and then I realized our destination was the dreaded bank of elevators. My head was spinning, from both the beer and the fear, as I looked around, desperately hoping to find a stairwell I could duck into. Walking down forty flights of stairs would be a cakewalk compared to stepping into that glass elevator again.

Seeing I had slowed, both Jake and Trish held back for a moment to let me catch up, each grabbing my arm as Dylan yelled from the elevator, "Our ride's here, people. Let's step it up." The two of them pulled me along, laughing, and we rounded the corner and stumbled into the elevator. I was hurled forward, due to inertia, my hands pushing against the glass of the elevator to slow my momentum. This gave me an unwanted and stomach-churning bird's eye view of the atrium and the dizzying distance to the ground. I involuntarily backed away from the glass, but the elevator door had closed and we were on our way, dropping with what felt like great speed.

And then we stopped. At the thirty-eighth floor. To let some more people in. Dylan and Jake had gotten into a conversation about elevators and the tallest buildings they had ever been in, none of which was helping my situation. I gulped, trying to breathe and coming up short. And then Trish's hand was on my shoulder.

"Are you okay?" she asked softly.

I shook my head. I was having trouble getting words out. "Heights. Not good with heights," I finally stammered.

She nodded sympathetically. "My kid brother had a similar problem. Couldn't go through tunnels. It was hell on family car trips. But this usually worked. Sing with me. Come on."

She started singing *Jingle Bells*, slowly and softly. Sweat was dripping down the back of my neck and there was a buzzing in my ears, but I did my best to concentrate and listen to her sing.

Jingle bell, jingle bells
Jingle all the way
Oh what fun it is to ride
In a one-horse open sleigh...

I did my best to sing along, my voice cracking and ragged, as she pushed on through the song, looking deep into my eyes as we sang. I started to breathe again and got caught up in the rhythm of the song, relieved to have something else to focus on as the elevator continued its plunge to the lobby. We made it through a verse, a chorus, and the next verse before the elevator finally came to a stop and the doors opened onto blessed, solid ground.

"What are you two singing back there?" Jake yelled as we piled out of the elevator.

"Eli was just reminding me of our school anthem," Trish lied, throwing a knowing smile in my direction.

"Really?" Dylan mumbled. "Sounded like a Christmas carol to me."

The valet brought their car first and we helped get Dylan into the passenger seat. He had mellowed in the warm night air and was probably asleep soon after we shut the car door. Trish handed a five to the valet and then turned to Jake and me.

"This was a lot more fun than it had any right to be," she said with a glance toward her husband, whose head was slumped against the passenger window.

"I'll look you up next time I'm in town," Jake said. "Or you could always come spend a weekend with me in LA."

"Yeah, that's not going to happen," Trish said with a smile.

"Never say never," Jake said.

"I'll see you around," she said as she got in the car. I was sure she had said it directly to me, but I sensed Jake would argue that point. We both waved as she pulled out of the hotel's shrub-lined driveway.

"She's a hoot and a half," Jake finally said.

"Of course, she is married," I reminded him.

"Sometimes that makes it more fun," he said with a grin.

"Yes. But she's married," I repeated, as much to him as to myself.

He gave his ticket to the valet as I watched Trish and Dylan, the not-so-happily-married couple, drive away. "Yes, Eli," Jake conceded. "She is married."

That was true, but only provisionally. The next time I would see Trish Lasalle, she'd be a widow.

CHAPTER 6

The ride home from downtown consisted almost entirely of a non-stop monologue from Jake. The subjects he covered alternated between his shame and embarrassment at bombing during his card trick, to his continued amazement at how beautiful and charming Trish was.

"You don't see a woman like that very often," he said wistfully as we made nice time heading south on Portland Avenue.

"Yes," I agreed. "Good thing you came back to Minneapolis. I understand Los Angeles is bereft of beautiful women."

"There are not as many as you might think," Jake said defensively.

"So many that you have to come all the way back here to find one?"

"I don't know about that," he admitted. "But I will admit I have started looking outside of LA County." He turned left on Forty-Eighth Street. Two blocks and one right turn later, he deposited me in front of Chicago Magic.

"Still can't believe I screwed up that trick so badly," he repeated for the umpteenth time as I opened the passenger door.

"It's just a matter of practicing," I said.

"I practice all the time," he countered.

"Yes," I said, "But practicing in front of a mirror is not the same as practicing in front of an audience. You need to get some actual crowd time under your belt. As Mac King always says, 'Whoever has the most stage time wins.'"

"And how does one do that?"

I thought about it for a second. "Well, I could always get you into a First Thursday show."

"What's First Thursday?"

"Once a month, my uncle and his cronies take over the Parkway Theater," I said, gesturing to the movie theater next to Chicago Magic, "and put on a show. It's not highly structured or, for that matter, particularly well advertised. It's just a chance for them to get in front of an audience and keep their magic muscles limber."

"First Thursday," he repeated quietly. "That might be a good idea. When is it?"

"Surprisingly, it's on a Thursday," I said, although my joke went right over his head. "And, as it turns out, it's this Thursday."

"And you can get me in?" he asked, clearly warming to the idea.

"I'll see if I can pull some strings," I said as stepped out of the car.

"Great. That's just what I need," Jake said, considering the opportunity. He then smiled his million-dollar smile up at me. "Well, as we say in the business, I'll see you on the set." I closed the car door and he executed a sharp u-turn, hitting the gas and just making it through the third second of the yellow light.

Not only did I fall asleep the moment I got into bed, I'd be willing to bet I was already in REM sleep before my head hit the pillow. It had been a long day ending with too much alcohol and way too much proximity to a forty-story vertical drop.

I was exhausted, so I can probably be excused for not hearing the front door to my apartment as it opened and closed. I also didn't hear the bedroom door open. And I didn't hear anyone walk across the room and lean over my bed.

The first thing I heard was my name, whispered softly. I immediately incorporated the sound into a dream, where I was backing away on the roof of a super-tall skyscraper, with only a thin railing separating me from what looked like a two hundred story drop. Someone called my name from somewhere above me, and then called it again, and then placed a hand on my chest—

I woke up with a start, grabbing the dream hand and realizing it was a real hand attached to a real wrist. In the dark room I could barely make out the silhouette of a figure leaning over me. She said my name again.

"Eli?"

"Megan?" I said, not sure if this was a new chapter in the dream or if I were actually back in my room.

"Yes."

I recognized her voice and could start to make out her features in the dim light. "What are you doing here?"

"I'm not here," she said quietly.

"You're not?"

"I'm not here."

"Okay..."

She leaned in and kissed me and I woke up enough to kiss her back. A moment later she was in bed alongside me and everything began to feel very familiar. Although somewhat rusty, we both got back in the rhythm very quickly and before I knew it, it was like she had never left.

Afterward, she lay next to me quietly, each of us listening to the other's breathing as our heart rates returned to normal.

"So," I finally said, "Here we are."

"I'm not here," she said.

"I think I could make a persuasive argument to the contrary."

She rolled over and kissed me, then jumped up and grabbed her clothes as she headed toward the door.

"I wasn't here," she said one last time, and then the door closed behind her.

I lay in the bed for a long while. And then for a while longer. And then for a bit more. Finally, I rolled over and went back to sleep.

* * *

The next morning I turned off the alarm when it started ringing, deciding I deserved to sleep in, if only for a bit. Once I finally rolled out of bed, I took a quick shower, spending most of its duration trying to clean off the recalcitrant ink spot on my hand from the previous night's reunion. I then made my way down the two steep flights of stairs to the magic shop, figuring Harry had already finished his breakfast and had opened the shop.

The lights were on in the store, but Harry was nowhere to be seen. I was about to turn around and go back up and check his apartment when the bell over the door tinkled. I turned, expecting to see Harry holding our traditional Saturday morning treat: a bag of warm croissants and two hot cups of coffee. No such luck. It was instead my ex-wife's relatively-new husband, Homicide Detective Fred Hutton.

"Morning Marks," he growled, his large frame filling the doorway and blocking the early morning sun.

"Homicide Detective Fred Hutton, to what do I owe the pleasure? Is this a personal call or are you here on business?" At one point I had promised to stop always referring to him by his full name and title, but some habits die hard. He didn't seem to care one way or the other.

"You attended a function last night downtown, a high school reunion?"

"I did. I did indeed," I said, getting a bit anxious about the reason behind his visit. "Is there a problem? Underage drinking, undocumented workers, excessive jaywalking or something more severe?"

"You spent some time with a Dylan Lasalle?"

"I did. Briefly. To be honest, I spent more time with his wife. But I did interact with him once or twice. Why? What's he done?"

"He's gotten himself killed," he said dryly.

* * *

Homicide Detective Fred Hutton is not, by anyone's estimation, a chatty guy, so it took me a while to pull the whole story out of him. The gist of it was that sometime around 2:00 a.m., Dylan decided to go for a late night run. His body was discovered by some early morning joggers, just a few feet from a running path near the Lake Calhoun condo he shares with his wife. He had been shot twice, once in the chest and once in the head. His wallet was found nearby, with ID intact but no cash or credit cards. He was assumed to be the victim of a mugging, but the police were contacting anyone who had interacted with him in the last day or so.

"He talked to a lot of people at the reunion," I said after some of the initial shock had worn off. "Well, he talked to a lot of women, at least."

"Yes, we have a complete list of all the attendees. Since I recognized your name on the list, I thought I'd make you one of my first stops."

"Well, I'm flattered, of course," I said, forgetting for a moment that humor and sarcasm were foreign to Homicide Detective Fred Hutton's experience. "But other than last night, I haven't seen him since high school, and even back then we never traveled in the same circles."

"What kind of guy was he?" he asked, flipping open a small notebook and then looking at me intently, waiting for my reply.

"Well, like I said, I didn't know him well, then or now."

"I've always known you to be an astute judge of character," he said with the straightest of faces. "What was your impression of him?"

"Well," I finally said, "I don't want to speak ill of the dead. But he was sort of a creep. Then and now."

"How so?"

I struggled to put the feeling into words. "I don't know," I said, groping for the right adjective. "I guess he always acted kind of...shady."

"Shady. I see." He made several notes, making me wonder what he was jotting down other than the word 'shady.' He looked up from his work. "And how well do you know his wife?"

"Really no better than I knew him," I admitted. "Although I did spend more time with her last night than with him."

"And why was that?" His question was completely straightforward and devoid of judgment, yet I couldn't help feel trapped by it.

"I don't know," I said. "He was playing the room, so I sat and chatted with her. She was popular in school, I always found her interesting..." My voice trailed off, not sure how this information could possibly assist him in his investigation.

"I see," he said, checking through his notes. "And how would you describe his relationship with his wife?"

"His wife?"

"You said you spent a good deal of time talking with her. What was your impression of the state of their marriage?"

"I'm not really sure it's my place to say."

He plowed on. "Did it seem strained in any way?"

I hemmed and perhaps even hawed to a degree before answering. "He'd had a lot to drink," I finally said. "And I got the impression that wasn't uncommon."

"Anything else?"

"He spent a lot of time flirting with other women. And I got the impression that also wasn't uncommon." There was an uncomfortable silence, at least for me, while he made some more notes. "So, that's what you think it was?" I asked. "A mugging?"

"Probably," he said, looking up from his notes. "The simplest answer is usually the right one."

"Occam's razor."

He nodded and almost smiled. "Yes, Occam's razor. When you have two competing theories that make exactly the same prediction, the simpler one is the better."

"What's the other theory?"

He waited a moment before responding. "That it was more

than just a mugging." He closed his notebook. "Thanks for your time."

As he reached the door, I felt the need to add one more, unrelated thought. "One more thing," I said.

He stopped and turned, waiting for me to complete my thought. I came out from behind the counter and cut the distance between us. There had been something I had been wanting to say to him for a long time, and this seemed like as good a time as any.

"I know we've never really talked about you. And Deirdre. The affair you two had."

He waited quietly for me to continue, no expression on his face.

"I just don't want you to feel like you owe me anything," I said. "Because of the affair."

"I don't."

"I don't want you to think that you're..." I struggled to find the right word. "That you're *beholden* to me."

"I don't."

"Because you aren't. Beholden to me."

"I know." He continued to stare at me. His face was expressionless, but in my mind I attached a flood of possible emotions to his blank countenance.

"Have a nice day," he said flatly as he left the store.

CHAPTER 7

The sight of a Renaissance village rising up out of the farmlands twenty miles outside of Minneapolis is odd in its own right. Take that artificial environment and layer on a movie crew, with their large trailers, enormous lights on wheels, and dozens of crewmembers in shorts and t-shirts, and an overwhelming feeling of temporal dislocation seems a natural response.

I'd driven the mile of dirt road that takes you from the highway to the grounds of the festival, traveling over bumpy grasslands you'd think would be smoother, given the thousands who drive and park along these makeshift roads each late summer and early fall.

I crested the last hill and saw the festival grounds below me—a tall, wooden fence and imposing gate separating the acres of pasture parking from the confined and dusty world of royalty, knights and ladies in waiting.

A bored security guard leaning against the main gate used his walkie-talkie to announce my arrival to a squawking voice at the other end. Moments later, a harried production assistant ushered me toward the row of Winnebago motor homes that lined one of the many dirt streets encircling the center jousting ring.

"I'm on route with a visitor for Jay One," she huffed into the walkie-talkie as we navigated around and between the motor homes. "He's in mid-interview. What's the ETA on his set time?" The response was piped directly into her earpiece, so all I experienced was her nodding along with the unheard voice. "Ten-four," she finally barked into the walkie-talkie, before re-attaching it to the hook on her belt. She stopped in front of one of the nicer motor homes and climbed the three built-in steps, knocking tentatively on the door.

"Ten minutes, Mr. North. And you've got another visitor." With that she jumped off the top step and disappeared behind the next trailer, her walkie-talkie back in her hand. "Yeah, yeah, I'm on my way," was the last I heard before she was gone.

I turned as I heard the motor home door swing open and was completely surprised by the voice that greeted me.

"Well, my stars and garters, if it isn't my favorite sorcerer!" The high British voice was unmistakable. I looked up to see Clive Albans, his tall frame scrunched awkwardly in the doorway. He jettisoned himself from the motor home and danced down the steps, landing in front of me in all his glory. As usual, he was dressed in a fashion all his own, mixing paisley and pinstripes and black and yellow checks with wild abandon. A silk polka-dotted scarf was wrapped around his neck. Before I knew it, he had engulfed me in an effusive bear hug, his cologne lingering like thick, oily smog.

Clive was a peripatetic journalist who dressed like Oscar Wilde and spoke like a fey character right out of Gilbert & Sullivan. I had met him the previous fall when he had been writing a freelance newspaper article on psychics and debunkers, but our paths had not crossed again since and I was surprised to find him still in town.

"I continue to turn heads with that trick you taught me," he said conspiratorially. "The one with the two coins."

"Scotch and Soda," I said, remembering his delight at learning the secret behind that old chestnut. "It's a classic, that's for sure."

"Yes, but I must stop by the shop and pick up something else to add to my repertoire," he sighed. "I've run out of people to perform for, and I need something new. You understand that need, as a performer: to fill the endless maw that is my adoring audience."

"Yes, that's the curse of the amateur magician," I agreed. "The old saying is a professional magician does the same six tricks for a different audience every day, while the amateur constantly has to learn new tricks to impress the same six people. Anyway," I continued, "stop by the shop and we'll find you something new that will shock and awe your audience."

"Shock and awe, exactly," he said. "But small enough to fit in a pocket, and nothing too difficult to master."

"So you want something that is self-working, but packs small and plays large?"

He nodded. "Exactly."

"You and every other magician on the planet. I'm sure I can find just the right item to help you out. And if I'm not there, Uncle Harry will look after you."

"If you're not there, I'll come back another day. Your Uncle Harry puts the fear of God in me. And this coming from a man who has covered three war zones," he added for emphasis. "Are you here to see Jake North? And if so, why? Dirt, please. I need the dirt."

"I'm sorry, Clive, there's no dirt. We went to high school together is all, nothing more sinister than that."

"Ah, well, I have to ask. I am a modern day Sisyphus," he continued, twirling where he stood, his head tilted back as he gestured toward an unseen mountain. "Rolling the large stone that is gossip up the unforgiving, uncaring slope each day, cursed to have to start again at the bottom the next with yet another unyielding stone." He stopped twirling, looking lost for a long moment.

"Well," he finally said, his head appearing to clear, "I'm going to hit the craft services table and then see what dirt I can find in the wardrobe tent. Isn't this exciting?" he added. "One of the great mysteries of our age: Who killed Terry Alexander? Not since Jack the Ripper has the identity of a killer been so wrapped in mystery. Who was it?"

He held up a finger for each of the suspects as he breathlessly named them. "Was it the angry and greedy manager? The former girlfriend and current onstage assistant? The insanely jealous new girlfriend? The rival magician in the troupe? Or the sociopathic local drug kingpin? Oh, goodness, it's such a juicy tale, bound to thrill the masses and fill the coffers! I love it!"

I remembered Harry's assessment, that it was a trick gone bad due to the incompetence of the performer, but since that view wasn't meant for public consumption, I kept silent on the issue.

It hardly mattered, as Clive had already disappeared down the row of motor homes, his high-pitched laughter echoing in the aluminum canyon.

"Ven si quieres, la puerta está abierta!"

It took me a moment to understand the voice responding to my knock was responding in Spanish. At least, it sounded like that language to my high-school Spanish-trained ear. Granted, all that remained from that education was my ability to inquire as to the location of Pepe's house and to comment excitedly about the pen's current location on top of the table. But it did sound like Spanish and the tone suggested I should come in, so I did.

Walking into Jake's motor home was not unlike walking into a miniature version of our magic shop. Magic posters lined the walls and every available surface was covered with decks of cards, jumbles of coins, and exotic-looking gizmos and gaffs.

"Hey, man. Qué pasa?" Jake was stretched out on the couch, but if I hadn't recognized the voice I'm not so sure I would have recognized him at all. He was in costume as Terry Alexander. His face was pale with exaggerated eye makeup and black lipstick giving him the look of a feral raccoon. He was dressed all in black, his hair was long, dark and stringy, and his bare arms were a mosaic of tattoos. He held a script in one hand and a pen in the other.

"Just doing a quick re-write of today's scene," he said, finishing with a flourish. "Trying to get some heart into this sucker, but it's an uphill battle."

"Sisyphean?" I suggested, thinking back to my conversation with Clive.

"Herculean," he responded, tossing the script on top of the table. "And old Mr. Williams said we'd never remember anything from our Classics class," he added with a grin. "Proved that old fart wrong. Or, I suppose I should say, demostró que pedo viejo mal."

"What's with the Spanish?" I asked. "That is Spanish, right?"

"Yeah, I'm not going all Method or anything, but Terry did learn to speak Spanish toward the end, so I thought I should do the same."

"Wow. You've learned magic *and* Spanish. Quite impressive."

"Yeah, if I could just learn to act, I'd have the hat trick."

"False modesty?"

"Or a dead keen assessment. Depends who you ask." He set the script down and looked up at me expectantly. "So, you've buried the lead. The cops think Trish shot Dylan?"

"You read the papers?"

"Who reads papers? It's all over the Internet. So they think she killed him?"

"Well, the detective I talked to didn't come out and say that, but that was the impression I got, yes," I said. "Killed him or had him killed. Something like that."

"Wow," Jake said. "Well, given his behavior, you'd be hard pressed to blame her."

"I suppose," I said. "But I don't think that would hold up in court. It doesn't look like self-defense."

"What's it look like?"

I thought about it. "It looks like a mugging gone bad," I offered. "But what do I know?"

"Well, at least one positive thing came out of it," he said, stretching and cracking his neck.

"What's that?"

"At least now she's single."

There was a knock at the door and I heard the strained voice of the production assistant who had guided me to the motor home.

"We're ready for you on the set, Mr. North."

"Gracias, estoy en mi camino," Jake shouted back as he pushed himself up from the couch, grabbed the script from the table and headed toward the door. "Come on," he said, gesturing toward me. "You can experience the magic of moviemaking first hand."

Magic might have been an overstatement. Tedium would have been a better word.

The next hour was spent shooting—and shooting and shooting—a shot of Jake walking across a dusty street, spotting a Venezuelan street urchin, and bending down to perform a small magic trick for him.

In my capacity as magic consultant to the star, I was called in immediately to oversee the simple card trick Jake had intended to perform. He demonstrated it for me under the watchful eye of the director—a husky twenty-something in a beard, wearing a Spiderman t-shirt—who grunted along favorably as Jake executed the trick. When it was done, they both turned to me. My facial reaction must have indicated my distaste for the illusion.

"What's wrong with it?" Jake asked, as he performed the trick again at double speed.

"Card tricks don't generally work on kids that young," I said, gesturing to the child actor who, for all I knew, may have been in his teens but looked to be no more than five years old. "Kids that age don't know cards. They don't know suits, they don't know values, and so changing one into another isn't really all that magical."

"At film school, they taught us never to say 'no,' unless you can follow it up immediately with a 'yes.'" The director stood back, waiting for the 'yes' he felt I owed him.

I pondered the situation for a moment and then dug into my show bag, which I'd retrieved from the car. After some rummaging, I found what I was looking for: a silk transformation.

"This is pretty simple," I said as I began to demonstrate the trick, "But it's visual and it's colorful and kids love it." I showed them the bright yellow silk, which I stuffed into my closed fist. I gave the fist a quick shake and then pulled the silk out again, but it had now changed to bright red. I concluded the trick by opening the fist, showing it was empty.

"Nice," the director whispered. "Colorful, visual, and I like how it corresponds to where Terry Alexander is at this point in his arc, in the midst of his personal transformation."

"Yeah, I like it," Jake agreed, rubbing his chin thoughtfully. "I just need to figure out the Spanish word for silk." He signaled to a production assistant who scurried over, an English-to-Spanish dictionary in his hands. Clearly this was a frequent request on the set.

"No, don't say silk," I said as Jake began to page through the dictionary. "Nobody says silk in real life, so the magician shouldn't either," I continued, parroting words I'd heard from Harry my whole life.

"How about bandana?" Jake asked, as he flipped to the front of the dictionary.

"That will work," I said, and once he'd found the right words, I set upon the task of teaching him the trick.

The trick, like the shot, was very simple: cross a street, see a kid, perform a quick illusion ("Mira este pañuelo amarillo!"), and then keep moving.

To my eye, Jake nailed it on the first take, but I'm not the director. The director needed to see it nearly thirty more times, with no discernible difference in the action I could spot.

So they did it again. And again. And again. After every take, the director would get up from in front of a video screen, one of many monitors shielded from the sun under a large, open-side tent, and amble over to Jake and the young actor for a whispered conversation.

He would then stroll back to his chair while another crew person announced "We're back to one, folks" through a bullhorn. As we neared the thirtieth take, I realized the person next to me was sighing, audibly and louder, every time the director yelled, "Cut!" Trying my best not to be obvious, I turned to see a short, dark-haired guy of about forty, dressed in khakis and a black polo shirt. He wore rimless glasses and held a black binder in one hand and a large cardboard coffee cup in the other. He was shaking his head and rolling his eyes and I was going to ask him if he was okay, but was interrupted by the sound of the director saying "Action" in a stage whisper that was amplified through the bullhorn.

Once again, Jake made his way across the street, saw the boy, bent down and began to perform the silk illusion. Before he was halfway through his question to the boy, he was drowned out by the director's amplified voice yelling, "Cut!" All action ceased while the director made the long trek across the outdoor set to his two actors for another hushed conference.

"He's trying to out-Kubrick Kubrick," the man next to me muttered.

"Excuse me?" I asked tentatively.

"Oh, it's these film school shits who think just because Stanley Kubrick shot a hundred takes of every shot, they have to emulate and surpass the master. Unless they leave the actors in tears, they're not getting to the reality of the moment, or whatever the hell it is he's looking for." He took a sip of the coffee and then immediately spat it out. "And, to add insult to injury, this frickin' scene—this whole frickin' sequence—isn't even in the script. I mean, my script."

"So you're the writer?" I ventured.

"Depends who you ask," he replied as he tossed the cardboard coffee cup in a nearby trash container like he was tossing a tear gas canister into a building full of terrorists. "I'm only the one who came up with the idea, I'm only the one who did six years of research, and I'm only the one who wrote twenty drafts of the screenplay. So, yes, in some circles, I would be considered the writer. However, here," he added, "I'm the jackass who keeps complaining.

"I'm not even allowed to stand by the monitor anymore," he continued, gesturing across the set to the video monitors the director was studying. "Why? Because Herr Kubrick didn't like that I kept sighing and shaking my head. And believe me, it was all I could do to limit myself to sighs and headshakes. A weaker man would have drawn blood, and not my blood I can assure you."

"So he's rewriting the script?" I asked quietly, remembering the work Jake had been doing in his motor home and the quick re-write we had improvised with the silk.

"Oh, would that he was the only person re-writing the poor pulpy mess that once was my script. I believe everyone in the cast and crew has taken a crack at violating my script, including the director's mother and her dog whisperer. All that remains of my original script are the page numbers and even those are now in the wrong order."

"And there's nothing you can do about it?"

"I am less than powerless. The schmuck who pours the dressing on the salad at lunch has more say in this process than the writer."

"Maybe this is an ignorant question, but then why are you here?"

He gave me a long, penetrating look. "Because when it all goes up in flames—and it will, believe me, it will—I want to see it happen. I may not be the one to throw the match on the kerosene-soaked edifice that is this movie, but I'm not going to miss watching the sucker explode."

I smiled weakly. "I've got to go," I said. "Um...stand over there." I backed away, but he didn't seem to notice. He just sat there, shaking his head and sighing.

"Hey, it's the debunker guy."

I didn't recognize the voice and I couldn't quite place the

woman who had approached me, although there was definitely something familiar about her. She was tall and rail thin, with spiked red hair and pale skin. Several tattoos were visible, poking out of various points from under her black tank top. She clearly saw the look of puzzlement on my face.

"I did your makeup for that Halloween show last year on public TV. You were the guy who hated the word Debunker, right?"

"That was me," I nodded. "And you're...Laura?"

"Close. Lauren," she said. "Good effort, dude," she added, punching my arm playfully. "You're a magician, right?"

"I am," I said.

"Can you make me disappear from this show?" Lauren said in a heavy stage whisper. "No, I'm just kidding." She started digging through the pouch that hung on a strap around her waist. "But, really, can you make me disappear?" She laughed and punched my arm again playfully. I could feel a welt starting to form.

"What is it about this movie that's making everyone so unhappy?" I asked quietly. "I just talked to the writer, I talked to one of the actors, even the production assistants seem cranky and stressed."

"Some movies just have a stink about them," she said as she adjusted the makeup items in her pouch. "And this one has a stench all its own. Everybody's mad and scared and irritable. It's a real drag. It pays good, but it's a real drag." She gestured across the set toward a woman dressed in what we used to call a power suit. The woman was furiously whispering into her cell phone.

"See the lady with the two hundred dollar haircut and the two thousand dollar suit? She's Donna, the producer. She's pissed at everyone, but mostly she's pissed at Walter," she said, gesturing toward the director, who was once again seated behind his bank of video monitors. "Walter is four days behind schedule, but every time Donna has tried to fire him, he's fired one of the department heads first, throwing everything into chaos, so she can't get rid of him."

She then tilted her head in the direction of the writer. "Stewart hates Walter, too, because Walter has eviscerated his script, rewriting scenes, adding characters. Stewart told me when they first started meeting on the script, Walter asked him what he thought were the four most important scenes in the movie. Stewart told him, and Walter has since cut all four of them out of the script. All the scenes we've been shooting recently is stuff Walter added—including the cute, cloying kid. It's driving Stewart out of his gourd."

"That's the impression I got talking to him just now."

"If you really want the dirt, get a couple drinks in him. He goes from a trickle to a flash flood in nothing flat. And if it's fireworks you're after, get him started on how casting a TV actor, not a real actor, was the final insult to his screenplay masterpiece."

She then pointed to a young woman sitting under the shade of an umbrella across the set from us. The woman, a long-legged, busty blonde, was wearing a skimpy sundress and oversized sunglasses. She was sipping a cola and reading a gossip magazine with a highlighter pen, stopping from time to time to mark a particular segment.

"Then there's Noël, the writer's ex-girlfriend and the female lead," Lauren continued, her dislike evident in her cold tone. "Casting couch stories in Hollywood are exaggerated, but I know for a fact she got cast because of her umlauts."

It took me a moment to understand the reference, but as Noël sat up and adjusted the straps on her dress, I understood Lauren's meaning.

"She got noticed by the producers because she was sleeping with the writer, but as soon as she got the part, she switched beds and started sleeping with Arnold."

She indicated an older, heavyset balding man in slacks and a Hawaiian shirt. He was also speaking heatedly into a cell phone. "That's Arnold. He and Donna, the other producer, are divorced but are producing together, which in itself is a trip and a half. They'd make *Who's Afraid of Virginia Woolf* look like a fluffy romantic comedy. I'm surprised they haven't killed each other yet."

I looked at Arnold angrily speaking into his phone on one side of the set and then at Donna, talking just as furiously into her phone on the other side. Unless I was mistaken, it looked very much like they were in a highly contentious conversation with each other via cell phone while standing fifty yards apart.

"Anyway," Lauren continued, "Then Noël dumped Arnold and is now shacked up with Walter, the director."

I glanced around at the people Lauren had pointed out to me: The angry writer. The psycho director. The warring producers. And the sex kitten actress. "So, is this a typical movie set?" I asked. "I mean, where everyone hates each other?"

Lauren laughed. "Honey, there's no such thing as a typical movie set—each one is screwed up in its own, special way. But this one is one of worst I've seen. I wouldn't be surprised if someone ends up murdered before we get to the last scene." Not hearing a response from me, she turned and saw what I'm guessing was a horrified look on my face.

"Don't worry, baby, I'm just exaggerating for effect. In Hollywood, no one actually kills anyone because of a movie."

"They don't?" I asked, feeling relieved.

"No, they want to keep you alive so they can really take their time torturing you. That's the Hollywood way."

Chapter 8

After a painfully slow six hours of watching them film the movie, I would have delighted in the rapid-fire pace of watching paint dry if it had been offered to me. I wasn't certain what my role on the set was, except to try to keep them from killing Jake, but if their weapon was boredom, they were well on their way to doing me in. I was in the throes of this lethargy when I glanced over to see that someone was sitting next to me in Jake's canvas chair and it wasn't Jake.

I recognized him as Arnold, one of the producers of the film who Lauren had pointed out to me earlier. He wore a loud and beautifully-tailored Hawaiian print shirt, which may well have been custom-made by a genuine Hawaiian. He was a large man, balding, with wisps of graying hair fighting it out on the fringes of his skull. He was whispering into his cell phone with a hoarse, angry rasp that conveyed more anger than if he'd actually been shouting at the top of his lungs.

"No, you are dead wrong, my friend," he hissed. "We are all about catering on this show and if the quality of the paté sinks below the baseline I established one more time, heads will roll. Do you hear me? Heads will roll." He pushed the END button on the phone and glanced over at me, shaking his head like the embarrassed father of an ill-behaved kindergartener.

"How tough is it to get liver paté right?" he asked and I shrugged because I genuinely didn't know the answer. If we were going to have a conversation—and it looked like we were—I hoped the questions would get easier.

"You're the new magic consultant, right?"

"Yes," I said, nodding, pleased we were now firmly in my conversational ballpark. "The magic consultant."

"So, what's your theory?"

"My theory?" I repeated. He'd just hit one out of the park. "My theory on what?"

"On who killed Terry Alexander," he said with a grin. "One of the world's great mysteries, never been solved."

"I think not being solved is the definition of a mystery," I suggested, but he didn't really seem to need my participation to keep the conversation rolling. He was one of those people who only needed a sounding board and if I hadn't been there he would have been just as happy talking to the tree behind me.

"That's the beauty of this movie," he continued. "A truly great, real-life murder mystery. Was it the ex-girlfriend, the manager, the current girlfriend, a wronged rival..." His voice trailed off dramatically. Given that I knew none of those answers were correct, yet I couldn't tell him why, I didn't know how to respond. But apparently a response from me was merely optional, as he kept talking.

"We're even considering releasing the movie with four different endings, each one with a different solution. Never been done before."

"I think they did that with *Clue*, the movie," I offered, but he didn't register any reaction to my voice.

"Groundbreaking," he continued unabated. "Each ending providing a completely plausible solution to the mystery. Never been done before."

"Actually," I offered, "The novel, *The Poisoned Chocolates Case,* presented a murder with six completely plausible solutions, and that was written back in the 1920s—"

"That's our marketing strategy," he said, skating right over my words like there was no sound coming out of my mouth. "That's the ticket. It will put this little movie on the map." He finally stopped talking and looked at me, apparently waiting for a reaction of some sort.

"Sounds like a plan," I finally said.

"Damn straight," he replied, as his phone began to buzz. "Because God knows we need something to put this movie on the map. Hell, anything." He got up, pushing his bulk up out of the chair. "Nice chatting with you. Try the paté," he added, beginning another harshly whispered conversation as he walked away.

Moments later I felt a vibration in my pocket, signaling I had in fact remembered to turn off the ringer. A crewmember had made that mistake earlier, and Walter's sudden rage was terrifying. He went from zero to insane in no time flat and it took Arnold, Donna and the assistant director to calm him down, each pointing out that the scene was essentially silent and that no harm had been done. Walter calmed down almost as quickly as he had exploded, laughing off the incident, but it left a sour taste and I made a mental note to always double-check the ring status on my phone.

I pulled the pulsating phone out of my pocket as I headed away from the set. The cameras weren't currently rolling, but I didn't want to feel Walter's wrath if I was the moron who was still talking when they called for quiet on the set.

I ducked behind a rustic shed and answered the phone. Before I was halfway through my "Hello," I was cut off by the rapid-fire barrage of words from the other end.

"Eli, honey, sweetie, I don't work for you, you don't work for me, we work for each other. We've got an opportunity, I dropped everything when they called, put people on hold, stopped answering emails, to make sure you're available, as my number one client, I don't work for you, you don't work for me, we work for each other, isn't that right?"

Before I could agree or disagree, the voice continued. "Anyway, it's a last-minute thing, a house party of some kind, tonight, in Kenwood, can't beat that, one hour of walk-around magic, paying top dollar, asked for you by name, let's hope you're available, are you available, sweetie?"

"Elaine, yes, yes, Elaine, I'm available, yes I am," I said quickly, suddenly taking on the speech patterns of my agent, a world-class mile-a-minute talker. I had to make a conscious effort to slow down, in the hope she would begin to mimic my more deliberate speech pattern. "So, let me make sure I have this right. It's tonight. In Kenwood. A house party. And they want some walk-around magic for an hour. Is that correct?"

"Right on the money, honey—"

Before she could continue, I swiftly cut her off, talking as slowly as I could. "That should be fine. Do you know what time they want me? And the address?" I drew out each word slowly.

"Yes, yes I do," she said, slowing to a more leisurely conversation pace. I could hear her shuffling papers around her desk. "I've got all the information. I'll email it over."

"That would be fine," I said patiently, like I was trying to calm a hyperactive puppy. "Are they paying me on the spot or did they pre-pay with you?" For someone who made her living off a percentage of what her clients made, Elaine was notoriously poor at tracking the actual flow of money.

"They said they'd pay you at the gig," she said, now sounding almost sleepy. "I told them you'd get me the commission. I said you were good for it. I'm sending the information now," she added.

True to her word, a ping in my ear signaled the arrival of an email. "Thanks, Elaine. Thanks for the call. And for the gig."

"I don't work for you, you don't work for me. We work for each other," she said. Like shalom, it had become her greeting at the beginning and end of every conversation, its meaning entirely dependent on its placement. The sound of a click and then no sound at all told me the conversation had ended and that Elaine had moved onto her next call.

I've often questioned my need for an agent, as most of my work comes to me direct, either from the website, a referral or repeat business. However, I've always liked the idea of having my own Broadway Danny Rose, even if she's actually a bottle-blonde from Anoka with a motor-mouth and a serious chocolate addiction. I was making a mental note to send her a box of her favorite Russell Stover candies along with her commission, when I rounded the corner of the shed and came to an abrupt halt.

Several yards ahead of me I was surprised to see Jake and Noël, the movie's lead actress, in the midst of what Harry would have called "the full canoodle." That's his charming old-world expression for kissing that has gone above and beyond a friendly greeting. They were wrapped in an embrace that looked to be headed from PG-13 to R, on its way to NC-17. They hadn't noticed my arrival, so I quickly stepped back behind the shed. I looked around for another exit route and as I did I was surprised to see Stewart, the writer.

He wasn't looking at me. He, too, had spotted the necking couple, but unlike me he didn't seem to be looking for an exit. He just stared at them, balling his fingers into tight fists at his side.

I turned the other way and spotted a path that would take me away from this mini-drama. Before leaving I took one last look to ensure I had gotten the details right. One more look confirmed it: Noël, current girlfriend of Walter (the director), former girlfriend of Arnold (the producer) and Stewart (the seething writer hiding behind the tree), had taken up with yet another person on the set.

Hollywood. Ya gotta love it.

Later that evening I pulled my car to a stop in front of the address for that night's last-minute gig. The large house sat among other impressively-large homes, nestled along a tree-lined parkway overlooking Lake of the Isles, one of Minneapolis' more lovely inner-city lakes.

The house, like its neighbors, could be called a mansion, but this was in the old-world definition, not like the McMansion behemoths that had sprung on lots big and small around the city. I couldn't imagine anyone in this neighborhood clipped coupons or clicked Groupons.

I let the car idle as I double-checked the address. Something seemed off and it took me a moment to realize that, for a house in the midst of an alleged party, there were hardly any cars parked nearby and only two lights burning in the mansion's windows. I had expected to see a steady stream of guests and the blur of valet parking staff as they ran up and down the street to park and retrieve each precious Lexus, Porsche and Hummer. Instead, all that was visible was a light over the front door, giving off enough wattage to confirm the address, and two other dim lights on the main floor. The rest of the house was dark.

I have learned, over the years, that a dark house is not always a true indicator you're at the wrong place. I am friendly with a married pair who constantly wage a war of lighting at their parties, with the husband insisting on bright illumination inside and out, while the wife opts for candles and mood lighting. Most times she is the victor and I have attended more than one party at their home where the lights were so dim, several guests hadn't bothered to come to the door, thinking they had arrived on the wrong night. Figuring that was the likely explanation for the low wattage at this house, I shut off the engine, grabbed my bag of tricks and made my way up the long walk to the massive front door.

The sound of the doorbell still echoed through the house when a squat and muscular man opened the door. He was the human equivalent of a fireplug with a neck nearly equal to the width of his shoulders and a tightly trimmed hedge of red hair covering his apparently flat head. He starred at me for a long, ominous moment.

"Hi," I stammered. "I'm the magician. I'm here. For the party. Tonight."

He gave me another long look, blinking slowly as if the words needed to be processed one at a time, then finally stood back and gestured for me to enter. I stepped into the foyer, a high-ceilinged room with a massive stairway straight ahead and several doors flanking both sides of the imposing hall. The house was dead quiet, with only the distant sound of voices and music barely audible, sounding like they were a long ways away.

Without a word he crossed the hallway and opened one of the large doors, turning and looking at me without any expression. Recognizing this was probably all the direction I was likely to be getting from him, I took a deep breath and stepped through the doorway into the dark room beyond.

The primary light in the room was supplied by the streetlights outside, which were filtering through a set of gauzy curtains that covered the large front windows. The streetlights offered a small but not really helpful dim glow, not nearly sufficient given the size of the room.

Once my eyes adjusted to the murky light, I saw there was in fact another light, if you want to call it that. It was a faint glow coming from a high-backed chair across the room. This also seemed to be the source of the voices and music, which were faint but getting louder as I approached the chair.

Looking around, I realized the chair seemed to be the only piece of furniture in the room. I suddenly realized why the entrance hall had seemed so large—it too had been devoid of furniture. I continued my trek across the large room, the hairs on my neck indicating I was as nervous as I thought I was.

Rounding the chair, I discovered the source of the light was an iPad, in the lap of a mere wisp of a man. He was as pale as a ghost, with skin pulled so tight over his slim frame it looked nearly translucent. His small frame was dwarfed in the large chair, and in the subdued light it was hard to tell where he ended and the chair began.

His thin hair was nearly as white as his skin and barely covered his small head. Ear buds hung precariously from his tiny ears as he smiled and nodded along with the images on the iPad. I couldn't identify the exact movie he was watching, but it was in black and white and one of the actresses on-screen looked to be Myrna Loy. Perhaps this seriously thin man was enjoying one of the *Thin Man* movies? Before I could consider this further, he looked up at me, his small dark eyes revealing a strength and energy the rest of his body could only aspire to.

"Ah," he rasped, his voice a throaty growl, gesturing to a chair across from him, bringing to two the number of pieces of furniture in the room. Three if you included the coffee table. "Mandrake has arrived. Welcome, sir, welcome. I trust Harpo made you feel sufficiently at home?"

"Um, sure," I said, moving as directed to the chair. "Harpo, yes, he did."

He touched the iPad screen and the soundtrack abruptly ceased, then set the tablet on the coffee table that sat between us. He watched me closely as I settled into the chair and placed my bag on the floor next to me. The glow from the iPad threw odd shadows on his already odd face.

"I'm here for the, um...party," I said, looking around the large room to see if perhaps a party had materialized in the last five seconds. "Was it tonight you wanted me or have I been misinformed?"

"I came to Casablanca for the waters," he said with a sudden and surprising burst of energy, a smile forming on his thin lips, revealing pointed and yellowing teeth beneath. His voice shifted, as if he were doing both sides of a conversation. "The waters? What waters? We're in the desert."

It took me a moment to recognize the quote. "I was misinformed," I repeated, this time adding a poor Humphrey Bogart lisp to my reading. "*Casablanca.* A classic."

"Ah, a movie fan. Excellent," he said, his smile growing into a large and grotesque grin. "I'm a fan of movies and movie fans. And magicians."

"Guilty as charged," I said. "On both counts." He stared at me for a long moment. I looked around the large, empty room, and then back in his direction, unnerved to see his gaze continued to be focused on me. "So, where's the party?"

"Excuse the, um, misdirection," he said, still grinning. "There is no party to speak of. I wanted to talk with you and thought paying for your time might be the most expeditious method of achieving that goal."

"Talk to me?" I parroted. "About what?"

"About whom," he corrected. "About our mutual, friend, the late Mr. Lasalle."

It took me a moment to make the connection in my mind. "Well, he wasn't really a friend," I began, but he waved a bony finger in my direction and I shut up. At that moment, it felt like the right thing to do.

"My reasoning is simple: I thought it prudent to speak to the person the police turned to so quickly after his untimely demise." He put a spin on the word "untimely" which produced an actual chill up and down my spine. "My understanding is you were the first person they approached."

"I'm sorry," I said, making my voice sound as polite as possible, "but who are you, actually?"

He smiled that spooky, toothy grin again. "For the purposes of this conversation, let's say I'm Mr. Lime, Mr. Harry Lime." He leaned forward, clearly testing me. My mind spun, trying to make the connection he seemed so sure I would get.

"Harry Lime," I finally blurted out. "Orson Welles. *The Third Man.*"

"Exactly," he said. "Harry Lime. Cuckoo clocks." The words rolled off his tongue in a manner just this side of obscene.

Another chill shot up my spine. "Okay, Mr. Lime," I said, keeping my voice steady and positive, "I don't mean to disappoint, but I really didn't know Dylan."

"As it turns out," he said, leaning back into the chair, "neither did I. In fact, to such a degree I had begun to call him Francis."

The reference was lost on me, but I pushed on, feeling a strong urge to put as much distance as I could between myself and the late Dylan Lasalle.

"No, you don't understand," I continued. "I wasn't a friend of Dylan Lasalle."

"Of course," he said, nodding in agreement, "I understand. As it turns out, not many people were friends with Francis. I would count myself in that number. But, be that as it may, we had our dealings and now he's dead and there are loose ends to be tied up. What sort of questions did the police put to you, if I may ask?" He folded his long fingers together, placing them on his pointed chin while patiently waiting for my response.

For my part, I was having trouble remembering just what questions Homicide Detective Fred Hutton had put to me. "Nothing in particular," I finally said, feeling his dark eyes boring holes through me. "I'd seen him at a high school reunion the night he...the night he was killed. They wanted to know who he had talked to, how had he seemed, that sort of thing."

"I see," the old man finally said, his voice now just a tad above a whisper. "So, tell me, who did he talk to? How did he seem?" He paused for a moment and then gave what he probably thought was a reassuring smile. It wasn't.

"Mostly he talked to the women at the reunion. He seemed upbeat, he drank a lot, and then he and his wife went home. That was the last I saw of him."

"That was the last most people saw of him," he said.

"I suppose so," I agreed.

"So, you and Francis weren't close?"

I shook my head. "Not now. Not ever. I hardly had anything to do with him in high school. And certainly nothing since then." I considered my answers so far and then added, "He seemed like a guy who was best avoided."

"Yes," the old man said. "But sometimes those types of people can be very helpful. In a pinch." He gave me another long look. "I thank you for your time, Mandrake. See Harpo on your way out and he'll see to it you receive your fee."

The speed at which I stood up clearly indicated how quickly I wanted to leave.

"Oh, there's no charge, um, Mr. Lime," I said, picking up my bag. "No show, no charge."

His voice stopped me in my tracks. "Oh, I won't hear of it,

Mandrake." The tone was warm but the underlying feeling was anything but.

"You will find," he continued, "once you get to know me, that if I offer you money you would do best to take it. And, in the case of our friend Francis, if you take my money, without my permission, you would be best to return it."

"But I didn't do anything to earn it," I said, almost pleading.

"Fair enough. Do me a trick."

"What?"

"Do me a trick."

"Okay, sure," I said, starting to feel the first warning signs of flop sweat. "What would you like? Cards? Coins? Rope?"

He smiled up at me, his eyes becoming thin slits. "Surprise me."

I sensed that in reality Mr. Lime was not a fan of surprises, but for the moment I took him at his word. I racked my brain for something—anything—I could do that would send me on my way in one piece. Uncle Harry always taught me, when in a pinch, go with the tried and true material. I wanted something surefire, I wanted something that would make Mr. Lime happy and most of all I wanted something that was guaranteed to get me out of there quickly. I also needed something that would play in the dim glow provided by the iPad on the table.

"Okay," I said. "To make it fair, we'll use your deck of cards. The one there, on the table."

He looked down at the table, then looked back up at me. "Mandrake, I don't have a deck of cards," he said, clearly puzzled.

"Sure you do, it's an invisible deck. I spotted it the moment I came in." I gestured again at the table. He looked again, then turned back to me, the beginnings of a smile forming on his thin, pallid lips.

"Oh, yes," he said, nodding. "I see it now. It's invisible."

"Great," I said, trying to take the nervous waver out of my voice. "Why don't you take the cards out of their box and give them a quick shuffle?"

He smiled up at me and then ever so gently, he mimed picking up the box, taking out the deck and shuffling it. "Should I cut it as well?" he asked as he completed the shuffle.

"If you wish," I said.

He pretended to cut the deck and then skillfully mimed squaring the cards. He looked up, patiently awaiting my further directions.

"Okay, I'm going to look away," I said. "While I'm turned away, I want you to fan through the deck, pick out one card, memorize it, reverse it in the deck and then put the deck back in its box. Got it?"

"I think I understand," he said, clearly beginning to relish his role in the trick. I turned away and could hear him chuckling, his laugh becoming a slight wheeze. After a few moments he said, "All right. It is done."

I turned back and he gestured proudly at a spot on the table where he must have set the invisible deck once he had completed his assignment.

"You picked one card and reversed it in the deck?" I asked.

"I did," he said. "Just as instructed."

"Well, you work with an invisible deck better than most," I said, going into my standard patter. "For myself, I sometimes need a little help seeing it. For that, I use some magic whiffle dust." I reached into the front pocket on my sport coat and then mimed sprinkling magic dust over the spot on the table. I placed my hand over the spot and turned to Mr. Lime. "Let's see if the whiffle dust has done its magic."

I removed my hand, revealing a card box where none had been before. Mr. Lime gasped, which is the desired response for that moment in the trick. "Now, what was your card, sir?"

"Seven of Clubs," he said confidently.

I pulled the deck from the box and spread the cards out before him, face up, so he could see all the cards. Only one card was face down. I pulled that card out and handed it to him. He turned it over. It was the Seven of Clubs.

"Very impressive, Mandrake. Very impressive. I believe you have earned your fee. And my admiration, which, believe me, holds a much higher value."

He was still chuckling over the card as I headed out of the room. I only stopped long enough for the silent thug in the hall—the aptly nicknamed Harpo—to hand me an envelope containing my fee in cash. I then nearly ran down the long sidewalk to my car and drove away without regard to public safety or the posted speed limit.

It wasn't until the house was several miles behind me that I stopped to consider some of the movie-related nicknames the man had seemingly pulled out of the ether. Harry Lime, the charming but morally corrupt character from *The Third Man,* seemed an apt moniker for my spooky host. His assistant had none of the charm of Harpo Marx, but shared his penchant for silent communication. Calling me Mandrake the Magician wasn't particularly clever, but was certainly in the same general movie realm as the others.

The only name I couldn't successfully connect was his nickname for Dylan Lasalle. I was still thinking about the name Francis as I parked the car and headed up to my apartment, glad to have the evening's bizarre gig safely in the past.

CHAPTER 9

"Did you enjoy your sojourn into the depraved depths of real Hollywood filmmaking?" These were the first words out of Jake's mouth when I answered his early morning call. I had just finished getting dressed, my hair still wet from the shower and jutting out in all directions. I squinted and rubbed some water out of my eyes, trying to remember where I had put my shoes. It's a small apartment, but some days it's the equivalent of a black hole for footwear.

"Enjoy? I wouldn't go that far, but it was intriguing. That's quite the dysfunctional bouillabaisse you've got brewing out there." I starting listing off the key players, to make sure I had them all clear in my head. "You've got Donna and Arnold, the divorced producers who hate each other and share a hatred for the director. You've got Stewart, the writer who hates the director and the leading lady, Noël, who is making the rounds through the above-the-line folks like a bad cold. And you've got Walter, the director with the explosive tempter who hates the writer and the producers. And I'm assuming one or more of that group hates you, if not all of them. In short, you've got a lot of unhappy campers on that set."

"Any one of whom would benefit from my untimely death," Jake said. "And it grows larger every day. But the simple fact is, while they may all hate each other right now, if this movie is a hit, it will be nothing but a love fest as they laugh all the way to the bank."

"And you'll be laughing as well?"

"Depends," Jake said. "If I'm alive, I've got net points right off the back end. But between you and me, if I'm dead, my interest in making money diminishes considerably."

"So, you still joining me for First Thursday?"

There was a pause on the other end of the phone. "Eli, after what happened at the reunion, I'm not sure I can ever get on a stage again."

"Oh, come on. Do five minutes. As my Aunt Alice used to say, whatever doesn't kill you makes you stronger."

"I feel like I already have enough things trying to kill me."

"Well, let's have dinner on Thursday and you can decide then whether to sign up for a slot or not."

Another pregnant pause on the other end of the phone. "Okay," he finally said.

"You sure you don't need me on the set today?"

Jake laughed. "Not likely. Walter fired the Key Grip and Arnold fired the caterer, so I don't think much is going to get shot today, least of all me. How are you going to spend your day off?"

I was going to say therapy, but it came out as "Oh, I don't know, running some errands."

"Sounds like fun."

"You have no idea."

By the time I headed downstairs, Uncle Harry had not only opened the store, but by the sound of laughter I heard, was already entertaining an early-morning patron.

I couldn't have been more surprised to see the customer was none other than Clive Albans. The British journalist, looking like a scarecrow dressed for a sixties-themed costume party, was seated on a stool while Harry stood behind the counter demonstrating a trick for him. I was surprised to see it was a variation of the trick I had come up with for Jake and the kid, but using a completely different method.

"Given your love of scarves and handkerchiefs, I think this

trick will serve your purposes well," Harry was saying in his distinct salesman patter. "If I may borrow your pocket square."

Clive, with wide-eyed enthusiasm, carefully plucked his chartreuse silk from his breast pocket and handed it to Harry.

Harry took one end of the silk and, making a fist with his other hand, began to stuff the silk into his clenched fist. "The secret of this trick," he said to Clive as he continued to push the silk into his fist, "is not only the magician but also the audience must believe it's possible for the handkerchief to vanish. Do you believe?"

"Oh, yes, by all means, I believe. Goodness, yes." Clive was nearly panting with anticipation.

Harry gave the silk one more firm push into the fist with his thumb and then pulled his hand away, placing his closed fist just inches from Clive's face.

"Do you believe?"

"Mr. Marks, you have my word I am in fact a believer."

"And so it shall be." Harry opened his fist, slowly uncurling each finger, finally revealing an empty palm.

Clive whooped and clapped his hands together in delight. "Oh, that's marvelous," he chirped. "I covet it. I must possess it." He looked over and noticed me for the first time. "Oh, Eli, it is a delight. A delight. It will provide the shock and awe I do so crave."

"Perfect," I said, heading toward the register. "The first sale of the day."

"Nonsense," Harry said, waving a hand dismissively at me as he packed the gimmick for the trick carefully into its container. "For our friend Mr. Albans, this is gratis. I guarantee we'll make it back ten-fold based on his continued good will."

For a second I thought I might still be dreaming. The idea Harry was not only giving something away, but giving it to a non-magician and a journalist to boot, was almost too outrageous to believe. My mouth slightly agape, I watched as he put the boxed trick into a bag and handed it across the counter to Clive.

"With my compliments," Harry said.

"Sir, you are too kind by half," Clive said as he took the bag.

"You have made my day, nay, my week. I shall delight in your largess and sing your praises to all and sundry." Harry walked him to the door, nodding and smiling.

"Thank you kindly, Mr. Marks," Clive continued as Harry opened the door for him, "For this lovely illusion, as well as the ideas and insight you have provided." He held up his small reporter's notebook, placing it with care in his front breast pocket, giving it a pat once it slid snugly into place. "You've offered some true food for thought, and I assure you I will masticate it thoroughly as I continue to digest your wisdom."

"Happy to help," Harry said, smiling as he held the door open a tad wider.

Clive tipped his hat to me. "Eli, good to see you again." And with that, he nearly skipped out of the store. Harry swung the door shut behind him, giving it an extra push until he heard the satisfying snick of the latch.

"Good lord, what a tiresome putz," he sighed as he headed back across the store toward me.

"Really?" I said. "It looked to me like the two of you were getting along swimmingly."

"A magician is an actor playing the part of a magician," Harry said, quoting a favorite phrase from the famous French magician, Robert Houdin. "And never more so than around the tedious Mr. Albans."

"So, what information did you give him that got him so excited?" I asked as Harry passed me. He picked up my iPad off the counter.

"Oh, Buster, I just verified some generalities he had misconstrued," he said with a long sigh. "By the way, your iPad needs charging. I'm going to make some tea. Would you like some?"

Not waiting for my answer, he parted the red velvet curtain that separates the front of the store from the back and disappeared into our workroom.

I watched him withdraw and then started rummaging around

behind the counter to see where the charger cord for the iPad had gone, wondering why the battery had run down so quickly.

"An irrational fear is just as terrifying as a real fear. To your brain, they are one and the same."

"Yeah," I said. "I think I read that in a fortune cookie once."

Dr. Bakke produced his first sigh in our session, undoubtedly inspired by my glib response and also by the sad realization there would likely be many more sighs to come.

"I think you know what I mean."

"I do," I said. "Half of my brain knew the fear was irrational and the other half was too busy being scared to death."

"My recommendation had been to only go up two or three floors at most."

"Tell that to the reunion committee. They clearly had other ideas."

"Did the breathing exercises have any impact?"

"I'm not sure," I admitted. "To be honest, I'm not sure how much actual breathing I was doing."

"So, you made it up to the ballroom—forty floors in a glass elevator."

"Do we have to discuss this?" I asked, feeling a bit queasy and weak-kneed at the memory.

"Maybe I'm wrong, but isn't that the primary reason for your visits here, to talk about this?"

Now it was my turn to sigh. "Yes, I suppose you have a point."

"And then you were able to come down forty stories, also in a glass elevator."

"Coming down was easier."

Dr. Bakke looked up from his pad. "And why do you think that was? The addition of alcohol?"

"Could be," I agreed. "I also had a beautiful woman holding my hand and singing Christmas carols."

"Christmas carols?"

I nodded. "It helped to take my mind off things."

He cocked his head to one side. "That's interesting. Which do you think had the greater impact: the beautiful woman holding your hand...or the Christmas carol?"

"I'm not sure. As my Uncle Harry is fond of saying, it's probably a horse a piece." I could tell from his blank expression that Dr. Bakke didn't have a relative who peppered him with such folksy kernels of wisdom, so I added, "You know, six of one, half dozen of another."

Dr. Bakke nodded and made another note. "It would be interesting," he said almost to himself, "to run a controlled experiment and put you under those same conditions twice—once with just the beautiful woman and once with only the Christmas carol option." He glanced over at me and I think he could register from my expression that experiments were not currently on my bucket list.

He made a note. "Well, if it turns out immersion therapy doesn't work, there are several other options we can pursue with your therapy," he said. "I think you're a good candidate for EMDR. And I also think you'd be a good subject for hypnotism." He stopped. "Why are you smirking?"

"Hypnotism," I said. "I'm sorry. It's a thing in my family. A prejudice against hypnotism, I guess you'd call it."

"A bad experience?"

"Sort of," I said. "My uncle had a bad experience and if he found out I was involved in hypnotism in any way, he would, well I don't know what the technical term is, but he would have a cow."

Dr. Bakke consulted his notes. "This would be Uncle Harry, the performer?"

"Yes, he's a magician," I said.

"And he had a bad experience with hypnotism?"

"Actually, it was with a hypnotist. His name was Oracle the Hypnotist. He and Harry shared the bill on several tours through the Midwest. This was years and years ago."

Dr. Bakke sat back, waiting for me to continue.

"Anyway, Oracle had this assistant, this girl he worked with. A really pretty girl and Uncle Harry was a young guy and he was, I think the term he used was, he was *sweet* on her. They had met at a party one of the performers had thrown and Harry thought they really hit it off. So he asked Oracle about her and Oracle said, 'Oh, no, Harry, she doesn't like you. She told me so. She doesn't like magicians and she doesn't like you.'

"So Harry was sort of devastated by this, and Oracle said to him, 'Harry, if you want, I could hypnotize her so that she likes you.' Well, Harry wasn't a big believer in hypnotism, but she was a pretty girl, so he said, 'Sure, go ahead.'"

I could tell Dr. Bakke was caught up in the story. He'd set his pen down and was leaning forward. He nodded for me to continue.

"So the next day, Oracle tells Harry he hypnotized her. Harry summons all his courage and goes up to her and asks her out. Well, she's delighted. 'Oh, that would be wonderful,' she says, 'thank you, Harry, I've been waiting for you to ask me out.' On and on like that.

"Anyway, so they go out, have a great time, and they start dating. Then Harry finds out from one of the stagehands that the girl had asked Oracle to fix her up with Harry. Turns out, Oracle had made up the whole thing about her not liking Harry and hypnotizing her. It was all a prank. When Harry found that out, he was furious, but what could he do? I mean, in the end, he got the girl, but he was always irked Oracle had tricked him, and as a consequence, he's had issues with hypnotists ever since.

"And the best part of the story," I added, "is he ended up marrying the girl and they were together for over fifty years."

"Charming story," Dr. Bakke said, but before he could continue I cut in.

"And there's more," I said. "Harry made the mistake of telling her, my Aunt Alice, the whole thing—about his conversation with Oracle and how he was tricked by him and how annoyed he was. And Alice never let him forget it. Sometimes, if anyone ever snapped their fingers around her, she would sit up, suddenly startled, and say, 'Where am I? Who are you? I was just talking to

Oracle and now where am I?' It drove Harry wild."

I smiled at the memory of Aunt Alice's little act and realized I hadn't thought about that story since she had died. "Anyway," I said, "let's leave hypnotism as a last resort."

"Not a problem," Dr. Bakke said, and then I think he noticed the change in my expression. "What's wrong?"

I shrugged. "I don't know," I said as I tried to put the feelings into words. "I just suddenly got sad."

"Because of the story about your Aunt Alice?"

"No," I said, shaking my head. "Because I just realized that I won't share a memory like that with Megan—something we laugh about for fifty years. And part of me sort of thought we would."

We were quiet for a few moments, and then Dr. Bakke softly cleared his throat before speaking. "I know you believe your experience last fall—the murders, being a prime suspect, and the dangerous situations you were in—were stressful," he said slowly. "But I'm wondering if this separation with Megan, which she calls a 'break,' but that you're registering more as a breakup—might actually be a greater stressor."

I thought it over. "It may well be," I admitted. "And her showing up the other night and then disappearing again certainly isn't reducing that stress."

"No it's not. And I think stress—like that, as well as what you experienced last fall—is what's behind these attacks. So, if you don't mind, let's spend a few minutes talking about you and Megan."

"Okay," I began, and before I knew it, my hour was up.

CHAPTER 10

As I left my appointment with Dr. Bakke, I checked messages on my phone and was surprised (pleasantly, I'll admit) to discover I had a phone message from Trish.

"Hi, Eli. It's Trish, Trish Lasalle, you know, formerly Trish Henry. You know, from high school? Oh, this isn't going well, is it?" She sighed, sniffled and then continued. "Well, charging forward, I was just calling to say I'm sure you've heard about Dylan."

This was followed by a long pause and for a moment I thought the message had cut off, then I heard a deep intake of breath and Trish continued.

"Oh, dear, I'm such a mess. Anyway, Eli, I'm really a bit lost right now and was just wondering if you were free to talk? Coffee or something, I don't know. Maybe tonight? Anyway, I'm bad at this. Call me when you get this. Or something." Another long pause. "Thanks. Bye."

I listened to the message again and then dialed her number.

"Hello, this is Trish," she said in a surprisingly upbeat tone when the phone was answered.

"Hi, Trish. This is Eli, um, Eli Marks returning your call," I stumbled, only to be surprised to hear her talking right over me.

"—so at the sound of the tone, oh, you know how this works. Leave a message. Thanks." This was followed by a delighted laugh, which was then followed by a familiar beep.

The contrast between the weepy woman who had left me a

message and the upbeat, vivacious woman who had recorded the greeting was not lost on me. The message I ultimately left was not emotional as the one she had left me, nor was it particularly one of my better efforts. I hemmed for a while, then hawed for a bit, finally combining the two into a barely coherent response. The gist of the message was I was happy to hear from her, was sorry to hear about Dylan, and yes, I would love to get together and chat but I was busy that evening. My rambling then took a sudden left turn as a thought occurred to me.

"Of course, now that I think of it, you may want to join us. Jake and I are going to an event, a performance I guess you'd call it, and then to drinks afterward. You could stop by for one or both, whatever works for you."

I continued jabbering in this fashion, surprised I hadn't been cut off by a message time limit. I remembered to give her the address and time for the show and then signed off in as upbeat a fashion as I could muster.

"So, anyway, I hope you're doing okay and if you want to stop by, it would be great to see you again." I took what was probably the first pause in my lengthy message, and then delivered a stellar closing line. "Um, that's all, I guess. Bye."

I hit the END button on my phone with such angst and self-loathing I would not have been surprised to find an actual indentation in the device when I pulled my hand anyway. Upon inspection, no such crevice was in evidence.

"I'm scared to death."

"Then don't go on. There is no requirement you go on."

"I mean, I'm shaking. Actually trembling. Look at my hand."

I dutifully looked at Jake's hand. In the dim light, I detected a faint if noticeable tremor.

"I haven't had stage fright like this since, since being in *The Music Man* back in junior high," he continued in a hushed, stuttering whisper. "I did Winthrop's first scene and entirely forgot to lisp. Everything I said came out in a British accent. I looked like an idiot."

I suppressed a smile, remembering that performance, where it appeared as if a cast member from *The Importance of Being Earnest* had wandered into Gary, Indiana to sing excitedly about The Wells Fargo Wagon in a clipped, crisp British dialect.

We were seated in the back row of The Parkway Theater, the movie house next door to our magic shop. I had spent a good deal of my youth sitting in the dark in this theater, consuming a healthy mix of classic films as well as more recent box office successes. Whatever raw movie trivia expertise I possessed could be traced to my time in this cavernous dark room.

While it still did an active business as a traditional movie house, The Parkway had incorporated a live element into its repertoire, showcasing stand-up and sketch comedy on its stage on a semi-regular basis. When that had proved successful, the ownership then instituted the First Thursday series several years back, which embraced what some might call the vaudeville arts. On the first Thursday of every month, performers were invited to sign up for a time slot to hone or sharpen their variety skills. The stage saw a wide range of participants, from burlesque to crooners to shadow puppets. And, of course, magicians.

In fact, for the last several months, Uncle Harry's pals in the Minneapolis Mystics had virtually taken over the First Thursday line-up, which offered them a great opportunity to dust off their acts for a new generation of appreciative audience members.

Currently on-stage were ventriloquist Gene Westlake and his acerbic puppet, Kenny. Dressed as an ersatz cowboy, Kenny was a surprisingly mean-spirited character, the exact opposite of his master, who couldn't have been a sweeter man. Gene had been grudgingly admitted to the Minneapolis Mystics forty years before, over the objections of some members who had bitterly complained, "If we let the ventriloquists in, what's next? Jugglers?"

Over the years, Gene had always been a source of support and encouragement to me in my career, while Kenny offered a seemingly endless tirade of insults that hit closer to home than I cared for. He was particularly hard on me when I was starting out and some of his comments about my act still carried a bit of a sting. It was that classic conundrum of liking one member of a couple and merely tolerating the other half.

Gene and Kenny finished up, as they always did, with a singing musical duet, demonstrating Gene's amazing skill. He appeared to harmonize with the puppet and he didn't use the tricks other, lesser ventriloquists employed, such as resorting to playing a pre-recorded track.

The secret, as he had explained to me years before, was he had mastered the art of Tuvan throat singing, traveling all the way to Siberia to take lessons from a Tuvan monk. That style of singing allowed one person to sing and sound like two people, which was perfect for Gene's act, although he went further than many people might have gone to learn the skill.

Gene and Kenny left the stage to a warm round of applause from the small but enthusiastic crowd and the emcee wasted no time introducing the next act: card maven Max Monarch. Max's theme song, *Shuffle Off to Buffalo*, played while he made his way slowly onto the stage. His careful navigation of the wobbly steps suggested a man who, if not used to falling, was aware of the implications if he did.

"I should just go take my name off the sign-up list," Jake whispered.

"That is certainly an option," I suggested.

"Why is this making me so nervous?" he hissed. "I mean, I've presented at the Emmys for God's sake."

"Wasn't it at the daytime Emmys, though?"

"The level of pressure is exactly the same."

Before I could respond, Max launched into his act.

Any indication Max might be beyond his prime vanished with his first series of card tricks, which involved summoning two audience members onto the stage and giving each a deck of cards to handle. Under Max's patient instruction, he produced some remarkable effects, culminating with selected cards appearing in each of the subject's various coat pockets. The demonstration, which maybe ran five minutes, so flummoxed Jake he spent most of it quietly moaning and shaking his head as he sunk lower and lower into his seat.

"How is he doing that?" he mumbled again and again. "I know how these things are done, I've studied this. How is he doing it?" He looked up at me accusingly. "You know, don't you?"

I hesitated, then nodded. He glared up at me. "And you're not going to tell me, are you?" I shook my head, giving him my best Mona Lisa smirk.

"Bastard," he grumbled. "Well, there's no way I'm going to try to follow that. I'm taking my name off the list."

He stood up to head over to the emcee, who was in charge of assigning performance slots from people who had signed up on the list. I watched him snake his way down the row, craning my neck around to see if Trish had shown up and taken a seat in the back. I didn't spot her in the small crowd. Jake made his way down the aisle to the emcee's position, just to the left of the stage. However, while making this short journey, Jake had clearly stopped listening to Max and was unaware he had just asked for a volunteer.

"Yes, you there. Thank you. Let's give the young fellow a round of applause," Max boomed from the stage.

Jake looked around, and his face registered what he'd gotten himself into. He turned left, then right, perhaps scoping out the exits, but it was clear he was trapped. He shuffled down the aisle, his head down and took the steps to the stage like a condemned man climbing the scaffold.

Max welcomed Jake to the stage, clearly not recognizing him as a semi-famous TV actor. He ushered him to one of the two chairs in the performance area and took the other seat, with just a small wooden table between them. He began to shuffle the cards and launched into the patter for one of his signature effects.

"Dead Man's Hand," he boomed, cascading the cards from one hand to the other. "That's what they called the cards that lay on the table after Wild Bill Hickok had been shot in the back. Eights and Aces, all black. The dead man's hand."

He handed the cards to Jake. "Give these a good shuffle, will you?" Jake obliged, while Max stood and addressed the audience, filling them in on the legend of the Dead Man's Hand. I had probably heard this routine a hundred times, but I never tired of his recitation as he outlined the final minutes of Will Bill Hickok at the poker table at Nuttal & Mann's saloon in Deadwood, South Dakota. How Bill always sat with his back to the wall, but on this fateful day Charlie Rich refused to change places with him—twice!—forcing Bill to sit with his back to the door. How the cards were dealt and how Bill was stone cold dead before he was able to place his first bet.

It was a great story and Max really knew how to tell it. Everyone in the room was hanging on his every word, with the exception of Jake, who was shuffling and re-shuffling the cards with a fierce intensity.

Max sat and watched Jake for a moment, clearly amused at the level of determination Jake was putting into his task. Jake finally looked up, realizing the room had gone quiet.

"Would you say the cards are sufficiently shuffled?" Max asked with wry understatement.

Jake nodded and held the pack out to him. Max shook his head and gestured he should place them on the table. "Mind if I cut the cards?" he asked quietly.

Jake looked from the cards to Max and back to the cards. He shook his head.

Max lifted the top half of the deck, placed it next to the first pile, and then completed the cut. "To keep this fair," he said to Jake and to the audience, "why don't you go ahead and deal. A simple poker hand. Four players. Five cards each."

Jake did as instructed, quickly dealing the cards and then setting the pack down on the table.

"In life," Max said as much to the audience as to Jake, "we must play the hand that is dealt us. That's true today just as it was the day Wild Bill Hickok was dealt his legendary hand. He had turned over four cards when the fateful shot was fired. Eights and aces, all black." He looked at Jake. "Tonight, one of us will be Wild Bill. And one of us will suffer his fate, with a gunshot wound to the back of the head."

Even from my seat in the rear of the theater I could see Jake gulp from Max's words. He sat up straighter in his chair.

"Let's see who will be our victim tonight." Max flipped over the cards in his hand. "A full house, nines and kings. Not a bad hand." He turned to the hand Jake had dealt to the right and flipped those cards over. "Nothing much, two pair. So far I have the winning hand." He smiled at Jake, who glanced from his hand, still face down on the table, to the other unexposed hand. Max flipped those cards over.

"Not much to speak of, some hearts, maybe the beginning of an inside straight. This player would probably be wise to fold." He set those cards aside and took a long look at Jake. "And now we come to you, my young friend. Would you be so kind as to turn your cards over, one at a time, and announce them as you do?"

Jake's hand hovered over the cards for a moment, and then he flipped the first one over. "Eight of Clubs," he said, with a distinct crack in his voice.

"Eight of Clubs," Max repeated. Jake turned over the next card.

"Eight of Spades," he said, clearly trying to put some power back into his voice and falling short.

"Eight of Spades," Max said in a loud, stage whisper.

Jake took a breath and turned over the next card. "Ace of Spades," he said in a flat voice.

"Ace of Spades," Max repeated quietly.

Jake touched one of the two remaining cards, then moved to the other, and then back to the first. He turned it over, a look of resignation appearing across his face. "Ace of Clubs," he said finally.

"Ace of Clubs. Eights and Aces, all black. The Dead Man's

Hand." Max took a dramatic pause, and then continued. "Poor Wild
Bill Hickok never did know what the next card was, for as he turned
it over..." He gestured to Jake to turn the card.

Jake picked up the card. Just as he did, a gunshot rang out.
And then someone screamed.

"I nearly wet myself from fear."

"What a coincidence. I nearly wet myself from laughing."

"You knew that was going to happen, didn't you?" Jake glared
at me. "You knew that routine ended with a gunshot."

"Well, yes. However, to be fair, I didn't know that's the routine
he was going to do when he dragged you onstage," I said, taking a
sip of my beer. "And in the interest of full disclosure, it wasn't really
a gunshot. Just a cap gun he had wired to your chair."

"I must have jumped four feet."

I couldn't help laughing. "At least. And you screamed. Like a
girl. It was magnificent."

Like the rest of the Minneapolis Mystics and many members of
the audience, we had retired to Adrian's bar for a post-show drink
and bull session. At another table, Harry and the rest of the Mystics
were trading barbs with each other and receiving compliments
from other patrons. At the moment, Uncle Harry was receiving
lavish praise for his routine with a spool of thread, a variation on
the classic Gypsy Thread routine he had made completely his own.
The woman spewing the praise was tipsy and kept leaning into
Harry in a fashion that he didn't seem to mind.

"The Gypsy Thread can be traced all the way back to Professor
Hoffman," he was saying to the very drunk lady. "I learned it from
Al Baker, but I have made modifications to suit my performance
style."

"You're cute," she said.

"Yes, well, that's a matter of public record," Harry replied with
a smile.

"I have a vague idea of how he pulled off the dealing for the

Dead Man's hand," Jake continued, "but that first trick with the two guys and the cards in their pockets. How in the hell did he do that?"

"Here's the thing you need to know about Max Monarch," I said. "He is literally one of the greatest card men. Ever. Harry told me that years ago, he and the other guys in the Mystics used to pull the same prank on Max every two or three weeks and every time it blew up in their faces."

"What did they do?" Jake asked with nervous curiosity.

"Oh, one of them would casually mention some card trick they had seen while out on the road. Some real knuckle buster that seemed completely impossible. They would describe the effect from the audience's point of view, confessing they had no idea how it had been done but that it was a killer effect. Max would nod along as they told the story, without making a comment. He wouldn't say a word, just sit there and nod. And then about two weeks later, he'd show up and perform the trick for them, flawlessly."

Jake shrugged. "What's the big deal? He reverse-engineered the trick. So what?"

I shook my head. "You don't get it. The trick never existed. Every time. They made it up out of whole cloth. They would conspire together to make up the most impossible effects they could think of—just mind-blowing stuff. Completely impossible. But they'd present it to Max like an existing effect, so he didn't know it was impossible. And then he'd go off and figure out how to do it. Every single time."

Jake gave a low whistle and stole a glance across the room. Max was holding court with Gene Westlake and some audience members. I couldn't hear clearly, but it sounded like he was complaining about how much of his day he spent sitting at red lights. The others were nodding in sympathy.

"So his opening trick," Jake said, look at me plaintively. "Not even a hint?"

"You want a hint?" I could tell it was killing him to nearly beg for a scrap of information.

"Yes, please."

I thought about it for a long moment. Finally, I said, "Two words."

He leaned forward.

I smiled at him. "Deck switch."

"He switched the deck?"

I shook my head. "Not one deck."

"Then what do you mean by deck switch?"

"Jake, in that trick, he switches the deck four times. Four separate decks are in play throughout the trick."

His jaw dropped comically, in a broad cartoon-like manner.

"I had no idea."

"That's what makes it a trick." I drained the last of my beer. "And here's a piece of advice Harry taught me. When you can't think of any possible way the trick could have been done..."

Jake was hanging on my every word. "Yes?"

"It probably involves a deck switch."

I got up to get another drink, gesturing to Jake to see if he was ready for a refill. He shook his head, lost in thought. I heard him mumble, "Deck switch, son of a bitch," as I headed up to the bar.

"Hi, Eli. Sorry I missed the show."

I looked up from my spot at the bar, surprised to see Trish standing next to me. Had I not being somewhat expecting to see her, I'm not sure I would have recognized her, at least not right away. She seemed much smaller than she had at the reunion, with no makeup and dark circles under her eyes.

"Oh, great, you made it," I said, just as the bartender handed me my beer. I looked to Trish. "Um, can I get you something?"

She sighed and considered this for a moment. "A glass of white wine, I guess," she finally said. I nodded at the bartender, who pulled up the nearest wine bottle, only to find it nearly empty. He held up his hand in a "wait a sec" gesture and headed down the bar.

"So," I said as we stood awkwardly at the bar. "How are you doing?"

She shrugged. "I'm not really sure," she said. "Still sort of numb, I guess."

"That would make sense."

An awkward pause. We looked at each other, and then looked away. The quiet, awkward moment got longer and finally we were saved by the return of the bartender, bearing a full glass of white wine. I added more money to the stack I had put down for the beer and handed Trish her glass.

"We're over here," I said, pointing toward a booth in the back.

"We?" she asked.

"Oh, just Jake. He was with me tonight at the show. He was supposed to go on, but got cold feet at the last second."

We made out way through the crowd toward the back of the room, but Jake was crawling out of the booth just as we arrived. He held his cell phone to his ear. "What does it say?" he barked into the phone. "Read it to me." He gave Trish a quick wave and then headed toward a quieter area of the bar, an intense look on his face and a hand over his ear as he strained to hear the voice on the other end of the phone.

Trish looked to me for some sort of explanation, but I just shrugged.

"Actors," I said, as I sat and gestured for her to take Jake's spot across from me. "They never miss a chance for a little drama."

She slid into the booth, took a sip of her wine and set the glass down. "So," she said. "You heard about Dylan?"

"Yes," I said. "I was shocked. Or surprised. Whatever the right word is. My ex-wife's husband, um, a friend on the police force stopped by and told me about it the next morning. The morning after the reunion. After it happened."

Trish nodded as if my ramblings were making actual sense.

"He just went out for a run," she said. "Sometimes he liked to do that, after we'd been out. There's a running path near our building. It runs alongside the train tracks. So he went out and I went to bed...and the next thing I know, the phone is ringing and it's the police. I had to go downtown. Identify the body..."

Her voice broke off. I reached across the table and patted her hand, not quite sure why that was considered a reassuring gesture but doing it nonetheless. She took a paper napkin from the dispenser and dabbed at her eyes. I got the sense she had been doing that a lot lately.

"That must have been difficult," I offered.

"Oh, Eli, you can't imagine. It was just so hard." She started crying for real now, her head down and shoulders shaking.

I was completely at a loss for what to do and was about to say something brilliant, along the lines of "there, there," when a voice to my left suddenly cut in.

"Hi, Eli, I thought that was you over here."

I looked up to see Megan standing by the table. She had come around the corner quickly and the expression on her face told me she hadn't noticed that I was sitting with someone. Particularly that I was sitting with a woman who was just this side of weeping uncontrollably.

"Oops, sorry to interrupt," she continued, starting to back away.

"Oh, that's okay," I said, quickly taking my hand from atop Trish's. "We were just, I don't know, talking."

Trish wiped her eyes again and composed herself, sitting up straight.

"I'm fine," she said to no one in particular.

Megan stood there awkwardly and I was feeling the same, not sure how to proceed. I thought maybe introductions might be the right way to go.

"Oh, this is Trish. Megan. Megan. Trish." My hands fluttered back and forth, gesturing to each person as I named them, looking like I was conducting an orchestra made up of fidgeting jackrabbits. The women nodded at each other and I quickly tried to fill the short silence that, at the moment, felt enormous to me.

"I went to high school with Trish," I said by way of explanation. I turned to Trish. "Megan owns the shop on the corner. Actually, the whole block, she owns the whole block. Which, as it turns out, makes her my landlady." I almost added a short laugh, then stifled it at the last second.

"I'll let you guys get back to...whatever," Megan said, continuing to back away. "I was just here with some girlfriends, celebrating, and I saw you over here and thought I'd stop by and say hi or something."

"Thanks," I stammered. "Thanks for that." She started to turn away, but I kept talking, so she turned back. "So, what are you celebrating?"

She looked from me to Trish and back to me. "My divorce," she said. "My divorce became final today."

"Well," I said. "Good for you. Congratulations. Good for you," I repeated for no apparent reason.

"Thanks." She turned away, then turned back. "Nice to meet you," she said to Trish. She nodded at me, almost smashed into someone walking by who was loaded down with drinks, sidestepped them and was gone.

I watched her go, then turned back to Trish. "She's getting divorced," I finally said.

"Yes, she mentioned that." She pulled another napkin out of the dispenser and dabbed at her eyes. "I hate crying," she said. I nodded impotently. "Then, when I stop crying, I feel guilty that I'm not crying. Basically, I'm a mess."

"I think that's understandable," I suggested.

I suppose you're right. Anyway, how are you doing?" she asked.

"Me? Um, fine, I guess. Aren't I?" I wasn't sure where her question had come from or where it was heading.

"After that elevator ride the other night, I don't know, you looked pretty pale. I know acrophobia can be pretty intense. My younger brother has claustrophobia."

"Yeah, you mentioned that."

She seemed surprised to hear this. "I did?"

"Yes, while we were in the elevator. Before the Christmas Carols commenced."

She smiled. "Did that help?"

"Yes, quite a bit. Thank you."

"I'm glad," she said softly. She dabbed at her eyes again and sighed. "Oh, it's been such a horrible week," she said. "The police have talked to me several times. About Dylan. And some of the people he associated with."

"So they think it might be more than a mugging?" I asked, remembering how Homicide Detective Fred Hutton had danced around that idea.

"They're not sure. Or, they're not telling me," she said with a laugh. "Probably trying to protect me. As if I didn't know Dylan hung around with some bad people. Some bad, bad people." She shuddered.

"I know," I said. "I think I met one of them the other night."

She looked up, confused. "What do you mean?"

"I was summoned to a house on Lake of the Isles, under the pretext of doing some walk-around magic at a party. But there was no party. Just this really creepy old guy."

"Who was he?"

"He called himself Mr. Lime, but I doubt that was his real name."

"What did he want? Did he know Dylan?"

"He said he did. He wanted to know what the police had asked me about Dylan. And he said something about Dylan taking some money from him."

She seemed to be taking this all in very slowly. "Dylan owed him money? That wouldn't surprise me. Oh, I wish I knew what this was all about." She picked up her napkin and dabbed at her eyes again.

She looked so sad and alone and helpless and I felt completely powerless, not sure what to say or do. I considered suggesting I could use my contacts in the DA's office to see if the police knew more than what they were telling her, but at that moment Jake returned to the booth, jamming his phone fiercely into his pocket. I slid over to make room for him, but he wasn't interested in sitting.

His face was bright red and a vein in his neck was pulsating.

"Jake, who was on the phone? What's the matter?"

"I'm a dead man, that's what's the matter."

"What?"

"I'm a dead man," he repeated, nearly shouting. "A dead man." He turned and pointed a shaking finger across the room at Uncle Harry. "And he's the man who killed me!"

For just a moment the bar got very quiet. And then all hell broke loose.

CHAPTER 11

Having breakfast with Harry has become a tradition ever since I moved back in after my divorce. Generally I'd wander downstairs to his apartment once I heard the familiar sounds of his early morning rituals coming from the rooms below mine. We'd share some coffee and the morning paper, although more and more I read it off my iPad while he's still a holdout for a traditional newspaper made out of actual paper. There generally wasn't much conversation, just the occasional comment about a newsworthy item or the short discussion of a plan for the day that lay before us.

On this particular morning, things were quieter than usual as we sipped our coffee and took bites from our respective toast slices. After the dust-up in the bar the night before, I thought it prudent to let Harry talk when he was ready to talk, and not to push the issue unnecessarily.

It had taken a while for me to understand what Jake was so upset about, as he was one of those people who becomes increasingly incoherent the angrier he gets, repeating the same key words over and over. In his case, the words were "dead man," "Harry's fault," and "dead man." While the words were certainly emphatic, they were not particularly insightful or helpful.

He finally calmed down, at least to a degree, and I got the story out of him. Apparently his PR person had called, saying his name had just popped up in a Google Alert from an online article about Terry Alexander. The article purported to prove that Terry's death had not been murder, but was in fact accidental. And, not only accidental, but that it was caused by the magician's own incompetence. There was no murder plot, no suspects, just a poor, pathetic performer who screwed up and died because of it.

The article, the PR person had told him, was written by one Clive Albans. And his primary source for the piece? A magician named Harry Marks.

Later, after things had calmed down a bit and Jake had headed back to his hotel, I went up to my apartment and searched online for the article. Jake's PR person had not been kidding. Clive's story spelled out in specific detail how The Bullet Catch was supposed to be performed. Then Clive showed where the mistakes had been made and why, with accompanying still frames from the video of Terry Alexander performing the trick for the last time.

While Clive made it sound like he was the one who had recognized the mistakes Terry had made, it was pretty clear all of his information on The Bullet Catch—and Terry's missteps—had come from Harry. And only Harry. No other magician was quoted in the article.

Two videos were embedded in the piece. The first was the shaky footage of Terry performing The Bullet Catch for the last time, with the new addition of voice-over commentary from Clive, along with freeze frames focusing on the key mistakes Terry had made.

Using his standard hyperbolic phraseology, Clive whispered his way through the narration, pointing out "Terry's first serious error" here and "his final miscalculation" there. A dramatic musical underscore had been added to the video, as had a new gun shot sound effect, replacing the faint "pop" from the original video.

The second embedded video was one I had not seen before. It appeared to be from an interview with Terry on a low-end cable access talk show, clearly recorded sometime after he had been exposed as The Cloaked Conjurer but before his self-imposed exile in Ecuador. The footage was grainy and the sound quality poor, but the video was mesmerizing. Although they cut to the inept host occasionally, most of the interview consisted of a too-tight close-up of Terry, looking drawn and tired. The video began mid-interview and it appeared Terry had been asked if he regretted his work as The Cloaked Conjurer.

"Every day," he said in a soft voice, just above a whisper. "I regret it every day. I made a mistake, I understand that. But does that one mistake need to erase the twenty-year career that came before it? I know I can put this behind me. But at what point will the rest of the world—the rest of the magicians of the world—put it behind them? How long do I have to pay penitence? At what point does the brotherhood opens their arms and say, 'All is forgiven? You are once again one of us.'"

He sniffled a bit and it was clear from the way his voice cracked there was genuine emotion behind his words. The video cut to the host, who seemed surprised at the level of pain apparent in Terry's words.

"So, where do you go from here?" the host finally stammered.

"Where can I go?" Terry said, as much to himself as to the host. "There is no place for me. I am adrift."

There was a long pause, an awkward cut back to the host, another shot of Terry staring into space, and then the video ended, frozen on the image of Terry Alexander, looking lost and alone.

"So, Buster, are you going to ask me about the damned article or are we just going to sit here all morning pretending nothing happened? Because if that's your plan, I'd rather go back to bed."

Harry's voice, surprising me from across the table, snapped me back to reality and breakfast. I set down the iPad I hadn't really been looking at.

"I figured you'd talk about it when you wanted to talk about it," I said. "Do you want to talk about it?"

"No, but I'd rather do that than sit here in silence."

"We usually don't talk during breakfast. How is today any different?"

"Today's silence is more...intentional. And annoying," he said, setting down the paper and picking up his coffee cup. "You want more coffee?" he asked as he crossed the small kitchen to the coffee maker.

"No thanks, I'm good."

Harry refilled his cup and then added a generous amount of chocolate milk to the brew, stirring it slowly as he made his way back to the table.

"The floor is open for questions," he said as he sat back down. He took a sip of his coffee—which at this point was basically coffee-flavored chocolate milk—then set the cup back in the saucer. He folded his hands and looked at me, the picture of innocence.

"All right," I said, leaning back and prioritizing my questions, which were legion. "Obviously my friend Jake is upset."

"Your friend Jake made that abundantly clear last night, loudly and at great length. He turned a pleasant evening into the verbal equivalent of a bar brawl."

"Well, can you blame him? You revealed the method behind The Bullet Catch in a national publication," I began.

Harry cut me off. "I revealed *one* method," he said sharply. "Only one method, and certainly not the best or cleverest version of that trick."

"This is sounding very much like the defense The Cloaked Conjurer raised about twenty-five years ago. And we know how well that was received."

"Be that as it may, I see nothing wrong in revealing the method behind that trick. It's an insanely risky trick. No one should do The Bullet Catch."

"Yes, I can agree with that, but you just told everyone and his brother how to do it."

"Yes, and now everyone knows how it's done, there will be precious little demand to see it performed."

I couldn't quite see my way around his byzantine logic. "Okay, let's skip over that part. Why did you tell all of this to, of all people, Clive Albans? You hate Clive Albans."

"Nonsense. I don't hate anyone. Hate is a very strong word."

"That may well be, but it's the word you always use in reference to Clive Albans. To quote you, for example: 'I hate Clive Albans.' Or, 'That pest Clive Albans came in the store while you were out. God, how I hate him.'"

Harry scowled. "Those may have been my words, but you're adding a tone I never used."

I sat back and rubbed my eyes. When I opened them, he was still staring at me like a kid forced to appear in front of the principal for a crime he didn't commit.

"Is that all?" he asked. "Or can I go down and open the store?"

"The store doesn't open for another half hour," I said, "and we're unlikely to see any customers for two hours after that."

"I have things I can be doing."

"Such as?"

He stared back at me, defiant. "Work-related things," he finally said. "Things having to do with work."

"Okay, let me ask you this." I leaned forward and tried to take any tone of accusation out of my voice. "Why did you tell Clive Albans how The Bullet Catch was done?"

"Because he asked."

"In the past you wouldn't tell him how the simplest trick in our shop worked."

"Perhaps he phrased his question in a nicer manner than some people I could name."

I took a deep breath and looked him straight in the eyes. "When you told him how The Bullet Catch was performed," I said, "did you know he was asking because he's doing a story on the movie they're making about Terry Alexander? The one Jake North is starring in? And did you realize if you exposed the method behind the trick, and the mistakes Terry made in performing it, you would destroy the mystery that is the basis of that film? That the film would no longer be a mystery about who killed Terry Alexander, but instead become a movie about an inept magician who died by doing a trick wrong?"

Harry stared back at me for a long moment. "Yes, well, I'm sure there's a market for that film as well."

I sat back, shaking my head. As Aunt Alice had said hundreds of times before, some days there was just no talking to him.

Jake answered his cell phone on the third ring with a whispered "Hello?"

"Jake, it's me, Eli."

"Oh, hi Eli," he said, still whispering.

"I just called to see how you're doing. After last night."

"I can't really talk. I'm sort of in a meeting. With the producers. The director. A handful of lawyers. A bunch of people."

"How's the mood?"

"Like Jonestown with bagels."

"Have they come up with a plan?"

"We're in triage mode." His voice, already a whisper, got quieter. "Some of the European pre-sale money pulled out, saying they invested in a mystery, not a remake of *Dumb and Dumber*."

"So Harry's article..."

"The producers are furious. He took the mystery right out of the mystery. We've got nothing. Walter, the director, has this lame idea of turning it into a goth musical, but that's not going to go anywhere."

"So what do you think they're going to do?" There was a long pause on the other end of the phone. "Jake, are you still there?"

"Yeah, I'm here," he finally said. "To be honest, I think they think there's only one thing that will keep this movie from becoming a colossal flop."

"What's that?"

"Something really newsworthy is going to have to happen. Something bigger than Harry's article."

"Like what?"

"Like the star actually dying."

I heard a click and then nothing. He had hung up.

Chapter 12

I visit my ex-wife about as often as I visit my dentist, and with the same level of enthusiasm. My dentist, who I've gone to my entire life, still hands out candy to anyone who has a perfect checkup. As the years have gone by, he's needed to hand out less and less candy to more and more patients. Not a bad racket, really.

My ex-wife also offers sweets, in the form of sour, hard candies that sit in a crystal bowl on the edge of her desk. In all the years I've visited her office, the number and relative positions of the candies has never changed. I imagine by this point they have all fused together into one tempting piece of sour, hard candy.

Which is also an apt, if overly harsh, description of my ex-wife.

Deirdre was not historically a happy recipient of the unannounced drop-in, but I figured catching her unaware might provide the greatest unedited flow of information. Warn her I was coming and she would want to know why and then clam up and make the trip unproductive. Show up without an appointment and she might start talking before she realized what she was doing.

After Trish had left the bar the night before—amid Jake's meltdown—I felt so bad about how she was feeling and the situation Dylan's sudden death had thrown her into. She seemed so helpless and lost, nothing like the vibrant woman who had dazzled me in high school and so brightened the reunion. Plus, after my forced meeting with Mr. Lime, I was more than a little curious about what the police knew, what they thought they knew, and where they might be headed with the investigation.

Since relations with Uncle Harry were strained from breakfast, I figured this morning was as good a time as any to dive in and start digging.

"Knock-knock," I said jovially as I knocked on the wooden doorframe to Deirdre's office.

"Busy. Go away," she replied without looking up from her desk.

"And thus did history's first attempt at the knock-knock joke end in abject failure," I said, ignoring her gruff anti-welcome and taking a seat in one of the two chairs in front of her paper-strewn desk.

"Seriously, Eli, take a hike. I've got a ton of depositions to go through and no time for your nonsense." She pulled back a wisp of blonde hair that had taken it on the lam from her well-coiffed hairstyle, and gave me a hard, unwelcoming look. It was like coming home.

"I'm fine, thanks, and how are you?" I asked, knowing I was pushing it but enjoying it too much to stop.

"What's it going to take for you to go away and go away right now?"

"Just one or two quick questions, pure and simple."

"Your questions are never pure and rarely simple."

"If Oscar Wilde had you as an attorney, he would never have gone to prison."

"If Oscar Wilde had you as a husband, he would have welcomed prison."

I gave her my biggest, broadest smile. "The magic never dies, does it?"

"Eli, what do you want?"

"Okay, all playful banter aside, your husband paid me a visit earlier this week," I began, but she quickly cut me off.

"My husband paid a visit to a lot of people this week. What's it to you?"

"I'm just wondering who else he talked to. Besides me."

She capped her pen and set it on the desk. "Why?"

"I'm curious."

"Yeah, you and a bunch of dead cats."

"I'm curious who else he talked to. What he found out."

"Why aren't you talking to him?"

"He doesn't like me."

"Nonsense. He adores you. In his own way." She gave me a long look. "Why are you curious?" I didn't answer and I made the mistake of looking down at my feet, which led to a longer, more intense look from her. "You're not canoodling with the widow, are you?"

"Hardly," I said. "And stay out of Harry's lexicon."

"Aren't you still going out with that psychic? What was her name?"

"Megan."

"Megan. Seemed like a nice girl. Sort of kooky, but you always had a thing for kooky."

"Present company excepted. Anyway, we're on a bit of a break."

"You broke up? I'm sorry to hear that." She looked genuinely concerned, which threw me.

"Being on a break is not the same as breaking up," I said, sounding far more defensive than I had intended. "We're just taking some time off. To reassess. And regroup."

"Well, I hope it works out, Eli," she said. "I really do."

"Well, thank you," I said, feeling any power I might have had in the conversation draining away quickly. I thought a quick subject detour might get me back on track. "Anyway, back when we were married," I said, "I occasionally helped you out on a case or two. I thought I could do the same here."

She looked ready to dispute this, but we both knew she couldn't. With my magician's knack for puzzles, I had actually been very helpful a couple of times, which may have had an impact on the speed with which she had risen in the department.

"Helped out?" she said, clearly trying to downplay my role in her success.

"Sure," I said. "Like in The Case of the Poisoned Pimento."

"You are the only person in the world who calls it that," she said flatly.

"But you have to admit, I did help," I countered.

"Yes, Eli, you did help," she admitted.

In that local murder case, a victim's last words had been recalled as "I'll live, I'll live," but I was the one who pointed out that he could have actually been saying "Olive." When a jar of poisoned green olives with the killer's fingerprints were found in the victim's refrigerator, the case was quickly closed.

"Anyway, I was wondering who else your husband spoke with about Dylan Lasalle's death."

She took the cap off her pen again. "Eli, I can't give you that information. He talked to some of the victim's work associates. He talked to your buddy Howard Washburn from the reunion. He did his job."

I cocked my head to one side. "He talked to Howard Washburn from the reunion?"

"Of course, after the scuffle he'd had with Lasalle, it seemed prudent."

"Of course," I said. "That does seem prudent. To talk to Howard Washburn. I would have done the same thing."

"But you know as well as I do the DA's office does not comment on open cases, not even to our ex-husbands. Especially to our ex-husbands."

"I know," I said, trying my best to sound contrite. "But I thought it was worth a shot. I'll let you get back to work." I got up and headed toward the door.

"And Eli?"

I stopped in the doorway and turned back to her. "Yes?"

"Spend less time canoodling with the widow and more time reassessing and regrouping with that Megan, okay?"

"You got it."

She gave me a quick 'thumbs up' and I returned it and doubled it, using both hands and both thumbs. And then I hustled out of her office, racking my brain, trying to figure out who in the world my pal Howard Washburn was and how to get in touch with him.

After digging out my old school yearbooks, I discovered that, amazingly, I had gone to school with Howard Washburn for twelve out of twelve years. Neither one of us ever really rose to the top of the pecking order and I don't remember our paths ever crossing. I looked long and hard at his graduation photo and could say with a clear conscience his face didn't ring a bell.

Once I knew who he was, I then turned to the more pressing question of where he was. I once again turned to the Internet, this time opening my rarely-used Facebook account. After much clicking and searching and scrolling, I was able to track him down. Howard Washburn's smiling face beamed back at me from his Facebook page. He still looked like his graduation photo, only now with the addition of several pounds and a few gray hairs. The "About" section on his page said he was the owner of Washburn International Shipping and Delivery, and moments later I had him on the phone.

"Eli Marks," he said with enthusiasm once I introduced myself. "Wow. That's a blast from the past. Fifteen years, huh? Where did it go?"

"Where did it go indeed," I agreed.

"I'm surprised I didn't see you at the reunion," he said, diving into the conversation like we were old pals who hadn't spoken in a week.

"Oh, I was there," I said. "We must have missed each other."

"Looks like it. My wife and I spent most of the night out on that Observation Deck. Hell of a view, don't you think?"

"That's what they tell me," I said. "I'm sorry I missed you."

"Me too, buddy. Me too. What are you up to these days?"

I was really being thrown off by his chummy attitude. I couldn't pick the guy out of a line-up and he was acting like we had been frat brothers.

"Oh, still doing the magician thing," I said.

"Really, you're still at it? Well, good for you. I remember taking some classes with you at that magic store back in like fourth grade or something—wasn't it owned by your uncle or something?"

"That's right. He's still at it." This was starting to drive me crazy. He's saying he took some magic classes with me and I don't have a single memory of the guy.

"Good for him, good for him," he said. "So what can I do for you, Eli?" his tone becoming a tad more businesslike.

"Well, Howard, I was calling because the police came and talked to me about Dylan Lasalle the other day."

"Yeah, they talked to me, too," he said. "Helluva deal, huh?"

"Yeah, it was very surprising," I said.

"Oh, not all that surprising," he continued. "The way that guy operated, something bad was bound to happen to him some day. It was just a matter of time."

"So you had dealings with him other than the scuffle at the reunion?"

"Oh, that was nothing," he laughed. "He'd had too much to drink or snort or something and he started getting handsy with my wife. I told him to back off and he exploded. He does that all the time."

"So, what was your relationship with Dylan?"

"The same one he had with anyone who'd made some cash after high school. He came to me with a business venture, a wild-assed idea. He hit up everybody who had disposable income. He must have hit you up once or twice."

"Not that I remember," I said, suddenly feeling a tad invisible myself. Apparently my post-high school success had not put me in a tax bracket that would make me of any interest to Dylan Lasalle.

"Well, the first time he came by, I gotta tell you I was sort of thrilled," Howard went on. "I mean, back in high school, he was a pretty big deal, whereas I don't think I made much of an impression outside of a select group of people. You know how you can tend to disappear in high school."

"Yes, I do. So did you ever end up working with him?"

This produced a pause from his end of the phone. I waited a few moments, and then said, "Howard, you still there?"

"Yeah, yeah. Eli, can I ask why you want to know?"

Now it was my turn to take a pause. "I'm looking into this for his wife," I lied. "Turns out, she didn't really know what he was into, and I'm trying to help her find some answers."

"Well, that's a decent thing to do. You see, Eli," he said, his voice getting quieter, "The police wanted to know the same thing. I was less inclined to talk to them, but since we go way back...and since you're doing this for his wife...I think we can talk. I don't feel comfortable doing it on the phone. Do you mind coming down to the office?"

I said that wasn't a problem and jotted down the address he gave me.

"It will be great to see you again, man," he said and I almost responded with, "It will feel like the first time for me," but he had already hung up.

Traffic getting into downtown was light, but something must have been going on somewhere, because the first two parking ramps I drove by had their red neon FULL signs flashing. I finally pulled into what I've always called the Dayton's Ramp, even though Dayton's department store had been closed for years and years. But in my mind, the ramp's name had never changed.

Up and up I went, passing FULL signs at each level. Finally, the spiral drive spit me out on the roof deck, which seemed to be the repository of all the empty stalls in the entire ramp. I pulled into one, stepped out of the car and froze.

In my effort to find a parking spot, I hadn't remembered the top of the ramp was wide open and put me ten stories above the sidewalk. The only thing between me and a ten-story fall—or jump—was a short retaining wall. The openness of the upper deck, the nearness of the short wall, and the glimpse I had of the height I had driven to all combined to make my head spin. I considered climbing back in the car and driving back down. I mean, I seriously considered it. It really seemed like my best option.

But, after several sessions with Dr. Bakke, I felt like the only way to get over this was to get through it. So rather than climb back into the relative safety of the car (because, I mean, really, what would keep me from driving straight through that wimpy retaining wall?), I did the more mature thing.

I ran from my car to the elevator like I was being chased by rabid weasels.

On the ride down in the elevator, I was able to catch my breath as the panic finally began to subside. I had stopped trembling but was still perspiring and would not have been surprised if passersby had commented on the loud racket my thumping heart was making. The suddenness of the attack had really taken me by surprise, and as I walked the short distance to the office building where Howard Washburn's company was located, I began to realize the impact these attacks were starting to have on my day-to-day life. I made a mental note to talk to Dr. Bakke about ratcheting up the therapy, while at the same time I made another note to find a better way of describing it.

Washburn International Shipping and Delivery turned out to be a small office on the fourth floor of one of the older buildings in downtown Minneapolis. Once upon a time it had been a Masonic Temple, but for dozens of years it housed an eclectic mix of arts organizations, non-profits and small oddball businesses that somehow defied the ups and downs of the economy.

The company name was stenciled on the glass of the office door. I turned the wobbly doorknob and would not have been surprised if it had come off in my hand. It didn't, and I stepped into the reception area for Washburn International Shipping and Delivery. "Reception area" might be overstating the case. The cramped room included a faded, saggy-looking couch, an old wooden desk, and stacks and stacks of cardboard boxes with foreign stamps and instructions scrawled across most of them.

"Hello?" My voice cracked a bit, so I said it again, louder this time. There was no response. A door at the far end of the room led either into a closet or another office. There was a light coming from that room, so I figure it must be an office.

"Howard? It's Eli," I said as I crossed the room. The office door was ajar, so I gave it a slight push and peered into the office, getting what turned out to be my first and last look at Howard Washburn. Finally seeing him here in person, I did have to admit I sort of recognized him. He did look a tad familiar. Everything, of course, except for the bullet hole in his right temple.

"Hey, Marks, you must have Homicide on your speed dial by now," said Homicide Detective Fred Hutton's partner, Homicide Detective Miles Wright. Then he smirked at his own line as if Don Rickles himself had said it on a Dean Martin Celebrity Roast.

"Detective Wright, you are a funny, funny little man," I said dryly. I was seated on a folding chair someone had found and set out in the hall outside the offices of Washburn International Shipping and Delivery. Wright had made several trips in and out of the office, along with a number of people who I assumed were part of the Homicide investigation unit.

I'd used my cell phone to report the body and the response had been swift: Uniformed cops followed by the Homicide detectives followed by a representative from the District Attorney's office. That representative was my ex-wife. She'd only made a cursory remark to me on her way into the office, but I had been told to please wait, as she wanted to speak to me before I left.

And so I sat. And I thought.

I thought about Howard Washburn. I thought about how his body looked so still, slumped in his chair, his head tilted back at an odd angle, his face lit by the cool glow from his computer monitor. For some reason, he had been wearing gloves, gloves that would have been perfect for keeping your hands warm on a blustery winter day. But in early summer, they would more likely been stifling and uncomfortable.

While waiting for the police, I had carefully stepped around his desk to see what was on his computer screen. It was clear one of his last actions had been to open a new, blank Word document. The final words he had typed glowed out at me from the monitor: "Im sorry."

The computer program had thoughtfully underlined the first word in red, letting him know he'd made one final spelling error. I shook my head when I read it, making a silent promise. If I ever choose to end it all, I will make sure the second-to-last thing I did on this Earth would be to proof my suicide note. Because, I mean, come on.

Deirdre came out of the office, conferring with her husband, Homicide Detective Fred Hutton. She had hyphenated her married name with his, something she hadn't done with me, giving her the mouthful name and title of Assistant District Attorney Deirdre Sutton-Hutton. I once asked her if she did it for comic effect; the language with which she replied suggested otherwise.

"So, we're not calling it suicide, we're not calling it murder," he was saying in a low voice as they stepped into the hall.

"For the time being, until we get the reports back, I'd prefer we don't call it anything but a suspicious death," she said, not bothering to mimic his quiet tone. "And the less said to anyone about it—and I'm talking about the press here—the better."

I recognized the finality of her tone and apparently so did Homicide Detective Fred Hutton, for he turned and went back into the office without another word. Deirdre glanced over at me and then pulled a compact from her stylish but efficient purse. She made a quick check of her hair and makeup, returned the compact to the purse and turned her attention to me.

"Eli. So here we are again."

"Yes, here we are." I stood up. I sensed where she was headed and decided the best offense might be a strong defense. "Look, I can't possibly be in any trouble. I found the body, I reported it. End of story."

Deirdre gave up smoking years ago, but I could tell by her body language she would not have had turned down a proffered cigarette at this moment, assuming I had one to proffer. Which I didn't. I dug into my pocket and found a pack of gum. I offered it to her and she waved it away and began walking toward the elevator. I followed.

"As you know," she said, "I'm not one for gossip, but I have to tell you that for the ex-husband of the Assistant District Attorney to continually find himself at crime scenes..."

"*After* the crime has been committed," I offered in my defense.

"Yes, your timing is appreciated," she said. "Not helpful, but appreciated." She pressed the call button for the elevator. "But be that as it may, your continued appearance at crime scenes is 'setting tongues to wagging,' as I believe your dear Aunt Alice used to say."

She had nailed Aunt Alice's phrase and we both couldn't help but smile. Aunt Alice never had an unkind word for anyone. I remember when the subject of Hitler had come up when I was a kid, the worst she could say about him was 'that man was bad news.'

"Well," I said as the elevator door slid open, "It's not as if I'm doing this on purpose." I held the door for Deirdre and pressed the button for the lobby.

"My question is, why are you doing it at all? What exactly brought you to the office of Howard Washburn this afternoon?"

I thought it best not to tell her she was the one who had steered me toward Howard Washburn. So instead I told as much of the truth as would keep me in her relatively good graces. "The same reason your husband went to talk to him—to find out about what was going on with Dylan Lasalle."

"And did you find out anything?"

I was surprised by the question. "Why would you think I might?"

"Because I've found oftentimes people will tell their friends things they won't tell the police."

"Actually, when I talked to him on the phone, he said there was something about Dylan he wanted to tell me."

"What was it?"

"He didn't want to tell me on the phone. And by the time I got here, he had become considerably less talkative. As you may have noticed."

We stepped out of the elevator and made our way through the cramped lobby. I held the massive glass door open for her and we moved out onto the humid air and traffic sounds of Hennepin Avenue.

"Where are you parked?" I asked.

"Dayton's ramp," she said, gesturing down the block. It was nice to see I wasn't the only one who hung onto that old name.

"I've gotta tell you," I said. "When I spoke to him on the phone, he didn't seem in the least bit sorry. Gabby, but not sorry."

She glared at me. "Did you read what was on his computer?"

"I was waiting for the police and there was no other reading material in the office."

We walked quietly for a few moments. Finally, she sighed and said, "Okay, so what does your gut tell you?"

I suppressed a smile, glad to see that in her own way she was acknowledging that I could be helpful, if only on occasion. "Well, if it wasn't a suicide, it certainly was made to look like a suicide."

"Yes, I think it was supposed to look very much like a suicide. But some parts don't fit." We stood on the corner and waited for the light to change. "Why, for instance, was he wearing gloves when he shot himself? Explain that."

"Probably for the same reason the assistant was dressed like a clown in Morrit's famous Donkey Disappearance illusion."

Deirdre looked over at me like I had started speaking another language. "Say what?"

"It's this really old trick some of the smarter people in the magic community were trying to reverse-engineer," I explained. "Because there are written descriptions of the effect, but nothing on how it was done. And one of the guys—I think it was Alan Wakeling—pointed out the effect required an assistant dressed as a clown. And, he concluded, the only reason you would dress him like a clown would be because you needed to switch him with someone else, also dressed like a clown."

"And this applies to my question how?"

"The only reason he was wearing gloves was because someone else was wearing gloves. That is, assuming it wasn't a suicide."

She stopped in her tracks. Thankfully, we had made it across the street, so no cars ran into us, but several other pedestrians gave us dirty looks as they were forced to suddenly maneuver around us.

"So, someone else shot him while wearing the gloves," she mused. "Then they took off the gloves and put them on Howard Washburn, because the gloves would show traces of a recently-fired gun. Traces which would not have been found on his bare hands, if he hadn't pulled the trigger himself."

"It's a theory, but for that matter, so is the idea of the second clown."

"There might be traces of DNA on the inside of the gloves."

I shrugged. "Maybe, but anyone smart enough to switch the gloves was probably also smart enough to wear thin plastic gloves under the gloves." She nodded in agreement and we continued walking.

"This is a very frustrating case," she finally said. Her tone had lost all of its official harshness, leaving only her normal, everyday level of harshness. "We were right on the edge with this Dylan Lasalle, and then he goes and gets himself killed."

"Right on the edge of what?"

We had reached the parking ramp and the elevator doors were just opening as we approached. We stepped in and Deirdre punched the floor button with far more effort than was necessary.

"Dylan Lasalle was a really shady character, Eli," she said as she turned to me. "We were never able to pin anything on him, but he traveled in nasty circles with some really bad people. And then, about two weeks ago, he started making overtures."

"He was a composer?" I knew the joke was a bad one, but it was out of my mouth before I could stop. Surprisingly, Deirdre didn't let it faze her.

"His attorney started asking us questions, about making a deal, getting immunity, turning state's evidence. He wouldn't get specific, but said he was just testing the waters. He said his client was looking for a way out and wanted to know if we'd provide it."

"A way out of what?"

She shook her head. "We don't know. We were supposed to meet with him this week." The elevator door slid open and she stepped out. I turned and followed her, and then I realized, with a suddenness that took my breath away, that we were on the roof. I stood there, frozen.

"This is me," she said. "Sorry, I should have asked what floor you were on."

I could see straight across the flat roof to the short retaining wall that surrounded the ramp roof. The stumpy wall was on my left and on my right and my knees began to buckle. I turned to go back into the elevator, but the doors had already shut. I closed my eyes tightly.

"Eli, are you okay?"

I took a deep breath, thinking about the breathing exercises I had gone through with Dr. Bakke. That seemed like a long, long time ago.

"Eli?" There was a distinct and foreign note of concern in her voice.

The breathing exercises didn't seem to be working and I felt like I was gasping for air. "Deirdre, I need to ask a favor," I was able to finally sputter out.

"Sure, what do you need?"

"Can you take my hand?" My eyes were clamped shut, but I extended my right arm in the general direction of her voice. My hand hung in space for a moment, and then I felt her hand clasp mine. The relief was palpable.

"I'm having something of a panic attack," I explained, turning to her so she could see my eyes were closed. "The first thing I need you to do is walk me to my car."

"Eli, if you're having a panic attack, I don't think you should be driving."

"I agree. Which brings us to the second thing I need you to do. I need you to drive me, and my car, down to the bottom of the ramp. Once I get off the roof, I think I'll be okay."

Amazingly, Deirdre didn't question any of this. With a gentleness I hadn't felt from her in years, she took my keys and guided me toward the car.

Even with my eyes closed, I could sense how close I was to the retaining wall and the edge. "Open the door, please. Now would be good. Or sooner than now, if you can manage it."

"Just about there," she said softly. I heard the snick of the passenger door unlocking, felt the edge of the door as she opened it, and then I ducked down to climb—really, climb, like a monkey—into the car. Once inside, I heard the reassuring sound of the passenger door closing.

I settled into my seat and found and fastened my seat belt. Through it all, I kept my eyes shut tightly, but in my mind's eye I could see through the windshield, could see the useless retaining wall, and could sense the distance between my body and the ground ten floors below.

Not a moment too soon, Deirdre was in the driver's seat, the car was started, and I felt the vehicle back away from the wall, and then turn toward the exit.

After we had circled down and down for several moments, I peeked one eyelid open. We were probably at about the fifth floor, but the tight space of the downward spiral was already helping me to relax. I looked over at Deirdre and could see she was alternating between looking where she was going and looking at me.

"Well," she said, "this is new."

"I'm just trying it out to see if I like it. Renting with an option to die."

"Seriously, Eli, are you seeing someone about this?" Her tone was sharp and demanding, which in anyone else would have been off-putting. But for Deirdre, it was the closest thing she had toward warmth.

"Yes, I'm seeing a therapist."

"How often?"

"Frequently. Actually, in about an hour."

We had made it down to ground level. Deirdre pulled the car into an empty handicap spot. "Are you sure you're okay to drive?" she said as she shifted the car into park.

"Now that I'm on the ground, I'm good to go," I said. "Still pale around the gills, but really, I'll be fine."

She gave me a long hard look. "Okay, but send me a text when you get to the therapist."

"Thanks, but I'll be fine. Do you want me to give you a ride back up to your car?"

She shook her head and then paused. "You take care of yourself," she said, swinging the car door open and sliding out.

I was taken aback. It wasn't exactly warmth, but it wasn't the coolness she usually projected.

"Thanks," I said, my voice coming out as more of a whisper than intended. "That really helped."

But she was already out of the car and heading toward the elevator.

Chapter 13

"Eli, let's think of your subconscious as a balloon."

"Is this a magician metaphor? Are these balloons in the shape of animals?"

Dr. Bakke ignored the comment and plowed ahead. "And think of stress as just one of the gases that fills that balloon. If the balloon gets too full of stress, something has got to give somewhere. Hence, your attacks."

"So, these 'hey, let's throw ourselves off a high building' thoughts are just like holes in a balloon?"

"Essentially."

"Well, given that it happened again today and in front of my ex-wife no less, I think we need to patch that balloon. And pronto."

"Well, if you want to continue with the metaphor, a patch is just that—a patch. I think it would be better to find a way to keep from overfilling the balloon."

I spread my hands in front of me in a posture of supplication. "I'm all yours."

"I believe what's happening to you is that your subconscious has taken an existing fear and, in a sense, super-sized it."

"Like a Coke at a movie theater?"

"Sort of. Before these major panic attacks began, can you think of experiences in your recent past where you experienced acrophobia?"

"Well, let me see," I said, thinking back over the last few months. "I was at a party last year where the porch had a glass or acrylic floor, it was see-through. I was only up a couple of stories, but I didn't care for that."

Dr. Bakke dutifully made a note. "Any other instances?"

"Well, last fall when Megan and I almost died, I took a heck of a tumble down a steep incline. It was a big hill, maybe three or four stories high."

"That could be significant," he said.

"Well, sure, but that took five seconds. I'd spent the previous hour trapped in a cave in pitch darkness. Why don't I have super-sized claustrophobia?"

"Because you didn't have claustrophobia to begin with. You had a minor fear of heights, which has now blossomed into a major fear of heights. And it's starting to get in the way of your day-to-day life."

"You could say that," I deadpanned. "So, what do we do? Dig back into my childhood?"

He shook his head. "I'm not a big fan of that."

"Sure, that's because for you it was only five minutes ago."

"I think our best course of action," he said, keenly ignoring my remark, "would be to continue with the immersion therapy, just not to the extreme that you took it at your high school reunion."

"Understood," I said. "I'm for any plan that gets me back to my previous level of acrophobia, or that can get rid of it altogether."

"That's fine, but you may get even more than that," he said. "Remember, sometimes our greatest fear is actually our greatest strength."

"Again with the fortune cookies," I joked, but I'd later find that the good doctor's little piece of wisdom was closer to the truth than I might have imagined.

I left the building where Dr. Bakke had his office in a bit of a daze. The events of the day had taken their toll, and then an hour of sharing my feelings on top of that had contributed to a definite feeling of lightheadedness. Given all that, I think I can be excused for not noticing more quickly I was being followed. But I should have really caught on faster, because my stalker was not being subtle by any means.

A black sedan followed me through the parking lot. It moved silently and slowly behind me as I made my way to my car. And I mean right behind me, about two feet behind, matching my speed with precise deliberation.

I finally recognized there was a car on my heels and stepped aside, moving closer to the other parked cars, but the sedan continued matching my pace. I slowed down even more, and so did the sedan. I stopped and the car mimicked my action. I glanced over at the car but couldn't see any occupant in the front or the back, due to windows that looked to be tinted well above the legal limit. I sped up, trying to get to my own car that much sooner, but the car increased its speed as well.

I clicked the remote lock for my car and pulled the driver's door open with a bit more sense of panic than I had hoped to exhibit. I slid into the driver's seat, shut and locked the door and turned on the ignition in what resembled one continuous action. As I was about to put the car into reverse, I glanced at the rearview mirror and saw the black sedan was still there, directly behind me, blocking my exit. I turned to look at the side view mirror for other options and found myself face to face with Harpo.

Sadly it was not Harpo Marx, who would have been a delightful and welcome surprise. Instead, it was Mr. Lime's henchman, the soundless fireplug, whose bulldog face was nearly pressing against my window. In keeping with his namesake, he silently jerked his head toward the sedan.

I sat there for a long moment, considering my options, realizing I had precious few. I shut off the ignition, opened the door and stepped out of my car, wishing—as it would turn out, not for the first time—I had skipped this year's reunion altogether.

I was directed into the back of the sedan by Harpo, who held the door open for me with a steely persistence. I peered into the dim light and finally recognized the bony Mr. Lime in the murky space.

"Come in and chat with me for a moment," he said.

"Do I have a choice?"

"Free will? Yes. A choice? No. Get in."

I hesitated and he smiled up at me. "Mandrake, if our plan was to hurt you, it would have happened much, much earlier and right now you'd either be recuperating in the hospital or in the morgue experiencing late stage rigor mortis."

With that comforting statement, I settled in the back seat. Harpo shut the door and returned to his post behind the wheel.

"How was your therapy session?"

Mr. Lime asked the question with a tone that almost suggested genuine interest and concern. However, his broad smile, with his translucent skin and lips pulled back tight across his face, cancelled any sense of warmth immediately. "So, your therapist, he's a good one?"

"Have you been following me?"

He smiled again. "I think the answer to that question is fairly obvious," he said, shaking his head. "But, to put your mind at rest, we're not making a career of it."

I stuttered for a moment, but could only come up with, "Why?"

He shrugged. "You talk to people. People talk to you. We'd just like to be part of the conversation."

"Then why don't you talk to the people who are talking to me?"

"Well, I enjoy your perceptions. And, in the case of our friend, Signor Ferrari, talking is on the list of things he will never be doing again."

I had a pretty good idea he meant Howard Washburn, but once again he stumped me with the movie-related pet name he had assigned.

"You mean Howard Washburn, right?"

Mr. Lime just smiled at me as I struggled with the name.

"Ferrari. Ferrari. It rings a bell."

"And swats a fly," Lime added wryly.

The image flickered through my mind and I struggled to grasp it. Finally it came to me. "Sidney Greenstreet. *Casablanca.*"

Lime nodded. "Signor Ferrari. A charming but corrupt businessman, not above playing both sides of the street, as long as he benefits in the end."

"But Howard didn't benefit in the end."

"Not so much, no." He nodded at me, which I assumed meant I should continue my recitation.

"Well, you know, I didn't really talk to Howard. Only on the phone. By the time I got to his office he was..." My voice trailed off.

"You gleaned no insight from the brief telephone encounter?"

"Not really. As I told the police..."

"Yes, you talked to the police. We'll get to that. Let's stay focused on what Signor Ferrari may have imparted." He extended a hand, gesturing for me to continue.

"All I really got from him was he'd had some business dealings with Dylan Lasalle and he wasn't comfortable discussing them over the phone."

"Prudent choice." He rubbed his hands together and seemed unhappy with the results. "Harpo," he said. "My hand cream."

The words were barely out of his mouth and the servant had already picked up a small white tube from the front seat and passed it back to the old man. Mr. Lime squirted a small amount of lotion on his hands, capped the tube and handed it back up front. He looked up at me as he spread the cream evenly across both of his pale, bony hands, with particular emphasis on the tips of his skeletal fingers.

"One of the many, many downsides of aging," he said by way of explanation. "Dry hands. Persistently dry."

"Perhaps you should wear gloves," I suggested.

He looked up at me sharply, then his face settled into a more benign countenance. "I do. Many days I do," he said.

"Well," I stammered, "You're not alone. It's also a problem for magicians. Of all ages," I added. "Dry hands can make it hard to work with cards."

He looked up, his eyes alert. "Do you have a product you could recommend? I find most over-the-counter remedies to be too greasy."

The sudden change in topic nearly made my head spin. "Um, yes. I can't think of the name of it now, but there is a good one out there." I shook my head. "Just can't think of the name right now."

"I would love to hear of it," he said, taking a handkerchief from his breast pocket and giving each of his bony hands a quick once over. "When you think of it, please pass it along."

I recognized I had no direct method of contacting him, but decided not to mention that particular issue.

"So," he continued, handing the slightly soiled handkerchief up to Harpo, "You said you spoke to the police. Did they offer any insight?"

"On Howard Washburn? Or Lasalle?"

"Ferrari. Francis. I'd like to hear whatever transpired."

I was unclear as to the proper path to take, so I admit I took a quick jog down the one of least resistance. "The police seem to think Dylan was trying to work out a deal with them before his death. They didn't give me details. In fact it sounded as if they didn't actually have many details," I added quickly.

"Francis, Francis, Francis," Lime said quietly. "And what of his wife, the lovely Phyllis Dietrichson?"

"You mean Trish?"

"A word of warning, my young friend," he said, his raspy voice sounding almost warm. "In this life, we all have a little Walter Neff in us. The less we let him out, the better off we are likely to be. But enough of this intrigue," he said, playfully clapping his hands with such force I feared for a moment they might shatter like fine crystal. "It's time for another card trick."

"Oh, Mr. Lime," I said quickly, patting my pockets more for show than might have been necessary. "I'm afraid I didn't bring any cards with me today."

"Not even your invisible deck?" he asked, the hint of a twinkle looking quite out of place in his eyes.

"Not even that one," I said, shaking my head.

"Not to worry," he said excitedly. "We brought our own. Harpo, the cards if you please."

Once again, the servant had anticipated the request and already had the cards in hand. He handed back a card box that looked to be as old as Mr. Lime, if not older. The corners of the box were crushed and worn, providing an ample preview of the distressed cards I found within. I removed the sorry cards from the box and gave the deck a quick Hindu shuffle, feeling immediately how soft and pliable the vintage cards actually were.

The poor condition of the deck instantly eliminated a large number of possible illusions. I tried a one-hand shuffle, which felt like I was shuffling a deck of soggy saltines. The deck felt light, which was either from how worn and ragged the cards were, or it might indicate we were shy a few cards. Mr. Lime cleared his throat quietly and I begin to improvise like mad.

"Well, let me see," I began. "This is a variation on a very popular trick in magic circles. It's called 'Dr. Daley's Last Card Trick.' Actually, this is closer to Eddie Fector's version, which he called 'Be Honest, What Is It?'" I continued, getting caught up in a mental spiral of accreditation. "Which in itself is very similar to David Williamson's 'The Memory Test,' although I've made some adjustments of my own," I added, my words trailing off.

"Sounds intriguing," Mr. Lime said with a sick smile. "Why was this Dr. Daley's last trick?"

I rarely name this trick while performing it, so I was caught off guard by the question. "He died after creating it," I explained.

"May you have better luck."

A chill ran down my spine but I pressed on. "Pick a card in your mind—just the value, not the suit," I said as I flipped the deck over and began to sort through it quickly.

Mr. Lime touched a finger to his chin and looked up at the dome light, then smiled at me. "A queen," he said. "I would pick a queen."

"Excellent choice," I said as I scanned the deck and was

mercifully able to find all four queens. I culled them from the deck and spread them in front of him. "Red or black?"

He gave it much more consideration than I felt was really required, squinting as he considered his options. His eyelids were so thin I was convinced I could see his steel green eyes right through the skin. "Black," he said. "I would pick black."

"That's interesting," I said, setting the two red queens aside. I held up the Queen of Spades. "In the world of magic, the Queen of Spades indicates intelligence. An intellectual."

Mr. Lime smiled as if I had complimented him directly. I held up the other card.

"The Queen of Clubs, on the other hand..." I said this with a smile, because it was in fact in the other hand. Mr. Lime offered a grim smirk at my attempt at humor. "On the other hand, the Queen of Clubs indicates intuition. This minor demonstration will pit your intelligence against your intuition. Hold out your right hand, palm down, and pinch your thumb and index finger together."

He did as instructed. I turned the two cards face down and switched them slowly, back and forth, between my two hands. This was no three card monte move. He would have no trouble following the cards. I placed one of them, still face down, between his thumb and index finger.

"Now, using your intelligence...and your intuition...which card am I holding and which card are you holding?"

He considered for a moment, more for dramatic effect than actually needing to think about it. "I'm holding the Queen of Spades. You are holding the Queen of Clubs."

I turned my card over. The Queen of Clubs. He turned his over and smiled. He was holding the Queen of Spades.

"Excellent," I said, taking the card from him and shuffling the two cards back and forth, much faster than before. "That was your intelligence at work. Now we will test your intuition." I took one of the cards and placed it back between his fingers. I held the other card, its face to my chest. "Using your intuition, tell me: Which card are you holding? And which card am I holding?"

He thought about this for a long moment. He had a look of real concentration on his face. I glanced toward the front seat and could see even Harpo was studying us closely in the rearview mirror.

"I believe," he said, choosing his words carefully, "that I hold the Queen of Clubs."

"And that would mean I hold the Queen of Spades?"

He nodded emphatically. I took my card and placed it on top of his, pulling the card out from his finger grasp as I did. "I believe, in this one instance, your intuition has failed you," I said. "For not only do you not hold the Queen of Clubs...but neither do I."

With that I turned the two cards over and set them on the seat next to him. He gasped, gaping at the two cards: The Queen of Hearts and the Queen of Diamonds. He looked up at me, his eyes wide.

"Intelligence. Intuition. Neither one is entirely fallible," I said as I reached across the seat and picked up the two cards I had set aside. I looked at him for a long moment, then turned the cards around, revealing the Queen of Spades and the Queen of Clubs.

Mr. Lime clasped his hands together, looking as thrilled and delighted as an aging psychopath can look. "Wonderful," he whispered. "Just wonderful."

I handed him the cards. "Then I think we're done," I said, reaching for the door handle.

"Yes," he said. "Mr. Marks, I think we are done."

I opened the car door and tried to mask my eagerness at getting out.

"Except," he said, and I froze, one foot in the car and one foot out. I turned back to him.

"Yes?" I asked weakly.

"All I need is the name of that hand cream. And then I think we can call it a day."

My mind was blank and the more I pushed to remember the name the further it receded into my unconscious.

"I'll give you some time to think about it," he said, "And then I'll be back in touch. In the meantime, I will trust you to employ your own intelligence and your intuition to the greatest degree possible. Yes?"

My head made a movement that resembled a nod as I crawled out of the car. I stood up completely and turned to close the door. My last image of Mr. Lime was of him caressing the four queens. He was making a sound that, from where I stood, sounded like purring. Then the door was shut and the car roared across the parking lot.

At that instant it hit me.

"Papercreme," I yelled. "It's called Papercreme Fingertip Moistener!"

But the car had already turned the corner and was gone.

CHAPTER 14

I sat in my car for a while after the sedan had driven off. It had been an eventful day and I felt a need to process all that had happened. I noticed my phone sitting on the passenger seat and turned it on, discovering it had been quite active while I was sharing my feelings with Dr. Bakke and being vaguely terrorized by Mr. Lime.

The first message was from Deirdre, asking if I'd made it home okay after our adventure in the parking ramp. Her voice was free of any sarcasm and she actually sounded concerned and almost warm. I listened to the message twice, just to make sure it was really her.

This was followed by a message from Harry, asking me to call him. The phone registered three calls from him, all coming from the store, but he had only left one message. I tried the store and then his cell and got no answer from either.

The third message was from Jake. It was short and to the point: "Eli, call me when you can. Things have gone from bad to weird out here."

Finally, the phone had logged a call from Trish, but she had left no message. I looked at her number for a long time, wondering not only what she might want, but why I was so drawn to helping her. Before I allowed myself to dig too deeply into my motivations, I hit the Return Call button and after three rings she picked up. Once again, she sounded like I had interrupted a crying jag.

"Oh, Eli, hello."

"Hi. I saw that you had called," I said.

"Yes, I was upset, I'm sorry."

"No reason to be sorry. What's going on?"

"The police just talked to me about the death of someone Dylan knew. They said you knew him too. They asked me some more questions about the night Dylan died and I'm really starting to think they suspect me of killing him or something."

"Oh, I'm sure that's not the case," I said, not even coming close to convincing myself. "Would it help if we got together and talked?" I suggested, again resisting the urge to plumb my motivations too deeply. Sure, she was in pain, and sure, she could use a friend. But she was also my high school crush and she was still attractive and now a widow. Before I could compare myself too closely to Jake, she answered.

"Oh, Eli, that would be very nice. If you don't mind and I'm not interrupting something..." Her voice trailed off and I could hear her sniffling quietly on the phone.

"Not a problem. I'm not doing anything right now, if you want to grab a coffee or something?" I suggested.

"Coffee at this time of day will keep me up all night," she said with a sigh. "And I'm already having enough trouble sleeping. But there's a coffee shop down the street from here that has a nice selection of teas."

"And where is here?"

"Oh, of course," she said with a short and unconvincing laugh. "I'm volunteering at St. Paul House, down on Washington Avenue on the north side of downtown," she said. I had never been there, but had seen their building for years as I'd driven by on the freeway, chuckling to myself that St. Paul House had chosen for some odd reason to locate in Minneapolis. At meal times, there was often a line around the block, even in what would be considered prosperous times.

"I know where it is," I said.

"My shift ends in about forty minutes. There's a Caribou Coffee down the block."

* * *

Rush hour was just starting, so it was thirty minutes later when I finally made it to the area, and I then spent five more minutes looking for a parking spot. I finally located one across the street from St. Paul House, which wasn't really a house, but instead a large brick warehouse space that had been converted over the years into a combination soup kitchen, food shelf and homeless shelter.

My timing couldn't have been better, as I spotted Trish coming out the front door. I locked my car and waited for traffic to clear in order to cross the street. She saw me and waved, and then turned to say hello to a group of three men who were just entering the facility. As a kid I would have called them bums or hobos, but times have changed and I recognized them for what they were: guys who had slipped between the cracks of society and were doing what they had to in order to get by. It was warm today, but I was guessing in the dead of winter, a place like St. Paul House was the only thing standing between them and freezing to death down by the river.

"I didn't know you worked here," I said as I finally negotiated the traffic and made it across the street.

"Well, I'm not on staff or anything," she said. "I volunteer here two or three days a week. Keeps me from going stir crazy in the apartment. Dylan doesn't—" She caught herself and re-started the sentence. "Dylan *didn't* like the idea of me working, because it got in the way if we wanted to take off for some place exotic on a moment's notice. Not that we ever did." She shrugged. "I guess it's going to take me a while to start getting the tense right. Come on," she said, forcing a smile. "I'll buy you that cup of coffee."

My coffee ended up being an iced coffee, as drinking hot liquids on hot days just seems odd to me. Trish was true to her word and went with a simple Earl Gray tea along with a slice of marble pound cake. In order to be sociable, I ordered a piece as well. At least that was what I told myself.

Once we settled into a table in the corner, there were some awkward moments, as neither of us was sure where to start. So I picked up where we had left off.

"Volunteering at St. Paul House," I said. "Good for you."

"It's oddly comforting to have this predictable schedule right now," she said. "I mean, to have a reason to get out of bed in the morning."

I nodded in understanding. "How did you get started here?"

"Well, my background is in non-profits, so when in doubt I always return to this world."

"Is that what you did after college?" Our discussion at the reunion had been so focused on tripping down memory lane I hadn't thought to ask about her career path.

"Oh, I did a million things after college," she said. "Trying to find myself. Pretty typical, right?"

I shrugged. "You're talking to a guy who's still using jokes in his act he wrote when he was fifteen."

"Well, obviously you found yourself at an earlier age."

"I'm not so sure. We sent out a search party once, but they came back empty-handed."

She gave this a laugh that we in the business call "polite."

"Anyway, for my first real post-college job, I ended up working at a non-profit. I didn't care for the cause, but I liked the work and felt I was pretty good at it."

"What was the cause?"

She lowered her head in mock shame. "I was Assistant Communications Director for the Dried Fruit Council."

"And their mission...?"

She sat up straight in her chair and recited it from memory. "To promote the nutritional value and health benefits of dried fruit to the American people."

"That's a pretty compelling mission," I said.

"It should be. It took a year and half and about two hundred thousand dollars in consulting fees to come up with it." She shook her head. "But that wasn't why I left. Ask me why I left."

"Why did you leave?" It was fun to see her lightening up, if only a little.

"Because I was asked to write the copy for a save-the-date card for a big fundraising event. And you know the name of that event?"

I shook my head, sensing a punch line.

"It was called 'Save the Date.'" She took a sip of tea and added, "You can not make these things up."

I smiled as I used the stir stick to move the ice cubes in my coffee. "Not to bring us down, but you had a visit from the police?"

Her smile disappeared and she nodded. "They said someone from the reunion killed himself. And he knew Dylan. Howard Washburn. Did you know him?"

I shook my head. "No, although he certainly seemed to think I knew him. He's in the yearbook, but I have no memory of him."

"That's what I told them. Dylan knew a lot of people I didn't know." She broke off a piece of pound cake and chewed it slowly. "All kinds of people I didn't know. And that I'm glad I didn't know."

"So they came and talked to you about Howard Washburn?"

She nodded. "This afternoon. They wanted to know my relationship with him, Dylan's relationship with him. They asked me where I was around the time he shot himself. And, of course, it was when I was on my lunch break, so in their minds I don't have an alibi. Just like when Dylan was killed. I was sound asleep in our apartment, but in their eyes I have no alibi." She brushed some crumbs off the tabletop. "It's like they really think I'm involved in this in some way. And the insurance money certainly doesn't help."

"Insurance money?"

She seemed surprised. "The police didn't mention that to you?"

I shook my head.

"A couple months ago, Dylan took out a life insurance policy for a million dollars. Didn't tell me a thing about it, which was typical of him and his approach to our finances. And then he dies and all of a sudden it's suspicious he bought the policy and named me as the beneficiary."

"Well," I said, trying to not look too surprised at this revelation. "A million dollars is a lot of money, even today."

She shook her heard. "It's not a million. It's two million, because of the double indemnity clause. Apparently, a mugging is considered an accidental death."

The words 'double indemnity' triggered a thought and I suddenly remembered the two names Mr. Lime had mentioned in the car. He had referred to Trish as Phyllis Dietrichson and warned me not to become Walter Neff. And I remembered that they were the two characters played by Barbara Stanwyck and Fred MacMurray in the movie *Double Indemnity*—a movie about a woman who murders her husband for the insurance, with the help of a sleazy insurance salesman. My memory of the film was sketchy, but I was pretty sure Walter Neff wound up dead at the end, a fate I very much wanted to avoid.

"What's wrong?" Clearly my face was registering a look that warranted the question.

"Do you remember that old movie called *Double Indemnity*, starring Fred MacMurray?"

"Mr. Douglas from *My Three Sons*?"

"Yeah, that's the actor, but he was not a very nice—or very smart—guy in *Double Indemnity*. It was a similar situation, a woman, an insurance policy..." My voice trailed off and I decided to shift the conversation back to the matter at hand. "Do you know who Dylan bought the policy from?"

"I would guess it was from the same guy we got all our insurance from—Roger Edison. You know Roger, he went to high school with us?"

"I remember him well. He was at the reunion."

"He was? I don't remember seeing him there. But I would guess he sold the policy. That's what I told the police."

"Okay," I said, sitting back in my chair. "So how did the police leave it with you? Are you a Person of Interest?"

"I don't know what I am," she sighed. "It's been a rough week. I'm crying a little less but feeling guilty about it more." She finished her tea, crumpled her paper napkin and placed it in the empty paper cup. "But enough about all that, I'm so tired about all that. How are you doing? You know, with your thing?"

It took me a moment to realize what she meant by 'my thing,' my mind sifting through several alluring options before realizing she was referring to my panic attacks.

"Oh, the same," I said. "I just came from therapy. Had a serious attack this morning at the top of a parking ramp with—of all people—my ex-wife. And let me tell you, there's nothing better for your ego than looking like a scared, simpering idiot in front of your ex-wife."

"Oh, I'm sure she didn't think that."

I thought back to Deirdre's behavior and smiled in spite of myself. "Actually, she was remarkably warm-hearted and caring about the whole incident. She must be mellowing with age."

"Was your divorce painful?"

"More for me than her, I think. She wisely had a spare husband in the wings, so she made the transition from married to not-married to married-again fairly quickly. She was always good at planning things."

Trish starred down at her empty cup, pushing it around the tabletop in a small circle. "I was going to ask Dylan for a divorce soon. At least, that was the plan. I think." She looked up at me, her eyes starting to water.

"Was he aware of that plan?"

"Who knows? I never really knew what was going on with him. Which I guess was our biggest problem—he had too many secrets and I didn't have any." She stared up at the ceiling for a long moment, then looked at me. I held her gaze.

"Why can't life ever be simple?" she finally said.

"Well, according to my Uncle Harry, life is only simple for simple people."

"You uncle sounds like a delightful man."

"Trish, you have no idea."

CHAPTER 15

"Is there something wrong with your cell phone?"

I could tell Harry was surprised to hear my voice coming from the top of the stairs. He was just opening the door to his apartment and he looked up the staircase, squinting at me. I was sitting in the dark.

"Hello there, Buster. Why are you sitting in the dark?"

"We're not talking about me right now. We're talking about you. And your cell phone. Did you perhaps lose it?"

He patted his pockets, finally pulling the phone out of his breast pocket. "It's right here. Do you need it?" He held it up toward me.

"Is it on?"

"Is it on what?"

"Is it turned on?" I hissed as I stood and slowly moved down the stairs toward him.

"Of course not. I don't want to wear out the battery." He slipped the phone back into his pocket and opened his door, stepping deftly into his apartment and out of sight. I sped up and made it into his kitchen before the door swung shut.

"Do you know how worried I've been about you? I've been to the bar next door, I called Max, I called Sam, I even called Abe. Nobody knew where you were."

"You should have called me," he said as he took off his windbreaker and opened the closet door.

"I did call you. Your phone was turned off!"

"Oh, that's right. Do you want some fruit? These bananas are right on the edge."

"So am I, but don't change the subject, old man. You left me a message this afternoon to call you."

"I did? Oh, that's right, I did. I needed a ride to the drug store. You didn't call back, so I went out to catch the bus."

"You've been at the drug store for the last eight hours?"

"Don't be silly. What could one do in a drug store for eight hours?"

There was something woozy about his attitude it took me a moment to recognize. "Have you been drinking?"

He shook his head and then nodded, holding up his right hand and demonstrating with his thumb and first finger the international sign for "just a wee bit."

I sat heavily in one of the three chairs that surrounded his small kitchen table and rubbed my eyes. When I opened them I saw he was now seated across from me. He was eating a banana. Another banana rested, unopened, in front of me on the table.

"Really, Buster, you should eat one. They're right on the edge."

"In the name of all that is holy, what is it going to take for you to tell me where you've been for the last eight hours while I've been sitting here going out of my mind?"

He arched an eyebrow at me. "Out of your mind?"

I shrugged. "Well, really, really concerned."

He smiled. "Thank you," he said. He took the last bite from his banana and then got up to throw the peel into the small trashcan under the sink. "Well, if you must know, I spent the evening in the company of two charming women."

"Two women?" He had my attention and he knew it.

"Two charming women," he said, stretching the word charming into about sixteen syllables.

I sat back in my chair. "Really. Do tell."

"I needed to go to the drug store to refill my prescription. I tried calling you and when you didn't answer your phone—I wonder from where you inherited that annoying trait?—I decided instead to take the bus. Minneapolis has, as you know, an extensive public transportation system," he said with a twinkle in his eyes that made me want to strike him. "I suspect by the time the light rail finally gets built in *this* neighborhood I'll be twenty years dead, but that's all well and good because the busses run on time and they run right past our shop."

"You're going to make me regret asking, aren't you? Can we cut to the chase?"

"So there I was, sitting on the bus bench, wondering about this and that, when a car pulled up, the passenger window was rolled down, and two attractive women asked me if I needed a ride somewhere."

"You got into a car with two strange women?"

"It's not like they offered me candy. And they weren't strange women. It was your friend the psychic, Megan, and her other psychic friend, Franny. Hardly the kidnapping type, I think."

"Megan offered you a ride?" I tried to take the incredulous tone out of my voice, but it slipped out right at the end.

"What's wrong with that? She didn't break up with me, she broke up with you."

"We didn't break up. We're on a break. There's a difference." I waved my hands, trying to clear the confusion out of the air in front of me. "But we're getting off the point. You spent the evening in the company of two psychics?"

Harry shook his head and leaned in conspiratorially. "Technically one psychic. I think we can all agree that, as a psychic, Megan is really, really terrible."

"But you don't even believe in psychics!"

"I don't have to believe in them to know when one of them is, frankly, not very good. Of course, I didn't say this to her face."

"Of course you didn't. So they drove you to the drug store." I gestured for him to get on with his story.

"Yes, and then they asked me if I wanted to continue on with them to dinner and, since I didn't have plans this evening, I agreed."

"So you went to dinner?"

Harry's face widened into an annoying grin. "Well, we never technically got around to dinner. We did what, in my day, we called a pub crawl."

"You went out drinking."

"Technically," he said, using that same word again, "We were wine tasting. Buster, did you know wine comes in flights?"

"Yes, I am aware wine comes in flights."

"Well, it was news to me. They are flights of fancy, let me tell you. So at each bar we'd order an appetizer and a flight or two and sip and compare. A very civilized way to spend an evening, if you ask me."

"Actually, I'm sorry I asked you. So you got soused with a pair of psychics?"

"Franny didn't drink. We called her the designated psychic." He gave the line a far bigger laugh than it deserved.

"So you got drunk with my girlfriend."

"She's not your girlfriend. You're on a break." Before I could respond, he stood unsteadily to his feet. "Buster, can you open the store for me in the morning? I think I may want to sleep in."

"Sleep in? You mean you want to sleep it off. Sorry, I can't. I need to be on the movie set with Jake."

"Well, that's fine," he said amiably. "The shop can stay closed. I can't imagine we'd have much foot traffic tomorrow. Good night, Buster." Before he rounded the corner to his bedroom, he turned back toward me. It took him a moment to remember why he had stopped. "Oh, yes. Can you shut the light off when you go? That's a good fellow."

I sat at the table for a while until I heard the steady snore that signaled he was asleep. And then I went up to my own apartment and climbed into my own bed. I pulled up *Double Indemnity* on Netflix on my iPad and watched it for a while. It was as good as I'd remembered it, but I fell asleep before it was over and never did learn if Walter Neff dies in the end.

* * *

"This place is spooky as hell."

It was early the next morning and Jake was whispering to me as we made our way down the craft services table, loading up on a breakfast of feather-light Western omelets, fresh fruit, yogurt and a wide selection of mouth-watering Danish. Around us, people were eating and laughing and getting ready to start their day of filmmaking.

"What do you mean?" I whispered back. "Everyone seems to be in a great mood."

"That's what I mean. It's weird. Look at them."

He gestured across the small clearing from where the food had been set up. Walter, the director, was laughing with the two producers, Donna and Arnold. Noël was hanging on Walter's arm. They were acting like they were private guests at the best cocktail party ever.

"Why is everybody so happy?" I whispered.

"Not everybody." He tilted his head to the left and I turned to see Stewart, the writer, glaring at...well, everyone. He clutched a Styrofoam cup of coffee in his hands, his eyes grim slits as he surveyed all the activity around him. He was giving the same look he'd given when both of us spotted Jake and Noël canoodling in the woods.

"The writer is still pissed off," I said, recapping the situation. "The plot of the movie has imploded, the producers have lost half their funding. Yet they're yucking it up." I turned to Jake. "You're right. This is weird. Why are they so happy?"

"Not sure. But my best guess is because they still have Plan B: Kill the leading man."

We grabbed some utensils and found two open seats at one of several picnic tables that had been set up for crew meals.

"So Noël is back together with Walter?" I asked as we settled into our seats.

"I didn't know they were apart," Jake said, using far more acting ability than I would have given him credit for.

"Oh, come on," I said quietly. "I saw the two of you. In the woods. You know."

He gave me a perplexing look that seemed genuine. "What?"

"The two of you. In the woods. Canoodling."

A look of recognition passed across his face. "Oh, that," he said, cutting into his omelet. "That was just acting."

"From where I was standing, that was an Oscar-worthy performance," I said, sounding far more like a fourteen year-old boy than I intended.

"We were rehearsing," Jake said. "We had a love scene coming up and that's what actors do."

"Wow. And they pay you and everything."

"Don't be a dork. Love scenes are hard to make look real and it helps if the two actors have already established some chemistry."

"Chemistry, right," I said, nearly snorting into my orange juice. "Pull the other one."

"It was actually sort of weird," he admitted quietly. "Noël and I have a bit of history. A couple years back, I dated her roommate out in LA and it ended badly."

"How badly?"

Jake shrugged. "My timing was bad. She was an actress, too. She'd had a run of bad luck with auditions, her career—such as it was—had tanked, and then I broke up with her. That was sort of the last straw. She quit the business and went back home to Ohio. Noël was super pissed at me."

He gestured toward Noël, who was laughing a little too loud and a little too long at something Walter had said. "You may find it hard to believe, but that girl has a temper on her. I mean, a Glenn Close in *Fatal Attraction* temper."

Before I could tell him that it was, in fact, hard to believe, he moved on to a new topic. "So, the police were out here yesterday to talk to me," he said. "Something about someone from the reunion that died. A suicide or something. Howard Washburn? I had no memory of the guy, did you?"

I shook my head. "Me neither," I said. "Although, from what I've heard, they don't really think it was a suicide. Actually, they seem to think Trish might be involved in some way. She doesn't have an alibi," I added.

"Interesting," Jake said. "Very interesting. First they think she offed her husband, and now one of his compatriots. She's a very busy girl."

"She didn't do it," I said too emphatically. Jake shot me a look. "She volunteers at a homeless shelter, for God's sake. She was homecoming queen. People like that don't commit murder."

"On the contrary," he said. "That's exactly who I would suspect if this were a movie."

"But it's not a movie."

"Neither is this, but we're still at it," Jake said, gesturing to the army of crew members who were wrapping up breakfast and preparing for their day of shooting. "Our central mystery has been blown out of the water, our main character is just a hack who screwed up, and now everyone and his brother knows the method behind The Bullet Catch."

"Well, they know one method," I said, biting into a strawberry that was way too big and juicy for this time of year. I considered the volume of pesticides I was consuming and then decided to throw caution to the wind and have another one. A hand shot in and grabbed my wrist as I reached for the second strawberry.

"What do you mean, *one* method?" I looked up to see Walter, the movie's director. He was holding my wrist tightly as I tried to pick up the strawberry. He wore his signature baseball cap and sunglasses. I couldn't see his eyes but I could sure feel his grip around my wrist. "There's more than one way to do The Bullet Catch?"

"Sure. I mean, it's like just about any magic trick. There are a lot of different methods to doing The Bullet Catch," I said, taking the strawberry from the plate with my free hand.

Walter hung onto my wrist. "There's another way to do it? That hasn't been revealed?"

I nodded while biting into the strawberry. I chewed it quickly, sensing he was looking for a prompt answer. "The audience may now know one way to do it because of that article, but you could simply use a different method and still fool them."

"So we could still fool them," he repeated quietly, finally releasing my wrist. "With another method." He stared up into the trees overhead. "The audience will think we're using the method they know and that's what they'll be looking for. But we won't. We'll use a different method." He turned and sat between us, the wooden bench creaking under his weight. He scratched at his chin thoughtfully.

"Magicians often did that after Terry revealed the method behind an illusion," I said, not entirely certain he was hearing me. "They'd just switch the method, which was double confusing for the audience, because it played on their preconceptions on how the trick was done. In many cases, it made for a more effective illusion."

"We'll do it all in one shot," Walter said, taking off his sunglasses and turning to Jake. "Seamless. From the moment Terry starts the act right through to when he gets shot. All one continuous take."

Walter then turned to me. His eyes were watery and bloodshot. "And you, Mr. Magic," he said, putting a chubby arm around my shoulder. "You will not only be our consultant on it, but I'm putting you in the movie. You, my friend, are the one who is going to shoot Terry Alexander."

CHAPTER 16

This new plan required an immediate meeting with the producers, Donna and Arnold. Huddled in the tented area that housed the video monitors—video village, as it was referred to by the crew—Walter outlined his plan for a new ending sequence for the movie that, in his mind, would put it on the cinematic map.

"It will be one continuous shot," he said breathlessly, "Taking us from the beginning of the trick, through each of the steps, right through to the final, fatal blast."

I noticed Jake wince a bit at Walter's choice of words, but he nodded along with the producers while the director made his impassioned pitch.

"Not since *Children of Men* has the cinema been graced with such a minutely choreographed set piece. *Goodfellas. The Player. Touch of Evil.* Those are the films that will be mentioned in the same hushed tones as our film." He stepped back and looked at them one at time. "We have the choice here, people, to make a movie or to make art. I, for one, vote for art."

"It will cost money that we don't have," Arnold said slowly.

"I'll cut my fee," Walter said.

"In half?" Donna ventured.

"By a third."

"How about your points?"

He shook his head. "Points demonstrate my commitment to this project. Points are sacred."

Arnold and Donna exchanged a look. "Give us a minute to talk about it." They retired to a corner of the tent and began to confer quietly. Walter turned to us and clapped his hands together gleefully. "This is going to be sweet," he said with a giggle.

Jake offered a halfhearted smile. A thought occurred to me.

"Walter," I began.

"Magic Man, speak," he replied dramatically.

"You know a lot about movies, right? Trivia and stuff."

"There is nothing about the cinema that is trivial," he said, continuing to intone his words. "But, yes, I'm a fount of useless information about movies."

"Great," I said, trying to think of the right way to phrase the question. "In the world of movies, what do you think of when you hear the name 'Francis?'"

"Easy. Frances Farmer. Brilliant actress, tortured soul."

I considered this. "Anything else come to mind around the name Francis?"

"Frances McDormand. Also brilliant. Much less tortured."

"What about on the male side of the equation?"

He thought about this for a long moment. "Well, Francis Ford Coppola, of course. Great filmmaker. Great winemaker. Could have retired after *The Godfather* and still been considered one of the best. Although," he added thoughtfully, "then we would not have experienced the stunning perfection of *The Conversation*."

He continued to ponder my question and was about to add to his list when Donna approached, with Arnold two steps behind.

"Here's our offer," she said. "Reduce your fee by one third, shave two days off the schedule, cut the helicopter shot and we've got a deal."

Walter took a deep intake of breath and his hand shot to his mouth at the mention of the helicopter shot. He stood very still for several seconds. Somewhere, I swear, I could hear a clock ticking. Finally he exhaled.

"You've got a deal. And I've got my shot. Let's put it on paper with blood."

The three headed toward the motor home that housed the

production office, Walter talking excitedly. Jake exchanged a look with me and I nodded. Before I could comment, Walter turned and yelled back at me.

"Oh, Magic Man, I forgot one, maybe the best one. When you're talking about old movies, the most famous Francis is a real ass. He's better known as *Francis the Talking Mule.*"

Filming shut down for the day, in order for Walter and his team to put together the components of their big finale. Before I left, I promised him I'd come back with another method for The Bullet Catch. The moment I said it, I realized I'd have to do it without Harry's help, as I had come to learn there was no greater enemy of The Bullet Catch than Harry Marks.

As I made my way across the barren field that served as the Renaissance Festival parking lot, I pulled out my wallet, searching for a business card I hoped I'd saved. I wasn't watching where I was going as I sorted through the various receipts and small-denomination bills that make up the desolate interior of my wallet. Consequently, I was taken aback when a foppish scarecrow suddenly lurched in front of me.

"Eli," the scarecrow hissed in a failed attempt at a stage whisper.

I yelped and jumped back, jamming my foot in a rut and neatly twisting my ankle. After a sharp grunt of pain, I finally steadied myself and looked toward where he had just been standing. There was no one in sight.

"Hello?" I asked tentatively.

"Eli," the voice hissed again. I followed the sound and turned to see the scarecrow cowering behind the Ford Fiesta was none other than Clive Albans. He was dressed in his typical potpourri fashion, a wild mix of stripes and checks and polka dots, with a madcap bouquet of colors sprinkled liberally throughout the ensemble. His eyes peered toward the main gate, and then back at me.

"Is it safe?"

I looked around, not seeing any threats on the horizon. "It appears to be safe," I said slowly.

"I must take precautions. I am *persona non grata* on these premises, I fear," he said. "Apparently, there are some who took offense at my article."

"You mean the article that ruined the mystery the movie is based on?"

"Yes, that's the one," he said, nodding and missing all the hints of sarcasm I had ladled onto my statement. "I was told in no uncertain terms to go and never darken their door again, so to speak."

"Then why are you here?"

He rose up to his full lanky height and leaned one long arm against the hood of the car, concluding the move with a prolonged, dramatic sigh. "Oh, Eli, it's show business. How can I resist?"

He scanned the horizon again and, convinced the coast was clear, lunged forward and was suddenly in my face. "Is there any dirt?" he asked breathlessly. "Any juicy gossip?"

"Clive, after what you've done, what makes you think I'd stand out here and dish dirt with you?"

"Because you're my brother," he said emphatically, mercifully taking a full step back.

"What?"

"Metaphorically, at least. We're in the brotherhood together, you and I."

"What brotherhood would that be?"

"Show business, dear boy. The business of show."

I pushed past him and continued across the field toward my car, taking care to put as little weight as possible on my throbbing ankle. "I've got nothing to say to you."

"Oh, don't pout," he yelled after me. "No one likes a pouter."

My answer took the form of me getting into my car, slamming the door, and spewing not nearly as much dirt and grass as I would have liked as I gunned the engine.

"Give Harry a hug for me," he said.

Then he disappeared across the field.

The search through my wallet had yielded the desired item: Roger Edison's business card. I gave him a call and he said it would be fine to drop by the office anytime. I was quick to explain I wouldn't be coming in to buy insurance, just to talk.

"That's okay," he said, chuckling over the phone. "I once sold $500,000 in life insurance to a guy who just came in to get change for the bus. So we shall see."

Roger's address put him in an office park near the Mall of America, so at the point where Highway 169 intersected Highway 494, I took the exit and headed east.

The office park consisted of a handful of seemingly-identical two and three-story buildings just off the freeway. The small lot in front of Roger's building was full, so I parked in front of a matching building across the street. As I walked back toward Roger's office, I noticed two blue-shirted maintenance men were standing by the large flagpole which stood majestically in front of the building. They were looking up the pole and I followed their gaze, up and up, to where a flag drooped sadly. The flag had evidently become twisted and tangled, and their efforts of tugging on the rope that raised and lowered the flag appeared to be having little effect.

"I bet I'm going to have to climb that damned pole again," said a voice behind me. I turned to see another maintenance man, in a blue work shirt that matched the others, striding along. The name patch on his shirt read "Doug."

"Climb the pole?" I said.

"Once it gets tangled up like it is now, that's usually the only solution."

As we walked, I looked up at the pole, which was probably close to three stories high. Even before my panic attacks I wouldn't have relished the thought of climbing it, but now the very thought of it tightened my stomach. And I wasn't comforted by the fact that my very out-of-shape thirty-something body was probably physically incapable of getting more than ten feet off the ground.

The guys at the base of the pole tugged ineffectually at the ropes and Doug, probably sensing they were making things worse, broke into a trot.

"Wish me luck," he yelled over his shoulder as he headed toward the pole. I gave him a weak wave and then headed up the sidewalk to Roger's building.

Of course, it wasn't really Roger's building. His was just one of the many businesses listed on the directory in the foyer. An indoor waterfall filled one wall of the lobby and I had the option of using the sweeping staircase or the elevator to go up the one floor to his office. Given my recent history with heights and railings, I opted for the elevator.

"Can I get you coffee or a soft drink?" his smiling receptionist asked once I had explained why I was there. I thanked her, said I was fine and went to grab a seat, but before I could pick a magazine to peruse, Roger bounded out of his office with an outstretched hand.

"Eli, twice in two weeks. We'll have to stop meeting like this."

"Thanks for seeing me on such short notice."

"What other kind is there nowadays? Hold all my calls," he said over his shoulder as he ushered me into his office.

"Yeah, whatever," the receptionist said and from my new vantage point I could see she was deeply involved in checking her Facebook page.

"My niece is filling in as my receptionist this summer before heading off to college," he explained as he pulled a chair up to the small table at one end of his office. "She's great in client-facing situations, but she seems to harbor a built-in resentment for management."

"Workers of the world unite," I said as I sat down.

"First talk of unionizing and she's back to babysitting. So, what brings you in today?" He held up his right hand. "No selling, I promise."

"It's about Dylan Lasalle," I said, and Roger's face shifted effortlessly from light and jovial to serious and concerned.

"A terrible tragedy," Roger said. "No one ever expects crime to hit so close to home."

I nodded. "I don't know how much you're allowed to talk about this," I continued, "but Trish was surprised Dylan had taken out such a large life insurance policy. I mean, without telling her. But, again," I added, "I don't want you to get in trouble talking about this."

"Eli," Roger said, patting me paternally on the arm, "This isn't like attorney-client privilege. I sold the guy some insurance, it's not a state secret. I mean, I've already talked to the police about it, so what's the harm in talking to you?"

"They've already questioned you?"

"One of their guys came by yesterday."

"Was it Homicide Detective Fred Hutton, by any chance?"

Roger turned his chair and consulted a business card on his desk. "It sure was," he said, holding the card up for me to see. "And what's the deal with him anyway? It's like Joe Friday, without the sense of humor."

"Homicide Detective Fred Hutton had a charm-ectomy."

Roger smiled at the image. "Well, surgery was successful. Looks like they got it all."

"So they asked you about the policy? And the double indemnity clause?"

Roger nodded. "They were all over it. I pulled my files and walked them through the whole thing. It was a very traditional policy, nothing special. Dylan did ask if it had a double indemnity clause, but he also asked a lot of other questions, so it didn't seem out of place at the time."

"Did anything seem out of place?"

"Yeah, as a matter of fact it did, but I didn't remember it until after the cops left and then I figured there might have been nothing to it."

I spread my hands, waiting for him to continue.

"When I was filling out the paperwork," he said, "I was asking him all the traditional questions—date of birth, social security, address, all that. And when I got to the part where I fill in the name of the beneficiary, I asked him if I should put in Trish's name. And he said the oddest thing. He said, 'Sure, why not. For now.'"

"For now?"

Roger nodded. "Anyway, he signed everything, passed the physical and the policy went into effect. I got my commission and didn't give it another thought."

I sat back in my chair, not quite sure what to do with this information. Always the professional conversationalist, Roger kept things rolling.

"So, pretty weird about Howard Washburn, huh?"

"You knew Howard?" For a moment I wasn't making the connection.

"Sure, we all did. We went to high school together."

I shook my head. "I know, I just can't place him."

"Well, to be fair, Howard didn't really stand out. I only remember him because he was one of my first customers."

"You sold him insurance too?"

Roger leaned in. "Eli, I sold him a ton of insurance. Way more than he needed. I still feel sort of bad about it."

I asked the obvious question. "Then why'd you do it?"

Roger shrugged. "I was brand new to the insurance business and wet behind the ears. I was making cold calls to everyone and his brother, trying to make some sales. I started paging through the yearbook and saw some likely candidates. Howard was the first person to give me any sort of positive response on the phone, so I arranged a meeting with him to talk about insurance."

"How'd that go?"

"Man, I still remember it, even though it was years ago. I guess you always remember your first." He gave a slightly risqué laugh, then continued. "We met for lunch at Liquor Lyle's. I'd never had much to do with Howard in school, but I was immediately struck with his need to, I don't know, fit in. Be part of the in-crowd. There was nothing I put on the table that day he wasn't interested in buying. And I was happy to sell it."

"What was he like?"

Roger thought about this for a long moment. "The key thing I remember about him was he wasn't memorable, if that makes any sense."

I nodded. "That's exactly how I remember him."

"It was sort of, I don't know, sad," Roger said. "But there was another quality I noticed at the time. I couldn't really put it into words, but he seemed like a guy who could easily tip."

"What do you mean, like more than twenty percent?"

Roger smiled and shook his head. "No, tip. Like, to one side or the other. I don't want to use dramatic terms, like go over to The Dark Side, but in his desperate need to please, I think it would have been very easy to screw with his moral compass. To tip him in whatever direction you wanted him to go."

Roger sat up and his big smile returned to his face. "Enough of the armchair psychology," he said. "Eli, is there anything else I can do for you?"

"Yes, one more question," I said as I stood up, sensing I had taken up enough of his time. "Who benefitted from all the insurance you sold Howard?"

"I haven't looked at the policies in a while, but I'm guessing it would be his wife, Sylvia." I was about to ask a question, but he shook his head and answered it before I could get it out. "No, she didn't go to school with us. Howard stumbled into that blonde bramble bush in college, God help him. You want her number?"

Given his description of her, I wasn't so sure I did, but I nodded and thanked him. Roger went three rounds with his niece and then finally got her to print out the contact information.

Upon leaving Roger's building, I was surprised to see an ambulance was parked by the flagpole, the lights on its roof flashing red and blue. From where I stood, I could see two EMTs were just loading someone into the back. He turned to look at me and I recognized Doug, the cheerful maintenance guy. His right arm had a seriously long and ugly gash in it, which one of the EMTs was hastily wrapping with what appeared to be yards and yards of gauze.

I looked up at the pole. The flag was straightened out and flapping freely in the breeze. I followed the rope down the pole, picturing how Doug had finished his work and probably slid down, perhaps gaining speed as he did. And then I saw the vertical cleat that was used to wrap the spare rope. One of the remaining maintenance guys was wiping blood off of it and I realized Doug's arm and the cleat must have intersected at great speed and proved to be a hindrance to his journey. A small adjustment to his right and it might have gone through one leg or the other or everything in between.

As the ambulance roared away, its siren blaring, I was reminded of our short conversation and was struck by a persistent, nagging thought: I probably should have wished him luck when I had the chance.

Chapter 17

"Sorry I'm late," I said. "I just spent fifteen minutes knocking at what I thought was the front door to your house. Turns out it was your garage." I gave a half laugh and Sylvia Washburn gave me a sour look.

I'd called her right after leaving Roger's office and although she was by no means enthusiastic, she said it would be permissible to stop by and talk to her for a moment. If I made it quick. Her tone struck me as odd. She sounded annoyed. Gruff. Impatient.

What she didn't sound like was a grieving widow.

The house, once I found it, was stunning. Buried deep in a swank neighborhood called Deep Haven, it was situated on the tony shores of Lake Minnetonka. The house—okay, let's call it a mansion—sat on a hill high above the lake and wasn't visible from the curvy road I'd used to get there. That may have explained my mistake with the garage, but trust me, the garage looked amazing. And the mansion even more so.

"I have people coming in thirty minutes, so we'll have to make this quick," she said, turning and walking into the house, not waiting to see if I would follow. She was tall and thin and blonde and coiffed within an inch of her life. Every hair was lacquered into place, her lipstick looked like it had been applied surgically, and her blood-red nails could have been painted with actual blood. Not since my fourth-grade teacher Sister Naomi had threatened me with a ruler had I met a more frightening woman.

"Our new maid of two weeks, Carmelita, quit suddenly yesterday and I could strangle her," she said over her shoulder as she made a sharp left out of the grand foyer through which we were trekking. I followed her, made the turn and found myself in a mammoth dining room, with a table set for at least sixteen with room to spare. A chandelier worthy of the Phantom of the Opera hung above the center of the table, around which two harried Hispanic women were furiously putting the final touches on the place settings. A quick count of the forks and spoons suggested at least a seven-course meal was planned. For what it was worth, my dinner plans were likely to consist of eating a bowl of Cheerios over my kitchen sink. Everyone defines haute cuisine in their own way, I guess.

Sylvia Washburn barked some words in Spanish to the two women. My high school Spanish was once again tested. She spoke with such speed and venom all I really picked up were the words for "faster" and "idiots." It was surprising Carmelita had lasted as long as she had.

"Twenty-eight minutes, Mr. Marks," Sylvia said as she made imperceptible adjustments to the women's work. She turned and gave me a glare that made me actually squint. "What did you want to talk to me about?"

For a moment my mind went blank and I would have been hard-pressed to provide my own name and address. Then, mercifully, conscious thought returned.

"Well, first, my condolences on your loss," I said.

She flicked something invisible off her sleeve. "Thank you," she said with no warmth. "Once again, Howard demonstrated his terrible timing. We'd had this dinner planned for weeks. He knew that."

"Were you married long?" I ventured.

"Too long by half, but I blame myself as much as Howard for that. Is that all you wanted, Mr. Marks? To extend condolences? Because, frankly, that could have been handled over the phone."

She made a move that suggested the front door was beckoning, but I held my ground. I've worked in front of my share of tough audiences and have developed skills for dealing with the drunk and belligerent. This may have been my greatest test yet.

"Actually, I was trying to get more information about Howard and his business. He and I chatted before his, um, accident, but I never got a really clear picture of how he made what was clearly a good living." I made an ineffectual gesture toward the surroundings, looking very much like someone selling something, badly, on late-night cable.

"Yes, Howard was a good provider, I will say that about him," she said. "Of course, I always told him if he would work ten percent harder I would be twenty percent happier, but it was like talking to a wall with him."

"What exactly was the nature of his business?" I pressed.

She gave the Deep Haven version of a shrug, exerting the least possible amount of energy to complete the action. "International shipping of some kind. Buying, selling. He was on the phone most of the time, I can tell you that."

"Do you have any more specifics?"

She could not have looked more bored. "Mr. Marks, our relationship was not unlike that of Jackie and President Kennedy. When he came home at the end of the day, I made a point of never discussing his business."

It took me a moment to realize she was comparing herself to the most famous widow of the past century without a touch of irony. I sensed I had reached the end of our conversational rope.

"I see," I said. "Well, thank you for your time, Mrs. Washburn."

"No trouble at all, Mr. Marks," she replied curtly, although I sensed that it had been a great deal of trouble for her, thank you very much. She marched back toward the front door and I followed. We walked quickly back through the foyer, her heels making a steady click click click. She held the front door open and turned a cold smile on me. "Enjoy your evening."

I stepped forward and a final thought occurred to me. "One last thing," I said, nearly slipping into a Peter Falk impression. "I was wondering, did you know Dylan Lasalle?"

There's a scene in the old movie, *The House of Wax*, where in the midst of a fire the villain's wax face actually cracks from the heat. That isn't literally what happened to Sylvia Washburn's face, but it looked to be the emotional equivalent. She looked at me and her expressionless face was suddenly filled with several waves of emotions. Then she regained control and once again all emotion disappeared from her visage.

"I was familiar with very few of Howard's business associates, but Mr. Lasalle and I did meet on a handful of occasions," she said, choosing each word precisely. "I was very sorry to hear of his passing. You've reminded me I really must send a card to his wife. It's Patricia, right?"

"Trish, yes," I said. We stood for a moment in silence. I was thinking she had something to add, but apparently she didn't share that sentiment.

"Thank you again, Mr. Marks. I really must prepare the house for my guests." The door shut with a solid finality.

I walked back down the lengthy, twisty driveway to my car and sat in it for a long while. I thought about the garage that was nicer than most people's homes. I thought about Howard Washburn and how he so desperately wanted to be liked. I thought about how my only real memory of Howard was going to be of him seated at his desk with a bullet in his brain. I thought about how easy it was for some people to tip. And I thought about the dinner party that was about to start without him and about the wife who would miss her last maid more than her sad, late husband.

It was at that point I shook myself out of my reverie, started the car and headed home. I was damned if they were going to catch me crying in Deep Haven.

Mack the Knife was playing on the jukebox when I walked into Adrian's and it was the perfect antidote to my encounter with Sylvia Washburn. As expected, Harry was seated in the back. It was likely he who paid a quarter to spin his favorite Bobby Darin song; he's been known to invest as much as three dollars in one sitting. It delights him, but the repeated playing tends to drive the other patrons crazy.

I expected to see a gaggle of Mystics at the back table, but this evening only Max had joined Harry for a beer. As I approached I could tell they were in the midst of their lifelong argument. They say most marriages are built on the same argument, repeated *ad infinitum*. The same was true of Harry and Max. Their argument revolves around what magicians have dubbed The Too-Perfect Theory. In a nutshell, it argues that the more perfect a trick appears, the more likely the audience will be to figure out the method. So, like every great piece of art, a trick needs a slight flaw in its design to draw the eye away from the method.

"For example," Max was saying as I approached their table, "if I do a trick with my cell phone, that's too perfect. It's a piece of technology and the audience is gonna be thinking, 'Well, there must be an app for it.'"

"But," he continued, holding up a hand to stop Harry from making a comment he didn't even look like he was going to make, "if I do a trick with *your* cell phone..."

"Good luck," I said as I sat down to join them. "It's never on."

"Buster, save me from this conversation," Harry said with mock terror. "Put me out of my misery."

"No way, old man. I'd wager that you were the one who poured the kerosene on the ember this time and it's your fault he's all riled up."

Harry grunted a response and the two continued their bellyaching while I stepped to the bar to order a beer. I didn't want them to realize it, but I actually enjoyed these arguments and over the years I'd learned a lot about the subtleties of magic from listening to them banter back and forth. When I returned, they had settled into a watchful silence. I sipped my beer as each of them looked around the bar and at the pretzels on the table and at me, but never at each other. *Mack the Knife* ended on the jukebox and then a second or so later it started up again.

"I will say this one last thing on the subject," Max interjected suddenly and I could see Harry's shoulders tense up. "And then I will call it a night."

"Please do that," Harry said.

"The final word comes not from me, but from Darwin Ortiz, who I think we can all agree knows good magic."

Harry grunted an assent. Max looked to me and I nodded enthusiastically. Darwin Ortiz was the real deal.

"Darwin said, 'If you can get people to ask the wrong question, you'll guarantee they never come up with the right answer.' And that, my friend, is all I need to say about the Too-Perfect Theory."

"Thank heavens," Harry said.

"Now I will take my leave of you fine gentlemen." Max looked at his watch. "Given the way the stoplights are timed in this city, I should make it home in an hour. I could walk it in twenty minutes, but with the fercockta stoplights, the drive will take me an hour." He got up, tipped a nonexistent hat at us and ambled out the door.

"You guys never get tired of arguing about that, do you?"

Harry smirked at me. "To tell you the truth, Buster, I'm entirely on his side. But where's the fun in that?"

He chuckled and sipped his beer. I took a handful of pretzels from the bowl on the table and we both sat there listening to Mr. Darin do the definitive version of *Mack the Knife*. For a brief second I thought of the dinner party going on right now in Deep Haven, and then put it out of my mind completely, sat back and enjoyed the rest of my evening with Harry.

I had just finished breakfast (Cheerios, over the sink) when the phone rang with the default tone. I've got a different ring tone for just about everyone I know. For my ex-wife, Deirdre, I had gone through a lot of options, finally settling on The Stones' *It's All Over Now*. Megan was originally assigned *It Had To Be You*, but right after she announced we were "on a break," I changed it to *Heartbreak Hotel*. She's never called, so it's never been tested since the day I set it. For other magician friends, I've used a variety of songs over the years: *Do You Believe in Magic, Magic Bus, Magic Mystery Tour, Magic Carpet Ride* and *Strange Magic.* Harry, of course, got *Mack the Knife.*

So when my phone rings and it's the default ring tone (*Hello* from *Book of Mormon*), I know it's either someone trying to sell me something or someone I don't know well enough to have taken the time to assign a ring tone.

It took me several seconds to find the phone, because it had slipped onto the floor next to my bed, and then under my bed when my foot hit it. Consequently I was a tad breathless when I answered.

"Oh, Eli, are you okay? I'm sorry to bother you. Oh, it's Trish, by the way."

"I'm fine," I said, sitting on the edge of my bed. "Just playing a quick game of floor hockey with the phone."

"Look, I'm sorry to bother you," she repeated.

"It's no bother," I said quickly. Although her voice still had a quaver to it, she didn't sound as weepy as the last time we had spoken.

"I just got a call from the police and it's sort of unnerved me," she said, "and I was wondering if I could ask a favor of you?"

"Sure, no problem, name it," I said, sounding way too agreeable.

"They say they want me to come downtown, so they can take an impression of my fingerprints or something. Oh, and they also need me to give a DNA sample," she added. "They said it's routine, it's just so they can have the information on file as they continue to investigate Dylan's death."

"I think that's very common with a spouse in these situations," I said, having no idea what I was talking about.

"Well, even so it's got me spooked and I was wondering if you have time this morning to come with me? You know, for moral support?"

I was trying to temper my eagerness, so I didn't answer

immediately, which she then read as hesitation on my part. "Of course, I know this is short notice," she continued, but I cut her off.

"No problem, Trish. I'm wide open all day. Do you want me to come get you and we can ride downtown together?"

"Oh, Eli, that would be great. Just great. Let me give you my address."

It took me a while to find a scrap of paper and even longer to find a working pen, but I finally got my act together and told her I'd see her in thirty minutes.

I realized, as I craned my neck and stared up at the condo tower, that I look at tall buildings entirely differently than I used to. Before the panic attacks, the condo tower on the Northwest shore of Lake Calhoun would have produced no other emotion in me than the envious feeling that I would never make enough money—even if I lived to be a hundred—to afford to live there. That thought was still in my head, but the primary emotion I was feeling as I walked up to the lobby door was a deep-seated hope Trish lived on the second floor, or better yet, on a rollaway in the lobby.

No such luck. The directory put the Lasalles on the twenty-ninth floor. I rang the bell and a moment later the buzzer buzzed and I stepped into the building. The elevator greeted me with a ding as I approached it, and before I knew it I was deposited on the twenty-ninth floor.

"I'm sorry, I'm just about ready to go," Trish said as she opened the door and then moved away, disappearing around a corner as I stepped into the apartment. I don't know what I expected, but I certainly didn't expect this. The place looked like a designer showroom, or like one of those celebrity homes in a magazine where everything looks perfect and completely unlived in.

It was an open floor plan, where the living room flowed right into the dining area which flowed right into the stainless steel kitchen. A hall around the corner led to what I assumed were bedrooms and bathrooms. Floor-to-ceiling windows lined two of the three walls. The third wall consisted of French doors that opened out onto a large balcony. I saw that and inched several steps backward, toward the safety of the front door. I felt a bead of sweat beginning to form on my temple as I worked on Dr. Bakke's breathing exercises.

"Can I get you anything?" Trish asked as she came back into the room. "Coffee? Espresso?"

"Ovaltine," I added hoarsely, completing the joke from *Young Frankenstein*, but this was of course lost on her.

"Oh, dear, I don't think I have any of that," she said slowly, her eyes scanning the kitchen cabinets.

"No, I'm just kidding," I said quickly. "Do you want to go?" I cocked my head toward the hall and the elevator beyond.

"Oh, I suppose we should get it over with," she sighed. I stepped into the hall and she followed. I pulled the door shut and started toward the elevator, but Trish doubled back toward her front door. She gave the door a hard yank until she heard a click.

"You have to yank it," she said. "It sticks." We then headed down the hall back to the elevators.

"What are you now, her chauffeur?"

"She wanted a ride, I gave her a ride. You know me, I'm a nice guy."

Deirdre snorted a short laugh and then took a sip from her cup. The coffee looked bad; I imagined it tasted worse. "Yes, Eli, you are that. And you know what they say about nice guys?"

I ignored her comment and turned my attention across the squad room. A policewoman was taking Trish's fingerprints, carefully rolling each fingertip across a computer tablet, checking the results on a video screen in front of her. It was a slow and deliberate process.

"How's the case coming?" I asked, deftly switching the subject.

"Slowly," she said, flipping open a thick file folder on the counter in front of us. She paged through sheet after sheet of paper.

"Turns out the gun that shot Dylan Lasalle was the same one that killed Howard Washburn. So there's that."

"Is that good?"

She looked up at me. "It's not good or bad. It just is." She continued looking through the file. "How's your thing?"

"Excuse me? Since the divorce was finalized, I think 'my thing' is no longer within your purview."

She rolled her eyes at me. "Your suicidal-scared-of-heights thing."

"Oh, that thing. About the same. I did some online research on it."

"What did you learn?"

"It turns out there are lots of other people with the same condition."

"Is that good?"

I gave her my best penetrating look. "It's not good or bad. It just is."

She turned over another report in the folder, revealing a crime scene photo. The moment I saw it, I made an involuntary sound, like a heavily suppressed yelp. Deirdre glanced over at me, and then realized the cause of my reaction. She pulled the photo out and placed it on the counter in front of me. It was clearly from Dylan Lasalle's crime scene.

"Yeah, this one's a real mess." She pointed at the photo as she continued. "First they shot him in the heart, killing him just about instantly. Then a shot to the head, just to be sure."

It was a grisly scene, even in black and white, with Dylan's body splayed across the running path, his face and chest a mass of torn flesh and blood.

"Is there a particular reason you're showing this to me?" I asked, turning the photo over. She turned it back right side up.

"Yes, to remind you of what we're dealing with here. Your high school sweetheart is connected to two unsolved crimes: A mugging that doesn't look like a mugging and a suicide that doesn't look like a suicide."

"So she's a suspect?"

"A person of interest," she replied. "For now at least."

"Have you gotten any more information about Howard Washburn's business and his connection to Dylan?"

"Only that he made a lot more money than his two-bit office would suggest, money I suspect he laundered heavily."

"With Dylan Lasalle's help?"

"That's what we think. Lasalle was likely carrying drugs or some other contraband in and out of the country for Washburn and possibly others. And we think recently Mr. Lasalle recognized the end was in sight."

"And that's why he was looking to strike a deal and maybe testify?"

"That's a theory."

"A talking mule," I said quietly.

"What?"

"Dylan was a talking mule."

Deirdre considered this and nodded. "Essentially."

I looked back across the squad room. The policewoman was just finishing swabbing the inside of Trish's cheek. She took the damp swab and placed it into an evidence tube, sealed it and pasted a typed label across the front. She nodded at Trish, who picked up her purse and crossed the room to us.

"Is that all you needed?"

Deirdre glanced up at her, quickly slipping the crime scene photo under one of the reports near the top of her folder.

"Yes, thank you for coming in," she said as she began walking her toward the door. I followed three steps behind.

"I know it's a hassle," Deirdre continued, "But having your fingerprints and DNA on file really helps in the elimination process. For example, some hairs were found on your husband's body and odds are they're yours, but if they're not, then that becomes a good lead."

"Well, if you need anything else, by all means let me know. And, of course, if you learn anything."

"You'll be one of the first," Deirdre said. "Now I'll release you into your driver's custody."

The joke, such as it was, took a moment to settle and then Trish gave it as polite a laugh as it deserved. I held the door for her and she went through it. I was about to follow, when Homicide Detective Fred Hutton made his way through the door. I held it for him, gave a nod to Deirdre and followed Trish to the elevator. The two of them quickly fell into a hushed conversation.

"Well, at least it didn't take long," I said as I got to the bank of elevators. She had already pressed the down button. "If you have no other plans, maybe we could stop and have lunch on the way back to your place," I suggested.

"Sure," Trish said as the elevator door slid open. "Or I could make you a chicken salad sandwich." She stepped into the elevator.

The thought of trying to hold any food down while seated in that kitchen made me stop for a moment, halfway in and halfway out of the elevator car. I pictured being surrounded on two sides by floor-to-ceiling windows and on one side by French doors that led out to a twenty-nine story drop. I knew that was well beyond my current therapy goals. I stepped into the elevator.

"Let's stop at a restaurant," I suggested, deciding being forceful here would be better than lying in a fetal position on her kitchen floor.

"Sure, whatever," Trish said as the door began to slide shut.

A hand reached in at the last second and stopped the door in its tracks. After a moment, it slid open again, revealing Homicide Detective Fred Hutton. Deirdre stood alongside him.

"Mrs. Lasalle. Eli. Would you mind coming back into the office for a moment?" Deirdre said in a flat tone, the one I knew always meant trouble.

"Is there a problem?" Trish asked.

"You could say that."

CHAPTER 18

"Sylvia Washburn is dead?" I repeated my question, even though Deirdre had already answered it once.

"Yes. Last night. One of her maids found her this morning."

For a quick moment, I thought how Carmelita had wisely vacated that job at just the right time.

"How? Where? When?" I stopped just short of asking why and who, thinking that was not the path to go down at this moment.

We were seated in a small conference room, Trish and I on one side of the table, Deirdre on the other. Homicide Detective Fred Hutton leaned against the wall, in his standard glowering golem pose.

"She drowned in her Jacuzzi tub," Deirdre explained. "There are no signs of struggle in the bathroom, so we're proceeding under the assumption the death was from natural causes." She turned to Trish. "Mrs. Lasalle, were you acquainted with Mrs. Washburn?"

"Only slightly," Trish said quietly. "We'd been to their house once or twice. We weren't close."

Deirdre made a note of this and then turned to me. "And you never met her, right?" she asked in passing as she returned to her note taking. When I didn't answer immediately, she looked up at me.

"Actually," I said slowly, "I met her once. At her house. Last night."

This got the attention of Homicide Detective Fred Hutton. He crossed the room and pushed the door closed with his hand. He then sat next to Deirdre at the table and produced his own notepad from his suit coat pocket.

"Let's start at the beginning," he said as he flipped open the notebook and clicked his pen. "At the very beginning."

As interrogations go, I suppose it could have been worse.

They quickly decided they needed to separate us, putting Trish in one room and me in another. While she cooled her heels, I related to Deirdre and Homicide Detective Fred Hutton everything that had happened so far: my encounters with Dylan Lasalle at the reunion, my mysterious meeting with Mr. Lime at a house on Lake of the Isles, my phone call with Howard Washburn and subsequent discovery of his body. Deirdre took down the address of Mr. Lime's mansion and then continued with the questioning. I talked about my conversation with Roger Edison and recounted my misadventure with the Washburn's garage, before getting to the heart of the matter.

"And why did you go out to her home?" Deirdre asked.

"Like I said before, I was just trying to figure out the relationship between Howard Washburn and Dylan Lasalle."

Homicide Detective Fred Hutton grunted on his side of the table, but a look from Deirdre quickly silenced him.

"Why is that your concern?" Deirdre continued unabated.

"I was curious," I said, trying to keep any defensiveness out of my voice.

"Did Mrs. Lasalle ask you to make these inquiries?"

"No," I said. "I was looking into this matter on my own."

"And can we make the assumption Mrs. Lasalle is saying the same thing to Detective Wright in the room across the hall?"

"I can't see any reason why she wouldn't."

Deirdre gave me a long look. "But you've had no relationship with Mrs. Lasalle since high school, is that correct?"

"It is. And we really didn't have much of a relationship back then."

"You were acquaintances."

"That would be putting it strongly."

"And you reconnected at the reunion?"

"We did."

She rolled her eyes, and then reached over and shut off the recording device that had been rolling since this 'official' interview had begun. "Oh, Eli. What are you doing?"

I looked around the room. "Is that an official question?"

"Did you have a crush on this woman in high school?"

"I'm not sure I should answer that."

"Oh, I see, the questions about the murders and the muggings and the suicides and the drownings, you'll answer those questions, but you want to take the fifth on whether or not you had a crush on her?"

"I'm not sure it's germane," I finally said.

"Why don't you let us decide what is and is not germane," she said, and then reached over and started the recorder again. "And where were you last evening between the hours of eight and eleven?"

"I was at Adrian's with Uncle Harry, listening to *Mack the Knife*."

This was too much for Homicide Detective Fred Hutton. "Nonsense, that song is only three minutes long."

"Not the way Harry plays it." That was going to be my answer, but Deirdre had beaten me to it. This resulted in a long look between the couple, the cold silence speaking volumes. Deidre closed her notebook.

"Finally, do you know of anyone who would have had any reason to harm Mrs. Washburn?"

I considered mentioning the household staff, but decided if any of them had committed the crime, they deserved to get away with it.

"No, I don't."

Homicide Detective Fred Hutton reluctantly closed his notebook, but he was clearly not happy about it.

* * *

After we'd made it through our respective interrogations, neither one of us was in the mood for lunch, so Trish suggested she'd take a rain check and I began to drive her home. Once we made it out of downtown, I took a right on Franklin Avenue, figuring going around the lakes might conclude the events of the morning on a more pleasant note.

"That Detective Wright really doesn't like me," Trish said as we crested the hill and Lake of the Isles came into view.

"Yes, well, you two are BFFs compared to how Homicide Detective Fred Hutton feels about me," I said. "He didn't like my alibi at all."

"Why not? You were in a bar, with your uncle, the whole evening."

"I think he didn't believe *Mack the Knife* can or should be played that often."

"Well, at least you have an alibi," she said. "God, I can't believe we're sitting here talking about alibis. How did I get into this mess?"

I had an answer on the tip of my tongue, but wisely kept it there.

It ultimately didn't matter, because a moment later she spit out the word I was thinking.

"Dylan," she said, as harshly as I'd ever heard her say anything. "That's how I got into this mess. Now, because of him, everyone thinks I'm a murderer and they're going to put me in jail and I'll never be heard from again."

"I'll come visit," I said.

For some reason, that made her laugh and then it made me laugh as well.

"Actually, at this point, you are unlikely to be arrested, let alone do any time," I said.

"Why do you think that?"

"Because like Homicide Detective Fred Hutton, I lived with

that Assistant DA and I know how she works. She's not going to push to have you arrested."

"Well, that's nice," Trish said. "At least someone out there thinks I'm innocent."

I shook my head. "Disabuse yourself of that notion right now. It's not that she thinks you're innocent. It's just that she knows she can't prove you're guilty. At least not in court. And I know that woman: she won't push for an arrest unless she is sure she can get a conviction. She never starts an argument unless she knows ahead of time she is going to win it."

"That must make things fun at home," Trish said with a trace of a smile.

"That's the central tension in their relationship," I said, turning off of Lake of the Isles Parkway, heading the car toward Lake Calhoun. "He knows who the bad guys are, but she won't prosecute unless she knows she can win. They really should consider getting into some therapy for that."

"But I will say this," I continued. "If someone is trying to frame you in these killings, they are doing a real half-assed job of it. I think the police and the DA's office are only interested in you because they have no one else to look at. Once they find another shiny object, they'll be done with you and start going after someone else."

"Well, given some of the people Dylan hung around with, I would think they have no shortage of other shiny objects."

Her mention of the people Dylan hung around with got me to thinking about Mr. Lime and his stocky, well-muscled assistant. They'd already demonstrated a keen interest and ability in tailing me. Had they followed me out to Sylvia Washburn's house, and then patiently waited until the party broke up to announce themselves?

I suddenly had an image of Harpo standing stock-still as he held Sylvia's head under the foaming water in the Jacuzzi, while Mr. Lime stood silently by, spreading hand cream on his bony fingertips.

Our arrival at Trish's high-rise condo knocked that image out of my head, at least for the time being.

"Are you sure I can't invite you up for lunch?" she asked as she swung open the passenger door. I turned my head and craned my neck, looking up at the building, imagining which floor in that too-tall building was the twenty-ninth.

"I'll take a rain check," I said. "Besides, I have a busy afternoon."

"Oh, do you have a gig?"

I shook my head. "No. I've got to figure out how to shoot a guy without killing him."

I spent the rest of that afternoon and most of the evening squirreled away in my apartment, doing research on other methods for doing The Bullet Catch. Normally I would have simply asked Harry and he would have given me a handful of feasible options right off the top of his head. But knowing his dislike of The Bullet Catch, I felt I was better off flying under the radar on this one, which meant cracking open the books and doing actual research.

I have a modest library of magic books and was able to sneak several out of the shop downstairs without Harry getting suspicious. But I knew the true mother lode of books would be found in my uncle's bookcases in his apartment, and there was no chance I could garner access to any of those volumes without alerting him to my mission. So I used the resources at hand, and some quick forays onto the Internet, working to assemble a suitable method that would look good on camera and keep Jake from being injured. Or worse.

I quickly discovered the downside to researching The Bullet Catch. With each method I found came stories of the many magicians who have died attempting the stunt. And these weren't just stories of amateur magicians who had gotten in over their heads. The majority of fatalities were magicians who had performed the trick for years, seemingly using well-practiced methods they considered to be foolproof. After I'd read over a dozen such stories, I set aside all the research and—using all the examples of what hadn't worked—I began to structure my own method I felt would work safely on camera in one long, continuous shot.

I took occasional breaks to clear my head. I spent some time emptying out my email inbox, which had become stuffed with spam that had cleverly weaseled past my filter, as well as legitimate emails I simply hadn't gotten around to reading.

Several emails pertained to the high school reunion. One was from the organizing committee, asking me to fill out a poorly-worded questionnaire about the event and my thoughts on future reunions. There were also several emails from the photographer at the event, each offering a better deal on the pictures he'd taken than the last, suggesting he wasn't getting many takers on the photos he had captured.

When I finished with that, I spent a long while staring out the window in my bedroom, which overlooks the roof of the movie theater next door. From this vantage point I can peer down through the small window in the theater's projection booth, where I can see a corner of the room and a portion of the back wall, which holds among other things, a small mirror. Over the years I've spent many happy and restful hours, trying to determine what movie they were showing by observing the way the lights and the shadows bounced around the small room. On this particular evening, I was unable to come to a conclusion about what movie it was, although I suspect it was in black and white.

When that no longer held my attention, I picked up the yearbook I had pulled out in my effort to try to remember who Howard Washburn had been. Flipping through the pages, I came across my own senior photo, which looked just as geeky as I remembered. Beneath the photo it listed my meager list of activities, including the chess club and the talent show. Like many others, I had chosen a favorite quote to conclude my entry. Mine was a favorite saying Harry had taught me, a maxim he felt all magicians should take to heart: "Don't run if no one is chasing you."

This foray down memory lane led me to search out the photos of Jake and then Trish and finally Dylan.

Jake looked movie-star handsome even at that young age, his head turned toward the camera from over his shoulder, an insolent grin on his face. Under his photo it listed all his high school activities, with a healthy emphasis on the drama club. He followed this up with his favorite quote: "Live fast, die young and leave a good-looking corpse."

Trish's senior portrait was also stunning, her clear eyes challenging the camera, her hands folded neatly in front of her. Her list of activities was twice as long as Jake's and included—in addition to her title as Homecoming Queen—a long list of all the charitable and service activities she had taken part in. Despite the lengthy list, the yearbook editors were still able to make room for a quote, in this instance attributed to Eleanor Roosevelt: "The future belongs to those who believe in the beauty of their dreams."

Finally I turned to the page that should have held the photo of Dylan Lasalle. His name was listed, but there was an empty space where his photo should have been. In the photo area were the words "No Photo Supplied." There were no activities listed under his name and certainly no insightful quote.

I paged through the book for a while and then went back to work on my assignment for the evening: Find a way to keep Jake's high school quote from coming true, at least on the film set tomorrow. It was well past midnight when I set my notes aside and crawled into bed. But sleep was elusive, and when it came it included repeated images of Harpo pushing Sylvia Washburn under the water, while Mr. Lime stood by, putting on gloves and smiling that toothy, cadaverous grin of his. It was not a restful night.

CHAPTER 19

"Now I know how the actors playing Amos and Andy must have felt."

"Any chance you could confine your references to those less than seventy-five years old?" Lauren said as she continued to apply the dark makeup to my face.

"You recognized the reference enough to criticize it," I countered, shutting my eyes while she worked on my eyelids.

"I'm a makeup person. Of course I get an Amos and Andy reference. You are a white man. I am applying makeup to give you the appearance of an Ecuadorian native. I'm just suggesting you might want to refresh your mental trivia bins. Even a lame reference to George Hamilton's tan would put you closer to the present day."

"This is a tough room," I muttered. "What happened to nice Lauren?"

"Suck it up," she said, twisting my head with her hand and starting to apply makeup behind each of my ears. "I'm under-staffed, overworked and have been on this picture for far too long. Nice Lauren disappeared about two weeks back."

"I'm just going to sit here very quietly," I said.

"Good plan."

We had done a quick rehearsal that morning and I had demonstrated to Walter, the director, the key steps in the approach I had put together for The Bullet Catch. Like the original version, it required Jake, as Terry, to pull two natives from the crowd. Under his direction, they would inspect the bullet, sign the bullet, and load the gun. Then one of them would fire the shot, bringing the show to a tragic conclusion.

The method I had developed took a sharp left turn from the method Terry Alexander had used and would, I thought, throw off track anyone who had read Clive's article.

Satisfied with my plan, Walter had sent me to makeup and sent the Assistant Director in search of an extra to play the other native. I hadn't known what to expect in the makeup process, but the best I could tell, Lauren had sprayed my hair black and was just about finished giving my skin a darker complexion.

"What can I do for you?" Lauren said to someone as they entered the tent. My eyelids were still clamped shut.

"Walter said to make me up like an Ecuadorian native," a familiar voice said.

"What? Now you're an extra?" Lauren asked, twisting my head to the other side, rubbing makeup behind my left ear.

"Not just an extra. I get to pull the trigger."

I opened my eyes and turned my head as much as Lauren would allow. I recognized Stewart, the writer, had taken the chair next to me. Out of the corner of my eye I saw one of Lauren's assistants throw a makeup bib over him and begin to prepare his blond hair for spraying.

"But I'm the shooter," I said, trying to turn my head to look at him. Lauren, who was just as strong as she looked, kept a firm grip on my skull, allowing virtually no movement.

"Not anymore," Stewart said, not even attempting to subdue his glee. "Walter said he thought he'd throw me a bone, after all the crap he's given me. I'm really looking forward to this," he added. He actually rubbed his hands together like a silent movie villain.

"I don't think that's a good idea," I said, once again attempting to turn toward him, but Lauren twisted my head back to her desired position. "This effect requires a level of training you don't possess."

"Oh, nonsense," he said. "I'm pointing a fake gun with a fake bullet at a fake actor twenty feet away. What could go wrong?"

* * *

"I'm really not comfortable with this," I said as I tried to keep up with Walter. He was following the cameraman around the set as they blocked out the shot. The cameraman wasn't so much holding the camera as he was wearing it. A harness encased his chest like a vest and a metal arm on a pivot jutted from the harness, with the camera securely clamped to the metal arm. A monitor below the camera allowed him to see the shot as he glided through the set, with Walter right on his heels.

"If you're uncomfortable, talk to wardrobe. They'll get you a looser serape. Although tell them I love that color on you."

"No, not my costume. I'm not comfortable with Stewart firing the gun in this scene."

"Oh, Eli, there's nothing to it. You showed me the process yourself. A monkey could fire the gun at that point and no one will get hurt."

"Unless he *wants* someone to get hurt."

Walter stopped looking at the image on the camera's monitor and looked up at me. "Are we still talking about the monkey?"

"No, we're talking about Stewart."

He thought about this for a moment and then shook his head. "Stewart can't hurt anybody. He's just the writer."

I wasn't so sure about that. Even at our first meeting, Stewart had exhibited a thinly-suppressed rage at what had been done to his screenplay and at the casting of Jake in the role of Terry Alexander.

I also remembered his reaction when we both separately came across Jake and Noël necking in the woods. His face had looked nearly demonic, starring daggers at Jake. And there had been a gleam in Stewart's eye when I left him in the makeup tent that made me seriously uneasy.

Walter and the cameraman had continued on their rehearsal path and were now on the other side of the large dirt clearing that would act as the staging ground for this scene.

"I love a martini," a voice said behind me. I turned to see Arnold, the producer, walking toward me, smiling an uncharacteristically large grin. Also uncharacteristic was his wardrobe. Instead of his usual freshly pressed Hawaiian shirt and very expensive off-white slacks, he was dressed not unlike myself, although about twenty percent better. Outfitted like an Ecuadorian townsperson, he had the addition of an impressively large hat and a slightly tarnished badge, which was displayed prominently on his equally prominent chest. Completing the look were a pair of mirrored sunglasses. Thrown as I was by his wardrobe, I was still trying to figure out why he was talking about martinis.

"Bit early in the day for a martini, isn't it?"

"Not the drink, my friend. The shot." He threw an arm over my shoulder and began to walk me along the perimeter of the set. "On a movie shoot, the last shot of the day is called the martini. Why, you ask?"

I hadn't, but that wasn't an issue with Arnold. "It's called the martini because the next shot is out of a glass...at the bar!" He laughed a deep and unsettling laugh. "And in this divine instance, not only is this the last shot of the day, it's the last shot of the production. After this, it's a wrap. And not a moment too soon, if you ask me."

Once again I hadn't, but again that didn't matter to Arnold. I did have a question, though, so I interjected it before he had time to start another soliloquy. "So you're an extra today?" I asked. "Sort of pulling a cameo, like Hitchcock?"

He shook his head and laughed. "I'm not just any old extra. I asked Walter if I could play the sheriff in this scene. You see, it will be my revolver that Terry Alexander borrows for his trick. His last trick," he added ominously.

"Your revolver? Your personal revolver?"

Arnold laughed. "Oh, would that it were, but no. It's coming from props." He continued to walk and to talk. "I gotta tell you it will be a great relief to finally get this monster in the can. I've produced some pain-in-the-ass productions in the past, but this has been a friggin' nightmare. You know the mystery is ruined, right? Right down the toilet."

He obviously still hadn't put it together that my uncle was the primary cause for this, and I felt no need to disabuse him of that notion at this late date. "Yes, it's a shame," I agreed. "So, what will that do to the marketing of the film? What approach will you take?"

"I have some ideas I've been playing with," he said, his voice dropping in volume, bringing it almost down to the level of an average speaker. "I think—depending on how things go today—we'll kick a few of them up the flagpole and see who salutes."

"And how do you expect things to go today?"

He took off his sunglasses and squinted up at the sun, then turned and surveyed the entire set before turning back to me. "I expect things to go swimmingly," he said, smiling as he put his sunglasses back on. "Just swimmingly."

While they continued to tweak the camera positions, I paced around the set, running the steps of the Bullet Catch method through my mind again and again, looking for any flaws in the plan. Even though a blank cartridge was being used, it could still cause damage. Actors had died when a gun firing a blank was shot too close to them, and at least one magician was injured when a joker stuffed some lead pellets down the barrel of a rifle containing a blank cartridge. The force of the explosion was enough to propel the pellets at the magician, causing injury but not death.

And then there was also the issue of someone substituting a real bullet for the blank. My plan made this impossible, I thought, but I had been wrong before. I kept running each step in the trick through my mind, searching for any holes in my plan.

I was so preoccupied with my thoughts I almost collided with Noël. She was just as at fault as I was, as she was looking into her iPhone as she walked.

"Oh, sorry about that," I said as I neatly sidestepped past her.

"No problem," she answered vacantly, continuing to look

intently at her phone. She stopped and ran a finger across the screen repeatedly, then held the phone up at arm's length from her face. She twisted her expression into a grimace, looking not unlike Munch's famous painting of "The Scream," if that painting's subject had been blonde and twenty-two. The phone's camera clicked and she altered the expression again, snapping another photo and then another. She then looked at the phone's screen, quickly swiping through these most recent photos.

As I looked at her, I remembered Jake's story about her heart-broken roommate and his claim that Noël had a temper of legendary proportions. Watching her innocently flipping through photos on her phone, I was still having trouble believing him. I was also having trouble figuring out what she was doing.

"So," I said, trying to find the best way to frame my question, "what are you up to?"

"Oh, just working on my scream face," she said matter-of-factly.

"Your scream face?"

"Yeah, I scream at the end of the scene, after Jake gets shot."

I wasn't thrilled with the way she had phrased that. "You mean, at the end of the scene where the character of Terry is shot?"

"Yeah. Anyway, when I first started out, I did a horror film—it was a vampire movie where the vampires could come out during the day and they didn't drink blood and they weren't actually dead."

"Interesting twist to the vampire legend," I said. "Could you kill them with a wooden stake through the heart?"

"Of course."

"That's good to know."

"I mean, that would kill anyone, right?"

I couldn't help but nod in agreement.

"That movie was way ahead of its time," she said. "Anyway, the director of that movie said I had a great scream vocally, but a terrible scream face. Since then, I've actually dubbed a lot of screams in movies you've probably seen. I'm kinda known for it."

"We live in a niche world."

"But now, any time I have to scream on-camera, I always rehearse my scream face, so it matches the volume and intensity of my actual scream. How do you like this one?" She held up the phone and I looked at the photo of her scream face.

"Very convincing," I said.

"Yeah, I like that one," she said as she walked away. "I think that's the one I'll go with."

The job of turning one hundred pale Minnesotans into one hundred Venezuelan villagers clearly was a larger task than originally anticipated, and so the day dragged on while we waited for the crowd to be properly coiffed and assembled. Walter and the cameraman blocked and re-blocked the shot as the sun moved across the sky, while Stewart wandered the set, twirling his gun in a poor imitation of Terence Hill's legendary *Trinity* character.

I camped under the shade of one of the sparse trees, surveying the set and again wondered what I had forgotten or where my Bullet Catch method might go wrong. As I mulled, I was surprised to see a familiar mop of unruly hair moving through the crowd, towering ever so slightly above the bored villagers. It was Clive Albans and he was being led through the set by Donna, the movie's other producer. He spotted me moments after I had spotted him.

"Eli Marks, what have you done to your hair? And your complexion? And your wardrobe?" He laughed at his questions and turned to Donna, who joined in the laugh a fraction of a second too late to make it convincing. The change in his attitude since the last time we'd met was striking. This was not the Clive I had seen cowering in the festival grounds' parking lot.

"Clive, I'm surprised to see you here," I said. "Really surprised."

"Never say never, that's what I always say." He stood back and gestured to Donna. "This lovely lady called yesterday and said, if I may quote, all is forgiven."

Donna smiled and nodded. She had clearly found her calling

behind the camera, because this woman was no actress. "Life is too short to hold grudges," she said, again smiling unconvincingly.

"Let bygones be bygones," I suggested.

"That's right," she said. "We're so excited about this last day of shooting and we just wanted Clive to be a part of it."

Clive wrapped a long arm around her shoulder. "We're a family again."

I cocked my head, looking from her to Clive. "Today of all days, you felt it was important to have a journalist on the set?"

She visibly winced at the word "journalist," but soldiered forward. "It's no secret this production has had its share of bumps," she said, choosing her words with care. "But I think after today, everyone will walk away with an entirely different feeling about this movie. And we wanted to make sure Clive was here to witness it."

She was clenching her teeth so tightly while she talked that for just a fleeting moment I thought it might be Clive they were planning to shoot at the end of the scene.

"It's a big day," I said.

"It will be memorable," she agreed.

"Historic," Clive added, and then wrapped his arm around Donna and led her away. "I heard someone mention the possibility of a martini? Or was I very much mistaken?"

The extras who had taken the gig with the hope of hanging out with TV star Jake North were disappointed to learn Mr. North was spending the day in his trailer and would not be signing autographs. To keep people away, they had even gone so far as to assign a production assistant to stand outside the motor home and vet anyone who approached. It took several moments for this production assistant to recognize me through my makeup and costume, but once she saw who it was, she allowed me to climb the steps and knock on the aluminum door.

"It's open," came Jake's voice from inside.

Over the past days, Jake's method-actor use of Spanish on the set had diminished considerably. I opened the door and walked into the dim trailer. All the blinds were pulled and the only light came from the sconces on the wall and a small light over the dining room table.

Jake sat in a recliner, strumming mournfully on a guitar. He looked every inch the spitting image of Terry Alexander from the grainy video of his final performance. He was gaunt and had dark recesses under his eyes. His skin was ashen and looked paler than any of the Scandinavians who had been made-up as extras this morning.

"You been to makeup already?" I asked as I moved some books off one of the chairs and sat down.

"No, do they want me?" he said, starting to rise up out of the recliner. I held up a hand.

"Not yet," I said. He stopped in mid-motion and then slumped back into the recliner. "How's it going today?" I asked, putting as much pep into my intonation as possible.

"It's going," he said. He strummed the guitar and I recognized the mournful tune of *The Man Who Shot Liberty Valance*. "How's it going out there?"

I shrugged. "Walter is chasing the sun. He keeps re-blocking the shot."

"So that's the hold-up?"

"No," I said, shaking my head. "The extras are too pale. They're working on it."

This produced a chuckle from Jake. "That's the downside of shooting in Minnesota."

We didn't speak for a few moments. I wasn't sure if I should raise the topic of the switch in shooters, but then Jake beat me to it.

"I hear Stewart's my new trigger man," he said with a wry smile.

"Yeah, I heard that," I said, trying not to place too much significance on it. "What do you think of that?"

Jake shrugged. "At the risk of sounding fatalistic, I'm not sure if it matters at this point." He stopped playing and took a moment to tune one of the guitar's strings. "I mean, if I get shot, the headline in tomorrow's paper is going to be my name, regardless of who pulls the trigger."

"You're not going to get shot."

He stopped tuning the guitar and looked over at me. "I can name a dozen magicians who were convinced of that. And they're all dead."

"You're not going to get shot," I repeated for emphasis and also because I couldn't think of anything else to say. There was a knock at the door and a voice said, "They're ready for you in makeup, Mr. North."

"Gracias," Jake said as he got up, leaning the guitar against the couch. "Me voy a morir pronto."

Although I still struggled with the language, I recognized enough Spanish to realize that instead of saying, "Thank you, I'll be there soon," Jake had instead said, "Thank you, I'm going to die soon."

I walked with him to makeup and on the way I corrected his translation. I also took the opportunity to set him straight on just how safe I had made The Bullet Catch. After I explained my latest plan, he laughed and slapped me on the back.

"You just keep thinking, Butch," he said, quoting a classic movie that also ends with the heroes getting shot. "That's what you're good at."

CHAPTER 20

"Quiet on the set please!"

Even though I had been on the movie set enough to have heard this phrase dozens of times, I was still always amazed at how effectively and instantly it worked. An immediate hush fell over everyone—cast, crew and extras—as Walter took the megaphone from the assistant director. He fumbled with the on/off switch and managed to create a screech of feedback before the assistant took it back, adjusted the volume, pointed to the TALK button and handed it back to Walter.

"Good people," Walter said through the megaphone, "we need to get this in one. One single, uninterrupted take. Not ten. Not two. One." He looked up at the sky for a moment, then pressed the TALK button again. "The sun is in the perfect position, but that moment is fleeting and we must seize it. And seize it we shall. Our time is now!"

His ersatz version of a motivational halftime speech concluded, Walter handed the megaphone back to the assistant director and took his seat behind the video monitor. The assistant director announced, "Places, please," through the megaphone and there was a flurry of activity as cast, crew and extras took their positions.

I found my mark—a small piece of blue tape on the ground—and the other extras gathered around me, forming the audience who would be witnessing Terry Alexander's final performance. Off to my left was Stewart, wearing a bright red poncho. A day's growth of beard had been added to his baby face, but it did nothing to dispel the look of eager anticipation in his eyes.

"Stand by, please. Rolling," the assistant director announced through the megaphone. Off to one side, the soundman responded with, "We have speed." Squatting behind the video monitor, Walter nodded to the assistant director, who held up the megaphone and declared, "Action!"

And suddenly it was happening. The crowd was applauding Jake, who was making a flourish after finishing an illusion in the middle of the village street with the help of Noël. He spoke in a practiced Spanish monotone, explaining what his next trick would be. When he got to the Spanish phrase for The Bullet Catch ("La Bala Captura"), the crowd murmured in anticipation.

Jake moved quickly through the crowd, the camera crew following in a tightly-choreographed series of movements. Jake first pulled Arnold, dressed as the village sheriff, from the crowd. Several words in Spanish were exchanged and, from my perspective, Arnold had morphed seamlessly into a cynical, small town sheriff with a chip on his shoulder toward this performing gringo.

After a short exchange, the sheriff produced his gun from his holster. He opened the cylinder and poured all the bullets out into his hand. Jake pulled one from the open palm and the sheriff placed the remainders in his pocket. I looked at the bullets he was keeping and the bullet he was giving away and as Arnold handed the gun to Jake, I detected a humorless glint in his eye. But before I could look closer, things were in motion again.

It was all I could do to keep my eyes on the gun, the selected bullet, the rejected bullets and the blur of hands as the exchanges were made. I was so caught up in the action I was actually surprised when Jake reached in and pulled me from the crowd. We locked eyes and for all the world, for that moment at least, I felt I was staring into the desperate eyes of Terry Alexander.

He spoke quickly to me and to the crowd, gesturing to the gun and to the single bullet in his hand. Noël produced a marker and indicated I should sign my initials to the casing. As I did, Jake again spoke to the crowd. Most of the words went by too quickly for my mind to translate them, but I did hear the Spanish equivalent of marksman ("francotirador"), said in a questioning tone.

On that cue, Stewart's hand shot up and I could see the camera crew had expertly anticipated the action, putting him right in line with Jake. The camera spun from Stewart to Jake, holding on him for a long moment. For a second I thought the scene had gone south, but Jake shouted "Si!" and the crowd cheered while Jake gestured to Stewart to step into the street.

Noël pulled me along and I joined the two men a moment later, putting the final touches on placing initials on the bullet casing. In honor of Harry, I had used the initials HM. I handed the bullet to Noël and she handed it to Jake. But did she? It was out of my sight for a millisecond, but I knew a millisecond was all it would take. But before I could react, the camera spun around the four of us in the middle of the street as Jake quickly recited what was about to happen, pointing to the bullet, to the gun, to Stewart, to a glass window which had been erected in the middle of the street, and finally to a point several yards on the other side of the piece of glass.

The camera was moving so fast and Jake was speaking so quickly that, although I was standing still, I couldn't help but feel a little dizzy due to all the action around me. I had tracked the bullet from the moment Jake had taken it from Arnold, and even though I had held it in my hands, for just a brief second I suddenly had doubts about it.

But it was too late to stop. Noël handed the bullet to Stewart. Jake opened the cylinder on the gun and Stewart inserted the bullet, showing the audience he was filling only one of the cylinder's chambers. Jake closed the cylinder, and the crowd was so quiet the click of the cylinder snapping into place sounded almost like a clap of thunder. Jake bowed low and dramatically as he presented the gun to Stewart. Then he turned and almost ran to the end of the street, tapping the glass in the suspended window as he passed it to demonstrate its veracity. All the while he yelled instructions to the crowd in Spanish.

Once he'd hit his mark at the other end of the street, he waved to Noël and she started the countdown chant. The crowd immediately joined in.

"Diez, nueve, ocho..."

As rehearsed, I stepped behind Stewart. He raised the gun, taking aim at Jake on the other side of the suspended glass. I held my breath, not by conscious choice. I was too nervous to actually breathe.

"Siete, seis, cinco..."

The chanting of the crowd grew louder. I squinted to get a look at Jake, but his image was distorted by the distance and the piece of glass between us. The rhythm of the chant was matching the beating of my heart. My mind raced through all the steps, checking and re-checking, uncertainty beginning to cloud my vision.

"Cuatro, tres, dos..."

I heard Stewart cock the gun and from where I stood behind him I noticed his hand trembled slightly. He reached up with his other hand to steady his aim. My mind flashed on a headline in tomorrow's Hollywood Reporter: "Actor Dies in Indie Incident." I shook my head to clear the image just as Stewart pulled the trigger.

"Uno!"

The gun fired and in nearly the same instant the glass shattered. Seemingly at the same moment, Jake was propelled backward, slamming into the ground with great force. The crowd cheered as we all moved toward him, Noël running from one side, me from the other. Stewart stood frozen on the spot, unmoving as I passed him.

Noël and I were the first to reach Jake. He was sprawled on his back, either unconscious or badly dazed. A small trickle of blood oozed out of one side of his mouth. But that was nothing compared to the mass of blood that covered the center of his chest. I could feel the crowd racing in behind me and the gasps as people saw Jake's prone and bloody body crumpled on the ground.

I looked over at Noël and, despite the horror of the situation, I had to admit it: She nailed both her scream and her scream face. Her preparation had clearly paid off.

A moment later, everyone was screaming.

CHAPTER 21

"He's dead," Stewart yelled.

The sudden use of English threw me for a moment. I turned to look at Stewart, who turned right back at me, pointing a trembling finger in my direction. "The magician screwed up and now he's dead. He killed Jake. He's dead!"

Stewart turned to the crowd, which was moving in on us, as he continued to shout, near hysteria. "The magician screwed up. Jake has been shot. He's dead."

He spotted Walter waddling toward us and the crowd parted to let him through. Stewart stumbled toward the director, grabbing onto his shirt.

"Do you see what you did?" Stewart whined. "Did you see? You and your stupid ideas and your stupid changes and now a man is dead. You as good as killed him."

Walter stared at Stewart for a long moment and then looked down at the body.

"There wasn't supposed to be blood," he said quietly.

"I know," I said.

"And yet, there it is."

"That's right, there it is!" Stewart said, grabbing Walter's shoulder. Stewart trembled in front of him, panting and near tears. "He's dead and it's your fault," he said.

Walter slowly shook his head. "No," he said.

"Yes. It's your fault," Stewart hissed.

"No, I mean, he's not dead," Walter said quietly. "He's fine." He gestured and Stewart turned to look.

Jake was just getting up, wiping dirt off his arms. He looked up and smiled his million-dollar smile at Stewart.

"Not a scratch on me," he said as one of the Production Assistants handed him a Diet Coke.

"But, but," Stewart stuttered, lurching toward us. "What about the blood? What about all that blood?"

"Yeah, what about the blood?" I asked. "Where'd that come from?"

"Oh, that. That's just the squib, under my shirt. You know, a blood pack." Jake waved at an older man, seated in front of a small table off to the side. "Henry over there set it off remotely, at the same time the bullet was fired." Henry tipped his hat to Jake and then began to reset his machinery. "I thought it would add a bit more verisimilitude," Jake added, taking a deep sip from the pop can.

"But you were shot," Stewart continued, his eyes scanning wildly, clearly trying to put all the pieces together. "I switched the bullet. I switched the bullet and you were shot."

I approached him slowly. "Yes, you did switch the bullet. But it didn't matter, because before you switched the bullet, I switched the method."

Stewart gave me a pained, puzzled look. "You did what?"

"You see, when the audience thinks they have an idea of how you do a trick, a lot of times a magician will do the trick again, but using a different method. Gets them every time."

"But I shot him," he said again, looking from me to Jake and then back to me. "I switched in a real bullet and I shot him."

"Do you need him to keep saying that?" I shouted

"No, we got it the first time." Homicide Detective Miles Wright stepped out from behind one of the ramshackle sheds on the edge of the street. "And you got it as well, right" He looked to the sound man, who's recording equipment was still rolling.

He pulled off his headphones. "Yeah, we got it, but there might have been a plane," he said, looking up and scanning the empty sky. "Can we get another one for safety?"

"How did you know it was me?" Stewart's voice had lost its whiny edge, but he was still out of breath from the recent dramatic events. Homicide Detective Miles Wright had just read him his rights and was in the process of putting the handcuffs on him.

"I honestly didn't know it would be you," I admitted. "Although you were certainly acting suspicious." This remark produced a snort and a headshake from Detective Wright.

"I wasn't really even certain that anyone was going to attempt anything," I continued, following the two men as Wright pushed Stewart toward a waiting squad car. "Certainly there were people with motives, but that didn't necessarily mean they were going to try something."

"You switched the method," Stewart mumbled, shaking his head sadly. "When did you switch the method?"

"Right after the last rehearsal. The only one who knew was Jake, because he had to handle half the sleight, while I handled the other half. I made it as foolproof as I could," I added, "but that's hard to do when you're not quite sure which fool is going to try something."

"You can say that again," Detective Wright said, skillfully guiding Stewart into the back of the squad car. He shut the door and turned to me. "Thanks for the tip on this one."

"Thanks for believing me," I said.

"Given the events of the last couple weeks," Wright said, "A nice solid arrest like this one will make a certain Assistant DA I know very happy."

"And how often does that happen?"

"You can answer that better than me," he said with a grin.

"Well, give her a hug for me next time you see her."

Wright just shook his head and shuddered, and then turned and headed toward his car.

* * *

"Champagne all around," Arnold yelled to the small, assembled crowd.

"That better be domestic champagne," Donna said, making it clear by her tone this was a joke on her part but that there was truth behind it.

"That's a contradiction in terms, dear," Arnold responded just as the cork popped on the first of what looked to be several bottles. "The only place one would find true domestic champagne would be in the Champagne province of France. And, regardless, we have much to celebrate. Fill your glasses, everyone, and then I'll offer a toast."

More corks were popped. I looked around at the small group of actors and key technical people who had been invited by Arnold and Donna for a parting celebration before the group officially disbanded. We were all standing in what had been the video tent, but the monitors, cables and cords had already been removed and packed onto one of the grip trucks. Outside the tent, crewmembers were wrapping cables and packing lights into cases, getting ready to move onto the next show.

Once everyone had a full glass of champagne in their hands, Arnold stepped to the center of the room and raised his glass.

"When I first started in this business..." he said in his booming voice.

"Oh, no, we're in for the long toast," Donna cut in.

Arnold acknowledged the laughter and waited for it to subside before continuing. "As I was saying, when I first started in this business, I had a great mentor and teacher. You would know his name if I said it, but he was essentially a private man. He taught me three things about being a successful producer and, for that matter, a successful human being."

The mood in the tent became respectful and quiet. Arnold played the moment, waiting dramatically before continuing.

"Number one," he said, turning and looking at each of us, "be the first one on the set each morning and the last to leave each evening."

We all nodded in agreement at this. I heard Noël whisper to no one in particular, "Yes, he does that. He really does."

"Number two: surround yourself with people smarter than yourself."

He smiled at his self-deprecating remark and this produced a murmur in the group, as we each silently acknowledged we did in fact feel smarter than Arnold.

"And three: never capitalize your equity on investments that include mutual funds, but always sell short on anything but oil and gas." Before we could fully grasp this idea, Arnold plowed forward. "But the biggest lesson I think I learned on our production is one I will take with me for the rest of my life. I believe it was Margaret Mead who said—"

"Oh, lord help us, he's going to quote Margaret Mead," Donna said. "Run, save yourselves!"

We all laughed and Arnold joined in, but only grudgingly. Once we had composed ourselves, he scanned the room to make sure it was once again safe to speak.

"As I was saying," he said, "Margaret Mead said, and I'm paraphrasing here, 'A small band of thoughtful people can change the world. In fact, it's the only thing that ever has.' Will we change the world with our little movie, our story of one man and his demons? Perhaps not. But will it make a difference? I think it might."

He raised his glass and we all followed suit. "To our small band of thoughtful people," he toasted and we all said "cheers" and took a sip of the crisp, cold champagne.

"And now a special moment of thanks to a visitor to our set and the man who made today's final shot not only one for the record books, but one that will be the delight of the entire PR team behind this movie. Mr. Eli Marks!"

He lifted his glass again and the entire group shouted "Hear, hear!"

"And," Arnold said loudly, still holding court, "one final word about the missing member of our little troupe, the troubled and misguided Stewart Claxton."

Everyone hushed and we became respectfully quiet. Arnold continued. "I don't think any of us understand just how difficult it is to be a writer and part of this creative process. There is, I would argue, no one more impotent than a writer on a film set."

"And not just on a film set," Noël again said to no one in particular. This produced a huge laugh from the group and then from Noël, who suddenly realized that she had said that out loud.

"Well, while we're thanking people and acknowledging everyone," Jake said as he stepped forward, "I just want to take a moment to thank all of you for putting up with me on this shoot. I know I was a pain some of the times, but like our friend Stewart, I was dealing with my own demons. Not the least of which was the delusion that there was a secret plan afoot to actually kill me in the last scene of the movie and use the subsequent flood of publicity as a marketing platform." He started to hold his glass up, but noticed the stares he was getting from the group.

There was a long moment of cold silence, and then Donna turned and punched Arnold hard on the arm. "Idiot," she hissed at him. "That's brilliant. Why didn't you think of that?" A moment later, she broke out laughing and then Arnold joined her and soon we were all laughing at Jake's silly idea.

I looked across the room at Donna and Arnold and although they had started the laughter, they seemed to be exchanging a look of regret at an opportunity missed. Or it might have just been my imagination.

It was late by the time I got home and I could see that the lights were off in the magic store as I parked out front. As I pulled out my keys to go inside, I noticed a large cardboard tube resting against the door. My name was scrawled on an envelope taped to the tube.

Once inside, I turned on the light by the cash register and

opened the envelope. Inside was a stiff, white card with embossed edges. In a spidery scrawl I saw the words, "For your consideration." It was signed "H. Lime."

Setting the note aside, I uncapped the cardboard tube. At first it looked empty, but I repositioned the opening toward the light and saw something tightly rolled up, clinging to the inside of the cylinder. I was able to pry it loose and pull it out without tearing it and I unrolled it across the top of the display case.

It was a poster for the movie "Laura," and by the look and feel of the paper it appeared to be an original. Illustrations of Gene Tierney and Dana Andrews stared out at me, with smaller images of Clifton Webb and Vincent Price balancing out the frame.

I looked at the poster for a long time, not sure why he had sent it and why he thought I would want it. Like everything else with Mr. Lime, it was a movie reference, but its purpose eluded me. I carefully rolled it back up and inserted it back in its cardboard tube, shut off the light over the register and made my way though the dark shop to the stairs.

The lights were on in the stairway and I could see a figure seated on the steps, halfway between Harry's apartment on the second floor and mine on the third.

"Hello?" I said tentatively as I made my way slowly up the stairs, wondering how I could turn the movie poster tube into a makeshift weapon on short notice.

"Buster," a voice said and I recognized it as Harry's, but he sounded uncharacteristically tired. "I tried to call you, but your phone was off."

"Oh, yeah, sorry," I said. "We have to turn it off on the movie set and I forgot to turn it back on."

"That's all right," he said softly. "It runs in the family."

I reached his doorway and looked up at him. "Are you locked out? You know there's a spare key in the store."

He shook his head. "No, I'm not locked out."

I continued up the steps toward him, noticing he looked very small and alone on the narrow staircase. "Is everything okay?" I climbed two more steps and we were now eye to eye.

"Buster, your Aunt Alice taught me," he said quietly, "when you have to give someone bad news, you must warn them first."

"Okay," I said, not at all sure where this was headed.

He ran a hand across his face and it continued across his head, doing nothing to calm his unruly hair. He looked me in the eye. He had clearly been crying at some point in the evening.

"Max," he said finally. "Max died."

Chapter 22

The wake for Max took place two days later at Adrian's. The bar had been such a long-time hangout for the members of the Minneapolis Mystics it seemed the appropriate place to gather and say goodbye. I didn't see much of Harry during those two days; he spent every waking hour organizing the event. I think having the various tasks to focus on helped him to deal with the sudden loss of his friend.

Due to the advanced age of most of the Mystics, it was decided an afternoon memorial would allow for the largest turnout. The owners of the bar were happy to pitch in and a sign on the door announced the entire establishment was 'Closed for a Private Event.' Not having an official function, I planted myself near the front door, acting as the informal greeter. This allowed me to either steer people toward Harry, or if he looked too busy with other guests, to steer them toward the bar and the food.

"I told you there'd be food."

The voice was as familiar as her sentiment. I turned to see a tiny, white-haired woman pushing her way through a bottleneck that had formed by the front door. She was dressed for winter even though it was close to ninety degrees outside.

"And I also told you it would be freezing in here," Franny continued, shouting over her shoulder. She spotted me and we both broke into bittersweet smiles.

"Eli, *boychick!*"

I bent down to hug her and she buried her face in my neck. "How is Harry doing?" she whispered.

"He's holding up," I said. "He's doing good."

"Good," she said, stepping back and giving me the once over from head to toe. "I had another ping about you the other day. I don't often get twinges off the line, but this one was solid and it was about you."

"Another ping about me?" While I wouldn't go so far as to label myself a believer, Franny's predictions hit more often then they miss, even if they do land left of center from time to time. Her last prediction that "the man who got shot was the man who got shot but he wasn't" seemed a fair, if garbled description of what had happened to Jake on the film set. So I always kept my mind as open as I can for Franny's pings.

"Yes, I washing the dishes last week and I suddenly got an image of you and the words, 'Stick to the lobby level.' Does that make any sense to you?"

"Yes," I said. "Yes it does."

"Well that's nice, because I couldn't make heads or tails of it. Now, I know I smelled food," she continued, perching on her toes in a failed attempt to see over the crowd. Even in a room full of tiny, old people, Franny's diminutive stature still put her at a disadvantage. I pointed toward a table which had been set up by the far end of the bar.

"There's food back beyond the bar," I said. "Help yourself. There's going to be a short program starting in about five minutes."

"Quick, let's get food and find a seat before both are scarce," she barked over her shoulder. Her companion had been trapped in a bottleneck of walkers and canes by the door and at that moment was finally able to maneuver her way into the room.

It was Megan.

We spotted each other at the same instant and so were spared that fleeting moment of hesitation of what to do before the other person sees you. We stood frozen in place for a second, and then simultaneously took a step toward each other.

"Eli," she said softly.

"Megan." We each took one more step, eliminating the small

distance between us. We then negotiated a hug, with each of us turning first one way, then the other, until we managed to execute what had once been a simple and frequent action. We held each other for a moment longer than I expected, and so I used the extra time to get a quick waft of her hair. We then stepped back, standing closer than strangers but not quite as close as lovers.

"Your hair smells the same," I finally said when no other thought was able to make the short jaunt from my brain to my lips.

"It does?" she said, suddenly self-conscious. "Well, I suppose it would. Still using Johnson & Johnson baby shampoo."

"If it ain't broke," I said. "As they say."

"Absolutely."

Another awkward pause.

"It was nice of you to come," I finally said.

"I liked Max," she said. "And I wanted to be here for Harry. How is he?"

"He seems to be doing okay. He's spent the last few days organizing all this," I said, awkwardly gesturing to the bar around us, "Which I think has been good for him."

"And how are you doing? You knew Max a long time."

Leave it to Megan to ask the question no one else had raised, even me. Everyone had been so concerned about how Harry was taking the death of his friend, no one had thought to ask how I was feeling about it.

"To be honest, it hasn't settled in yet," I said. "I've known Max forever. He taught me my first double-lift, then spent the next twenty-five years criticizing me for the way I did it. Max was someone who was always, I don't know, always *there*. So it will take a while for me to get used to a world where he's not."

Megan was nodding along as I spoke and I noticed tears had begun to form in her eyes. She closed the gap between us and gave me another hug, this one much more intense than the first. She then stepped back, wiped a tear away and looked around the room.

"I'd better find Franny," she said hoarsely.

"Find the food and you'll find Franny," I said.

She smiled up at me. "I'll see you later," she said and then began working her way toward the far end of the bar.

"Not a bad turnout."

I was adding more chairs to the back row, due to the surprisingly steady flow of people who were streaming into the bar. I looked over to my left and was surprised to see Deirdre. She pulled a chair off the stack in the corner and handed it to me to add to the new back row I was attempting to create.

"Why did Harry decide to have the memorial here in the bar and not in the theater next door?"

I placed the chair she had given me and made room for the next one she was handing me. "Because there are too many seats next door at the theater."

"Excuse me?"

I set the chair and turned to her. "It's a show business thing. Most performers would rather play to a small full house than a large house with empty seats. Harry always said 'magic is more magical in a packed house.' I'm surprised to see you here," I continued, straightening the row Deirdre had helped me create. I quickly calculated if it would be possible to add another row behind this one.

"Max performed at our wedding," she said, handing me another chair and readjusting my work to accommodate more people. "He was a crank, but a sweet crank."

"That he was," I said. I leaned on the chair for a moment. "You know, I had forgotten that he was one of the performers at our wedding. How many magicians performed all together? Eight?"

"Ten. And a mime."

I smiled at the memory. "Deirdre, you were very patient to have that many magicians perform at your wedding."

She shrugged. "That's the price you pay when you marry a magician. And speaking of marrying a magician, I saw your old girlfriend across the room. Is your new girlfriend coming as well?"

"What new girlfriend?"

"The widow Lasalle."

"She's not my girlfriend," I said, my voice nearly cracking.

"I'd keep it that way if I were you, until all the evidence is assembled."

I took another chair from her but didn't set it down. "Is Trish actually a suspect? I mean really?"

"Maybe. Maybe not. If you're wondering do we have enough evidence to book her, the answer is no, because if we did, we would have by now."

"But in your mind, she's still a suspect."

Deirdre took the chair out of my hands and set it in place at the end of the new row. "Her biggest problem right now is what I call The Last Man Standing syndrome. When just about everyone in her small circle is dead and there's not a scratch on her, that doesn't look good for her."

"What about Mr. Lime? Did you track him down?"

She shook her head. "The house where you met him is currently unoccupied and has been for months. The title search shows ownership belongs to about twenty different dummy corporations, set up like Russian nesting dolls, with nothing but air in the final doll."

"But he exists," I said, a little more emphatically than I had intended.

"Eli, I don't doubt he existed when you met him, but he's vapor now. For all we know, he's as dead as Dylan Lasalle and Howard and Sylvia Washburn." She made an unnecessary adjustment to the final chair. "Anyway, I'm going to go sit down."

I recognized her tone from the latter days of our marriage, with her body language basically screaming, "I'm done talking about this." She walked to the other side of the room, even though we had jointly created two new, empty rows in front of us.

I waved some latecomers in as Abe Ackerman took the small stage and began the process of us all saying goodbye to Max.

* * *

I don't think I've ever felt so sad and laughed so much at the same time. I have only vague memories of my parents' funerals, and the service for Aunt Alice had been a somber occasion indeed. But for nearly an hour, performer after performer had taken to the small stage in the back of the bar and regaled us with their stories of Max Monarch, the man and the legend. Max even had the best seat in the house: his simple brass urn sat on a chair, front and center.

I was late to get seated and thought I might end up standing in the back when an arm waved me over. Megan had saved me a place on the aisle. I slid into the seat and whispered a thank you. She nodded and I looked to see that Franny was next to her and Harry had taken a seat on the other side of Franny. He turned and gave me a wry smile and then we all turned our attention back to the stage.

The stories were personal, profound and profane and, because they were being recounted by performers with decades of stage experience, each story was a small, polished gem. There were stories of USO tours where Max clashed with Bob Hope, standing ovations at the Magic Circle in London, and late-night card sessions with Orson Welles at the Magic Castle in Los Angeles.

The final presentation came from the ventriloquist Gene Westlake. He took to the stage with his long-time puppet companion, Kenny. Neither one said anything for a few moments, and then Kenny nodded to someone offstage.

Recorded music began to play and Gene and Kenny started singing *Shuffle Off to Buffalo*, each taking a verse and then, amazingly, harmonizing on the chorus. While they sang, photos of Max appeared on the screen behind them.

It was miraculous, watching a man's life pass before our eyes, morphing from a fresh-faced teen with a cowlick to a skilled and sophisticated performer. Without even turning toward me, Megan handed me a tissue and then pulled another one out of her purse and passed it to Franny. I dabbed at my eyes and when I set my hand back down, Megan took it and gave it a squeeze.

She turned to me and smiled a sad smile, which I returned. I looked past her to see that Franny had gently taken Harry's hand and was rubbing it delicately. The two hands, with their matching age spots, looked good together.

After all the performers were through, Harry stood up and walked slowly to the stage. He looked a bit wobbly and I almost jumped up to help him make the final step up to the platform, but he made it okay on his own. He stood center stage for a long moment, squinting up at the stage lights I had set up that afternoon, and then he finally spoke.

"The first words Max Monarch said to me were, 'You know, you're doing that wrong.'" This produced a knowing chuckle from the crowd. Harry waited for the laugh to subside and then continued. "I, of course, disagreed with him, and we continued that argument, in one form or another, for nearly fifty years. I will miss it. And I will miss him."

Harry reached into his coat pocket and produced a magic wand. Even from where I was sitting, I could see this wand had some miles on it and would have benefited from a new coat of paint and some spit and polish. As he held the wand in front of him, I suddenly realized what he was going to do.

"This is the Broken Wand ceremony," I whispered to Megan next to me. She nodded, although I suspect she had no idea what I was talking about.

"The magic wand," Harry began to recite, holding and turning it for the audience, "is one of the oldest known totems. Primitive cave paintings have been found showing early man holding wand-like objects. In the world of conjuring and conjurors, the wand is considered to be an extension of the magician, part of him and part of his magic. When the magician dies, so does the magic in the wand. It ceases to hold meaning and becomes what it once was—a simple piece of wood."

With a sudden move, Harry snapped the wand in half. The action was so unexpected several people in the audience gasped.

"Today we will lay our friend Max to rest and with him will go the remains of the wand, which is also now, finally, at rest. It is our sincere hope Max, wherever he may be, is at peace." Harry looked down at the urn in the front row. "Goodbye, my friend. Looks like you found the one and only way to win our ongoing argument."

Organizing the funeral procession took longer than expected, due in part, I think, to the advanced age and diminished driving skills of many of the attendees.

Eventually, though, all the cars were lined up and ready to go, although to the casual observer most of the cars appeared to be driverless. It was only after looking more closely that you'd spot the gray hairs, oversized glasses and squinting eyes creeping up from behind the steering wheels.

Once everyone was ready, Harry sat next to me in my car, with Max's urn on his lap. The motorcycle cop who was to lead the process surveyed the group and started to mount his cycle, suggesting we were finally ready to go.

"Wait a second, I almost forgot," Harry yelled as he unsnapped his seat belt. "Buster, I can't believe I almost forgot," he repeated as he shoved Max's urn into my lap. I struggled to grasp it as Harry opened the passenger door and quickly climbed out.

Once out of the car he waved to the motorcycle cop and ran toward him. I couldn't hear what he was saying, but Harry handed the cop a sheet of paper and then executed a series of gestures. He pointed at the paper, he pointed at the street ahead of us, he pointed at the procession behind us, and then again pointed at the piece of paper. It must have made sense to the cop, for he nodded and then sat for a moment studying the paper while Harry returned to the car.

"What was that all about?" I asked as Harry climbed back in and shut the door.

"I worked out a special route for the procession," Harry said as he snapped his seat belt in place. "In honor of Max."

I handed the urn back to him. "What's so special about the route?"

"Funeral processions get to run red lights," he said, smiling for the first time in two days. "So I worked out a route that would allow us to run the maximum number of red lights between here and the cemetery. I thought Max would get a kick out of it."

The motorcycle cop gave us all a wave and the procession pulled away from the curb and began our short journey to Lakewood cemetery. In all, we ran seventeen red lights. I suspect Max would have loved it.

Chapter 23

I think I share the same sentiment that most people have toward bagpipes. I wouldn't say I hate them, but I can't imagine going to an evening of bagpipe selections. Not even if they were performed by the equivalent of Jascha Heifetz on the Stradivarius of bagpipes. If such exists.

Harry is the rare exception who can't get enough of bagpipes. However, he is also a realist who recognizes his is clearly the minority position. That being said, I know he really wanted a bagpipe rendition of *Amazing Grace* at the cemetery as a final tribute to Max.

To appease all parties, he landed on an elegant solution. As Max's urn was lowered into the ground of the plot he shares with his late wife, Irene, we were treated to the distant strains of *Amazing Grace*. Harry had instructed the musician to stand on a nearby hill, about two hundred yards from the small hill we were perched on. The music was haunting and evocative, but most importantly it was distant. Blessedly distant.

While the urn was slowly lowered, I looked out at Lake Calhoun, which is adjacent to the large and sprawling cemetery. From my vantage point, I could just pick out Trish's condo tower on the far side of the lake. It was the tallest structure at that end of Calhoun and easy to spot high above the trees.

I thought about what Deirdre had said about Trish and the Last Man Standing syndrome and what she'd said about Mr. Lime.

I wasn't so sure he was dead, but I also wasn't surprised she hadn't been able to find a trace of him. He was like a sickly wisp of smoke, quick to appear and impossible to grasp.

Harry stood by my side as we all listened to the last strains of *Amazing Grace* and without even thinking about it, I put my arm around his shoulder and, after a few moments, he leaned into me and sighed.

"Twice in one day. It's like I won the lottery." Deirdre looked at me from behind her desk, her reading glasses perched near the end of her nose.

I stood in the doorway, not yet getting the sense I was approved for entry. "Can I come in?"

She nodded as she took off her glasses. "The DA's office is always glad to welcome the general public." I entered, eyeing the guest chair in front of her desk but not wanting to commit to it just yet.

"How was the burial?"

I shrugged. "Sort of odd. A bunch of ashes are stuffed into a two-hundred dollar tin can and then dumped into a hole in the ground. A peculiar custom."

"And this coming from the same fellow who once tried to convince me of the value of buying matching cemetery plots for our second anniversary?"

"What can I say, I'm a romantic guy. And as I remember, it was a hell of a deal."

Deirdre chuckled. "My loss. How's Harry?"

"I think it was good for him to go through the ceremony and the rituals. He's still down, but I guess that's to be expected."

"So what brings you into the office?"

"I have a favor to ask."

"Give it a shot."

I wasn't sure how to phrase it, so I just blurted it out. "Can I look at the Dylan Lasalle crime scene photos again?"

She gave me a long look and I felt any warmth that might have existed suddenly drain from the room. "Why?"

"I have an idea. A theory. I'd like to check it out."

"Would you care to share that theory with me, and when I say 'me,' I mean the Assistant District Attorney in charge of the case and not your long-suffering ex-wife?"

"I'd rather not."

Another long pause. "Why?"

"Because it's probably stupid."

"It won't be the first time you looked stupid in front of me."

"And it certainly won't be the last. But this time, I'd rather avoid that."

We looked at each other for what seemed like a long time without talking. "Humor me," I said finally.

"Eli, I've been doing that, in one form or another, since the day we met."

I had to give her that. "Then once more won't kill you."

Sensing this was one of the rare arguments with me she was likely to lose, she rifled through a stack of file folders on her desk, pulling out one that was stuck in the middle.

"I see it's no longer at the top of the pile."

"It's not a cold case yet, but it's getting cooler every day," she said as she carefully opened the file. She flipped past pages of documents until she got to the photos and then placed the folder on her desk. She unhurriedly rotated the folder so I was looking at the photos right-side up.

I could feel her staring at me as I slowly looked through the images. They were just as graphic as I had remembered. I did my best to show no reaction as I reviewed photo after photo of Dylan's body, photographed from multiple angles. There was one thing I was looking for, one thing that should have been there. And it wasn't.

I got to the last image, gave it a long look, and then closed the file folder. I lifted my head and caught Deirdre's eye.

"Well?"

I shook my head. "Nope," I said. "Dumb theory."

"Would you care to share it now?"

I shook my head again. "Let's just forget we even had this conversation."

"Happily." She grabbed the file folder and placed it back on top of her stack of folders. "Anything else I can do for you?"

"No. Thanks."

"Give my best to Harry." She put her reading glasses back on and returned to her work.

"Okay," I said quietly as I walked out of her office.

As I stepped into the elevator, I wasn't thinking about how I had just lied to my ex-wife. Instead, I was thinking about high-school reunions and Max Monarch's skill with cards and old people with age spots holding hands. And I was thinking about a withered psychopath and a movie poster and a garbled prediction from an occasionally reliable phone psychic.

In short, I was thinking I finally understood what was going on and why nothing had happened to Trish. Or worse, why something was about to happen to Trish if I didn't get there in time to stop it.

The only thing I wasn't thinking was the likelihood I might be wrong.

CHAPTER 24

"Hello?" Trish's voice, filtered through the lobby intercom system, sounded stressed.

"Hi," I said, leaning toward the small holes in the silver plate on the wall. "It's me, Eli. I'm downstairs, in your lobby. I tried calling you on your cell, but I kept getting put into voicemail."

"Eli? Is everything okay?" She still sounded stressed, but now she seemed to be stressed about me.

"Oh, sure. I just wanted to talk to you. I got some insight. Today. Into Dylan's death. I think. Maybe." The more I talked, the less sure I felt.

"Oh, great. Why don't you—why don't you come up?" There was a click on the speaker, followed by a buzz by the door. I grabbed for the door handle and pulled it open, heading into the lobby and toward the elevator bank.

As I waited for one of the three elevators, I couldn't help but think of Franny's admonishment to 'stick to the lobby level,' and for a brief moment I even considered calling Trish again and asking her to come down. But then the middle elevator dinged, the doors slid open and I stepped in and pressed the button for the twenty-ninth floor. Before I could give it another thought, the elevator began its quick ascent.

"My, you're all dressed up."

I had forgotten I was still in the suit and tie I had worn to Max's memorial service. I hadn't expected to start the conversation talking about my wardrobe, so I was momentarily thrown off the plan I'd put together in the elevator.

"Yes, I just came from...ah...there was a memorial this afternoon. For one of my uncle's friends."

Trish had moved away from the front door, crossing the room to pull the only set of curtains that weren't already closed. It was nearly dusk outside and three lamps lit the living room. Hanging lights over the center island in the kitchen illuminated that part of the room.

"A memorial service. Sorry to hear that," she said as she pulled the curtain cord. "I remembered your problem with heights," she continued, gesturing to the curtained windows, "And thought you'd be more comfortable without the view."

"Yes, that's great," I said, stepping slowly into the room and shutting the door behind me. "That's very thoughtful."

She gestured toward the couch. "Can I get you something? Coffee? Iced tea?"

I shook my head as I sat down. The couch was less firm than advertised and I sank into the cushions rather further than I had anticipated. "No thanks. But if you want something, don't let me stop you."

"No, I'm okay," she said, taking a seat on a matching chair across from me. I glanced around the room and noticed two suitcases on the floor by the hallway.

"Are you going somewhere?" I pointed toward the suitcases.

"No, I wish," she said with a laugh. "I was doing some cleaning and realized I have far too many suitcases. I'm not sure where they all came from. So I set a couple of the older ones aside to bring down to the homeless shelter."

I smiled. "I have a bunch of things I should unload as well, I guess. Who knows how it all piles up?"

We both laughed in agreement. After a suitable pause, Trish leaned forward. "So you said you had something about Dylan's death? I think you said insight?"

I shrugged. "Maybe. Some pieces sort of came together in my

head today. I went down to the DA's office and did some checking—without," I was quick to add, "letting them know I might be onto something."

"Okay."

I sat back, trying to figure out the best way to start what was feeling more and more like a wild-assed idea. Trish waited patiently while I gathered my thoughts. Finally, I leaned forward and just dove in.

"There's an idea in magic, raised by a really great magician named Darwin Ortiz, that if you can get the audience to ask the wrong question, you are guaranteed they'll never come up with the right answer."

"Okay." I could tell she was being patient with me, letting me present my idea before asking any questions.

"For example," I went on, "if you get them thinking you're using sleight of hand, they'll never realize a card trick is essentially self-working."

"All right," she said, drawing the words out. I sensed I needed to get to a point of some kind.

"So, the question we've all been asking is who killed Dylan, right?"

She nodded in agreement.

"But the problem we're running into," I continued, "is no one is getting anywhere with that question—not you, not me, not the police. But I think that might be the wrong question, and that's why we can't come up with the right answer."

"So, what is the right question?" Trish said quietly as she leaned forward, moving to the edge of her chair.

"I think the correct question is, 'Is Dylan really dead?'"

It seemed to take her several moments to absorb the meaning of the words. "Is Dylan really dead?" she repeated.

"I was at a memorial this afternoon for this magician, Max Monarch, a really terrific card magician. And one of his signature moves was a deck switch."

"What's that?"

"It's exactly what it sounds like—at some point in a performance, you take a deck of cards that has been thoroughly examined or shuffled by an audience member. You take it and, unbeknownst to them, you switch it with a cold deck, which is a deck you've prepared in some special way. And I think that's what Dylan did—he switched decks."

"He switched decks? I'm not sure I understand."

"Well, not literally, of course." I was gaining traction and started to dig in. "Look, remember when we were at the reunion and they stamped our hands with an ink mark as we came in?"

She nodded as she thought about it. "Something about keeping interlopers from coming in and eating our food. I think it was supposed to be our school mascot, but it really just looked like a black smudge."

"That's right. And we all got one. I even looked at the photos that pushy photographer is trying to sell online, and you can see everyone got one. And I also remember it took me about ten minutes to wash it off the day after the reunion."

Trish continued to nod. "Yes, I remember how annoying it was."

"Well," I continued, "I looked at the crime scene photos of Dylan's murder again this afternoon. The police were very thorough about the photos—they shot every part of him. And there wasn't a mark on his hand. Either hand. No stamp."

Trish sat back as she considered this. "Maybe he washed it off before he went out jogging?"

"Maybe. Maybe. But it seems unlikely. You said you both came home and he went out immediately for a run. He didn't take a shower or anything before he left, did he?"

Trish shook her head. "No, no he didn't." She got up and crossed the room, picking up one of two wine glasses on the kitchen counter. She opened the refrigerator and brought out a bottle of wine. She uncorked the half-full bottle and was about to pour when she stopped. "But I identified the body. I went downtown and identified the body."

"I know. But I think Dylan found someone about his same height and build, switched clothes and then shot him." I suddenly remembered Franny's odd psychic prediction: 'The man who got shot was the man who got shot but he wasn't.'

I had made the assumption that it referred to Jake and the character he was playing in the movie. But in retrospect I think she saw right through Dylan's staged mugging and the scenario he was trying to create for the police. Dylan was the man who got shot but he wasn't.

"They said he was shot first in the heart, and then in the head," I continued, trying to keep my thoughts focused on recounting my theory for Trish.

"In the face," Trish corrected. "It was horrible."

"It certainly was," I agreed, remembering the photos. "Under those circumstances, it's completely understandable you'd think it was Dylan. In fact, I think he was counting on that."

She finished pouring the wine and held the bottle up to me. I shook my head. She set the bottle on the counter and headed back toward her chair. "So if Dylan is alive..." she began, taking a sip as she sat down.

She left her sentence hanging, so I finished it. "If Dylan is alive, then suddenly the other murders make sense. He was in business with Howard Washburn and maybe Washburn knew about his plan to fake his death."

"And Sylvia Washburn?"

"Well, given her reaction when I mentioned Dylan to her, I think they may have been having an affair. Maybe," I added in an effort to soften that blow.

"With Sylvia Washburn," Trish said quietly. "That makes sense. I suppose I shouldn't be surprised."

"And maybe with those loose ends tied up, Dylan really has disappeared. Mr. Lime said something about Dylan taking some money that belonged to him."

Trish interrupted. "Mr. Line?"

I shook my head. "No, Lime. That's not his real name, just the name he told me. He's this creepy old guy that knew Dylan and had some sort of dealings with him."

Trish sat back. She took a sip of wine and repeated the name quietly. "Mr. Lime."

"Anyway, he said Dylan owed him. I think it might have been money, something from one of his courier jobs. Maybe Dylan has taken that money and is really gone for good."

"You keep saying 'maybe,'" Trish said.

"Well, I say maybe because there's always the chance he considers you to be a loose end that still needs to be tied up." I sat back, again sinking in further into the couch than anticipated. "But since he hasn't made any attempts so far, I think that's becoming less and less likely."

Trish considered what I had just told her. "And you haven't shared this theory with the DA or the police?" she asked.

I shook my head. "Not yet."

"Why not?"

"Because," I said, "if Dylan really is gone, that's a good thing for you. The police have no further leads and this is quickly turning into a cold case. I think if nothing else surfaces, they'll file it away as unsolved."

"And what happens if you tell them your theory?"

I shrugged. "Maybe nothing. But if they think Dylan is alive and on the run, that could blow this thing up even larger than before. If he's crossed state lines, that might pull the FBI into it. It could get big."

Trish smiled. "And you prefer the version where Dylan is gone and I'm free and clear?"

I returned the smile. "I do. I think you've had your share of bad guys."

"I think you're right. Thank you, Eli."

"No problem. And, as long as Dylan is convinced there are no more loose ends, I'd say everything is going to be fine."

"The problem is," said a voice behind me, "that now I have one more loose end to clear up."

Trish rolled her eyes. I tried turning around, but that was harder than anticipated as I was being swallowed by the couch. I was finally able to prop myself up against a cushion and turned to see who this new voice belonged to. In my gut, I already knew.

Standing in the hallway, with a gun in his hand, was Dylan Lasalle.

Chapter 25

Trish was on her feet in an instant and she was surprisingly angry. "For God's sake, Dylan, he wasn't a loose end until you stepped out of the bedroom. You just made him a loose end. Every time I think you've been as stupid as a person can possibly be, you find a way to go ahead and top yourself."

"But," Dylan said, "he had it figured out. He had most of it figured out."

"Yes, and he wasn't going to do anything with that information, because he thought it would make my life worse if the truth came out. Were you listening at all to what was going on out here?"

"Some. Most. I heard most of some of it," he mumbled.

It was absolutely Dylan, but I'm not sure if I would have recognized him if I'd bumped into him on the street. I guess that was the idea. He sported a shaggy brown beard and his previously blond hair was now a mousey brown. But it was clearly Dylan, as evidenced by the macho swagger and insolent attitude that had been his trademark.

"Perfect," Trish snapped. She turned sharply and headed back to the kitchen. She set her wine glass on the counter with so much force I was surprised it didn't break. "Just perfect. We're a half hour away from hopping on a plane and you have to take care of one more of your idiotic loose ends."

"But he figured it out," Dylan repeated.

"And what about Howard Washburn? He didn't figure it out, but that didn't stop you from shooting him."

"He could have figured it out."

"Oh, nonsense. Howard Washburn couldn't figure out a three-piece jigsaw puzzle. And I suppose you thought Sylvia was going to figure it out as well?"

"Well, once she saw me, she instantly figured it out."

"And why did she see you?"

Dylan lowered his head.

"Because you went to her house," Trish answered for him. "And why did you go to her house?"

Again Dylan was silent, although just the slightest hint of a grin started to break through.

"One more for the road? How was it you put it?"

"Once more for old time's sake." He gave this response his best 'aw shucks' charm, but it was evident Trish wasn't buying it.

"Idiot. Complete idiot." She looked at me and I was sort of surprised she remembered I was still in the room. "Eli, what did the police call Dylan's death?"

My mind was whirling, but somehow I was able to pull an answer out of the maelstrom in my head. "A mugging that didn't look like a mugging," I said.

"And they would have left it at that," she said, moving back toward Dylan with such ferocity he took two awkward steps backward. And keep in mind, this was a guy with a gun in his hand.

"But then," she continued, "you had to add a suicide that didn't look like a suicide and a drowning that didn't look like a drowning." She got up in his face for a long moment, then shook her head and walked away again. "Idiot," she mumbled.

There was a long, tense pause. I don't know why I did it, but I decided to add my two cents to the discussion.

"My Uncle Harry has a saying," I said quietly. They both turned and looked at me, probably surprised I was entering into the fray. "He says it to magicians all the time, particularly ones who try to hide things the audience isn't even looking for. This is the expression: 'Don't run if no one is chasing you.'" I let the words hang in the air.

"But I didn't run," Dylan began, but Trish cut him off sharply.

"You were dead. The police were buying it. Or they were buying it enough. You didn't need to kill anyone else."

"Oh," he said quietly, apparently beginning to understand. I looked at them, in an apparent standoff, and then something dawned on me. It occurred to me it was in my best interest to get out of that apartment as quickly as possible.

"So," I said, repositioning myself on a couch that provided about as much stability as an under-filled waterbed, "You two are getting on a plane?"

"That was the plan," Trish said. "The insurance money has come through, so we can pay back Dylan's, um, employer."

"Mr. Lime?"

Trish couldn't hide a grimace. "I believe we're talking about the same person. We don't say his actual name around here, so sure, we can call him Mr. Lime."

"Why did Dylan owe him money?" I knew it wasn't really my business, but I wanted to get all the elements of the story before whatever was going to happen happened.

"That's a good question. Why did you owe him money?" Trish asked, turning to Dylan. He glared at her but didn't answer, so Trish turned back to me.

"Gambling. Gambling with a psychopath's money. I don't recommend it." She ran a quick hand through her hair and scanned the apartment. "So now we're in a position to get him off our backs for good, leaving us free and clear," Trish said.

"Well, I'd hate for you to miss your plane on my account," I said, trying to get up out of the couch as casually as possible. The couch was not providing any help in my effort. "You probably have more packing to do, so I'll just skedaddle and get out of your way." I was pretty sure I had never used the word skedaddle before in my life, but was hoping I might still have many opportunities to use it in the future. If I had one.

"I'm sorry, Eli, but that's not going to work." Trish said, and then she gave me a hard look. "First, explain to me why you're involved in all this?" she asked, sounding more than a little annoyed.

"Me?"

"Yes, you."

"I was trying to help you," I said lamely.

"Really. You were trying to help me." Her voice had taken on a scary, cold edge. "At what point did I ask for your help?"

I thought back over our various conversations. I shook my head. "You didn't."

"No, I didn't." She turned back toward the kitchen island, grabbed the wine bottle and added more wine to her glass. "Jesus, it never ends with you guys, does it? All through high school, it's 'Trish, can I help you with this?' and 'Trish, can I help you with that?' If I wanted your help, believe me, I would have asked for it."

"But you kept talking to me about it," I protested. "You called me and had coffee with me and asked me to go with you to the police station." I was having a little trouble grasping her sudden anger with me of all people.

"Think it through, Eli. Your ex-wife is with the DA's office. I was looking for information. That should be clear by now." She took another sip of wine, shaking her head in disgust. "What is it with you guys when you're face-to-face with a pretty woman? Trust me, every encounter with an attractive woman is not a come-on."

"He was coming on to you?" Dylan sounded more surprised than angry.

"No more than everyone else," she said. "Now we just need to figure out what to do with him." She threw a look at Dylan, who snapped to attention and turned the gun in my direction.

"Trish, I don't need to tell anyone anything about what we've discussed here tonight," I began, aiming for a casual attitude and falling short.

Trish cut me off. "No, Eli. We can't take that chance. You weren't a loose end until my brilliant husband walked into the room, but you're clearly a liability now. And one that needs to be disposed of."

"I could shoot him," Dylan suggested. "I could shoot him right now. The police come, you tell them he broke in and was going to attack you. Self defense. They'd buy that. They'd buy that in a minute."

"No, they wouldn't," Trish scoffed. "I mean, look at him."

I believe she had meant it as a rhetorical command, but that didn't stop Dylan from giving me the serious once over.

"Oh, yeah," he said when he'd finished his assessment. "I see what you mean."

"Hang on," I started, but Trish was already onto the next idea.

"They wouldn't believe he had come to attack me," she said as she crossed the room. "But they might believe he came over to chat and had one of his attacks and jumped off the terrace." She opened the curtains that covered the sliding glass doors to their balcony.

Dylan was nodding along with her as she spoke. "That's right, he's got that thing, that heights panic thing. That would work."

"What?" I looked from Dylan to Trish. "You told him about my panic attacks?" I looked at Trish, genuinely hurt. I'm sure she could see it in my face.

"Sorry about that, but you know, there's hardly ever any secrets between a wife and her husband."

"Even a dead husband," I muttered.

Trish slid open the balcony doors and then continued to move through the room, opening all the drapes, revealing the expansive and expensive view from the twenty-ninth floor. "Yes, I think I can sell this. It has a ring of plausibility."

Despite the situation, I couldn't help but look out the windows. In fact, my field of vision had narrowed and the windows were really all I could see.

I couldn't see the ground directly below, but the view of the top of the Calhoun Beach Manor across the street and the street wending its way around Lake Calhoun told my unconscious all it needed to know: I was up high, up way high, with an open door right in front of me.

I tried to slip into Dr. Bakke's breathing lessons, but his words of instruction had flown out of my head. A weakness started to settle into my knees and although I was pretty sure I was breathing, my lungs were starting to become convinced no actual oxygen was entering my body.

I made a quick inventory of what I had in my pockets, in the hope that I was carrying something that could be fashioned into an impromptu weapon. A deck of cards, a couple trick coins, my car keys, my wallet, my phone and some invisible whiffle dust. Perfect.

I heard Dylan speak. "How do you want to do this?"

Trish responded from somewhere behind me. "How do you think? Get him out on the balcony and throw him over the railing."

I tried to find some amusement in their continued squabbling, but at the moment my mind and body were occupied with more important issues. I started to back away, not heading toward anything in particular, but instead trying to put some distance between myself and the French doors to the balcony.

"No so fast, magic man," I heard Dylan say. "You're headed the wrong way. Go out onto the balcony."

It came out as a whisper, but it was loud enough for them to hear it. I'm sure it surprised them as much as it surprised me. "No."

"What?"

"I'm not going out there. I can't go out there." I realized I was talking to myself as much as them, but I didn't have the energy to stop and explain this. In the back of my mind I heard Dr. Bakke's voice and what he had said earlier finally made sense: 'Sometimes our greatest weakness is actually our greatest strength.' I had a sudden realization. My intense, shattering fear of that balcony was the strongest weapon I had to keep myself from being thrown off of it.

I felt a sudden jab in the middle of my back, as Dylan prodded me with the gun. "Move," he said, sounding like the tough guy he had always pretended to be.

He shoved me with his free hand, propelling me several feet closer to the windows and the open door. This new vantage point gave me a bird's eye view of the ground twenty-nine stories below. I felt my stomach tighten and the spinning in my head ramped up from thirty-three to seventy-eight rpm. For a moment I was sure I was about to pass out, but then I realized passing out would likely be only a short-term solution and not a good one at that.

I felt Dylan's hand on my back, pushing me forward toward the opening. I placed a hand on either side of the doorframe and pushed back. The sweat that had formed on my brow started to trickle down into my eyes. Without an available hand to wipe it away, I resorted to squinting and shaking my head. I positioned my feet against the doorframe as well and for a moment I knew exactly how a recalcitrant cat feels when you try to push it into a pet carrier.

I could see the railing ahead of me and it looked surprisingly low, making me wonder for an odd instant if it was below code. The sweat cleared out of my eyes for a second and I got a sudden view of the street below. The perverse imp in my brain was suggesting in the strongest possible terms that jumping over the railing was in my best interests, and the pressure Dylan was applying to my back was simply an agreeable chorus to the voice in my head.

I suddenly realized it was as if the perverse voice had suddenly manifested itself into two-hundred pound brute who was doing his best to get me out onto the balcony and over the railing.

"How about if I just shoot him and then throw him over the railing?" Dylan huffed behind me.

"Brilliant," Trish said. "So I tell the police he shot himself and then jumped over the railing? I don't think they're going to buy that." She reached out her hand toward him. "Give me the gun so you can use both hands."

Dylan relaxed his efforts for a second to hand off the gun, allowing me to grab a quick breath. I had barely inhaled when he pushed against me again. I dug my nails into the doorframe. I may have begun to whimper.

"Eli," Trish said, her face very near mine, "it will be over in a second, trust me. And, deep down, don't you really want to jump? I mean, deep down, isn't that what your mind is telling you to do?"

I turned and stared at her.

"What happened to you?" I asked, my voice sounding surprisingly hoarse. "You used to be so nice."

"I'm the same girl I've always been, Eli. You just never took the time to really look, to really see me."

"I see you now," I whispered.

She looked into my eyes and I looked into hers and for just a second I could see the fury. I saw the anger and the selfishness and for the first time ever she wasn't in the least bit pretty or attractive.

"Yes," she said, "I believe you do."

The sweat was running down my face, my arms were aching and my legs were about to buckle. I looked back at the tempting railing and the street below. I looked at her smiling face and I started to feel tired. So tired. And then I saw the gun in her hand and a small voice in the back of my head started to sing, getting louder and louder.

"Everybody run," I sang quietly, remembering Julie Brown's novelty song from the eighties, "The Homecoming Queen's got a gun."

For some reason, this immediately made me feel a tiny bit better. And I remembered being in the elevator at the hotel and the strange power singing had offered. I kept singing in a hoarse whisper, but switched to a more upbeat number.

"What's he singing?" Dylan grunted as he stepped back and then smashed into my back. I gasped for a second, and then returned to singing.

"*Jingle Bells*," Trish said with a derisive tone.

"It would be weird to kill someone while they're singing *Jingle Bells*," Dylan said. "Make him stop."

"This is ridiculous," Trish hissed, handing Dylan the gun again. "Just knock him out. The head injury will get lost in the shuffle after you throw him over the railing."

I was halfway through the first verse, headed toward the chorus, using what little strength I had to keep my body on this side of the doorframe. I turned just in time to see Dylan swinging the butt of gun with great speed and force right toward my forehead.

Then I heard a gunshot and a moment later everything went black.

"So this is what it's like to be dead," I thought to myself. I had been swallowed into an inky blackness and was just settling into it, luxuriating in the warmth and the calm, when I was abruptly blinded by a white light.

Frankly, I was surprised. Annoyed by the brightness of the light, sure, but also surprised. I had never counted on an afterlife, so I was happy to discover that, apparently, you didn't have to believe to ultimately benefit.

"What's his name?" an unfamiliar voice said somewhere off in the distance.

"Eli," was the answer. There was something recognizable about that voice.

"Eli, can you hear me?"

"Humnhpghs," I said in reply, and then thought I should qualify that. "Yiftysd dugsfud," I added for good measure.

"I think he's starting to come around."

I don't know what I was coming around to or where it was, but I did know the blinding light was adding to a massive headache the started in the back of my head and traveled all the way down to my toes. I was suddenly glad I wasn't taller, because I figured it would have hurt even more. That's the way my brain was working.

"Eli, do you know where you are?"

The white light mercifully moved away from my eyes, leaving a white trail as it did. The darkness that had enveloped me had morphed into a muddy gray, with tiny spots of white light still burning into my brain.

"My head hurts," I managed to say, although the words sounded distant and echoed in my head.

"I would imagine it does, you got conked pretty hard. Didn't break the skin, though, but you're going to have a heck of a bump."

The murky gray faded away and was replaced with a young Asian man who was smiling at me just inches from my face. "Let's check those retinas once more," he said, again shining the white light directly into my eyes.

"Must we," I moaned quietly.

"There we go," he said, giving each of my eyes a quick flash with the light. "That's looking closer to normal. I think you're going to be okay."

"Can you tell that to my brain?" I mumbled. "It's offering a dissenting opinion."

The haze that was the sum total of my field of vision started to clear and I realized I was still in Trish's apartment. Somehow I had gotten to the couch, which as it had done before, was enveloping me deep into the heart of its cavernous cushions.

Another face appeared in my line of vision and it took at least three seconds for me to place him: Homicide Detective Fred Hutton.

"I don't think I've ever seen your face this close up," was all I could think to say. "It's sort of weird."

"It's no picnic on my end," he responded. "How are you feeling?"

"Like Pele just scored a goal with my head." I squinted, which might have been a mistake, and then I tried to sit up. As before, the couch fought me at every turn.

"Take it easy," he said, grabbing my arm and helping me to sit up straight. "We're in no hurry here. The show's all over."

I slowly took in the room. Trish and Dylan were gone, and in their place were police, both the plain clothes and uniformed variety. They were snapping photos, dusting for prints, looking through drawers and cupboards.

"What happened?" I looked back at Homicide Detective Fred Hutton. I might have been mistaken, but I think I noticed a look of concern on his face. It vanished as quickly as it had come.

"You want the long version or the short version?"

I squinted again and ran a hand across the back of my head,

instantly wishing I hadn't. "I could throw up at any moment," I said, "So let's go with the short version."

"Dylan Lasalle, who's not nearly as dead as we thought he was, clocked you on the head and was about to throw you off the balcony."

"Well, I'm guessing he was successful with the clocking," I said, "But what happened to prevent the second part of his plan."

"Simple," he said. "I shot him. In the ass."

And then, for maybe the first time ever, I saw Homicide Detective Fred Hutton smile.

"We got an anonymous phone call," Homicide Detective Fred Hutton said as we were riding down in the elevator.

"An anonymous call? From whom?" I immediately recognized the stupidity of the question. "I mean, who did they call?" I added quickly, hoping to cover the gaffe. "911? A precinct?"

He shook his head. "They called me directly. On my cell. Which is unlisted."

His look suggested that if I had any answers, now would be a good time to offer them up. I did my best to stare back at him blankly, which took no appreciable effort on my part.

"Detective Wright and I were nearby," he continued, "so we went up to the apartment. We heard what was going on through the front door and, since it wasn't closed completely, we pushed open the door and saw Dylan Lasalle swinging a gun at the back of your head."

"And then you shot Dylan in the ass."

"I used deadly force to prevent a potentially lethal assault," he said. "I fired low to disable the assailant."

"Well, however you want to put it, thank you."

He snorted at this, but I felt the need to continue. "We're even now."

Homicide Detective Fred Hutton turned slowly and looked at me. "Excuse me?"

"Well, I know you probably felt bad, you know, having an affair with my wife and all, and I just wanted you to know that now we're even."

"Marks, we were never uneven. Besides, I was just doing my job."

I smiled at him and nodded. "That's okay. I know you have to say that. But I just want you to know we're square now."

"We're not square," he said definitively as the elevator came to a stop. The doors opened and he stepped out, turning back to add, "If anything, you owe me one."

He headed through the lobby toward the front doors and I followed.

The circular driveway in front of the building was buzzing with activity. An ambulance was taking up the most space, with squad cars parked haphazardly around it, while a TV news van had created its own parking spot on the sidewalk. Lights atop the van lit up the driveway, while cars in the adjacent street slowed to get a glimpse and see what the fuss was all about.

Dylan was laid out on a stretcher by the back door of the ambulance. He was lying on his side and I noticed he was handcuffed to the metal frame of the stretcher. It appeared that even with his injuries he was considered a flight risk. Two EMTs grabbed the side of the stretcher and lifted, sliding it smoothly into the back of the ambulance. One of the EMTs climbed inside while the other headed toward the driver's seat. Before the back door closed, Homicide Detective Fred Hutton climbed in. I suspect he and Dylan would chat on their way downtown.

I started to head to where I had parked my car, but had to detour around one of the police cars. As I passed it, a voice called to me.

"Eli!"

I turned and saw it was Trish. She was seated in the back seat of one of the squad cars. I approached the car, not really sure if you're allowed to talk to someone in the back of a police car.

"You're in a police car," I said.

"Yes," she nodded. "They've asked me to come downtown and answer some questions."

"They *asked* you?"

"After a fashion." She held up her hands, revealing the handcuffs she was wearing. "I bet you know how to get out of these things," she said, adding a wicked smile.

I looked more closely at the handcuffs, and then up at her. "I do," I said. "But, more importantly, I know how not to get into them in the first place."

"Because you're not a bad boy."

"Decidedly not."

"How's your head?"

I instinctively reached up and touched the knob on the back of my head and then instantly wished I hadn't. "It hurts when I touch it."

"Then don't touch it."

"Good advice." We looked at each other for a long moment. She once again looked gorgeous to me, but I was surprised to find that I no longer felt in the least bit interested. I'm not sure if that counted as growth, but I was going to take it.

"What are you thinking?" she asked.

My head was sore, inside and out. "I'm thinking," I said, "that I'm really beginning to question my judgment when it comes to women."

"Oh, I don't know. Your ex-wife seemed nice."

"Yes," I conceded. "She has her days."

"And that woman we met in the bar. The one whose divorce had just come through. I liked her."

"Yes," I said. "I like her too."

We continued to look at each other. I had no idea what to say in a situation like this.

"Remember at the reunion," Trish finally said, "when I asked you how you did that one trick?"

I nodded, not really remembering but, as always, wanting to be agreeable.

"And you said," she continued, "that in your experience, people are often let down when they finally find out how a magic trick is done?"

"Yes, that's true," I said.

She looked over at the ambulance as it pulled out of the driveway and then she looked up at the apartment building. Finally she turned back to me.

"Now you know how the trick was done," she said quietly. "Sorry to let you down."

I didn't know how to respond, which is just as well for at that moment the squad car started up and began to head down the driveway.

I watched it go and then turned and looked up the side of the building. I craned my neck, finally spotting the balcony on the twenty-ninth floor. I then looked down at my feet and realized that, give or take a foot or two, I was standing exactly where I would have landed.

I unconsciously took two steps to the side, just to be safe. And then I began walking toward my car.

CHAPTER 26

"Man, she played you like a banjo."

"Played me like a banjo?"

"You know, like someone who was really good on the banjo. Wasn't Earl Scruggs good on the banjo?"

"I think so, yes."

"Well, she played you like Earl Scruggs played the banjo," Jake concluded, smiling broadly at his late-to-arrive analogy.

"I was taken in, yes," I replied flatly. "She fooled me."

"Suckered. One born every minute." Jake laughed and then did a quick flourish with his card deck, producing four kings, two in each hand.

"You're still playing with magic?" I asked, steering the conversation in a more appealing direction. I was putting away the tricks I had demonstrated earlier that morning, placing them in their designated spots inside the glass display case. Jake was leaning on the case, absently repeating his card flourish.

"Well, I spent so much time learning this crap, I'd hate to let it all go. You never know when someone's going to want to see a trick at a bar or party."

The bell over the door rang and we both turned to see an older, bearded man step into the shop. He looked lost and I was sure he was about to ask for change for the bus. Harry, adding receipts by the cash register, glanced up and greeted him with a smile.

"Can I do something for you today, sir?"

"Yes," he said hesitantly, sounding like he didn't use his voice much. "I was looking for some silks, if you have any. Nothing fancy."

"I have exactly the thing," Harry replied, gesturing toward a display at the far end of the counter across the room. "Well-made, not fancy, real workers you'll use for years and years." He continued with his sales pitch at a quieter tone as the older customer slowly followed him to the far counter.

Jake gave him a bored once-over, then turned back to me. "So how many people did she kill? Three, was it?"

"She may not have actually killed anyone," I said, lowering my voice in the hope might Jake would follow suit. "It sounds like Dylan shot Howard Washburn and drowned Sylvia Washburn. I'm not sure who shot the guy they passed off as Dylan."

"And who was that guy, anyway?"

"They're still working on that. Deirdre says the theory is it was someone from the homeless shelter where Trish worked. Somehow she coaxed him into meeting her out on the running path in the middle of the night."

"I'd meet her on a running path in the middle of the night," Jake said, winking broadly.

"I don't doubt it."

"And then—blam!"

"Something like that." I pulled the sliding door shut on the display case and began to straighten up the counter behind me.

"And then she goes down to the morgue to identify the body and she tells the cops, with a straight face, that it's her husband. Wicked. Wicked girl."

Jake grinned and flourished the four kings again. I was getting annoyed with the flourish and with him.

"Yeah, I guess that's what she did. So, when do you head back to LA?"

He stopped in mid-flourish and consulted his watch. "My flight is in a couple of hours. I just wanted to stop by and thank you for your help on the movie."

"No problem. It was fun. And different."

"It was that." He looked over his shoulder and then leaned across the counter. "I also wanted to let Harry know there are no hard feelings. About, you know, how he destroyed the Terry Alexander mystery and all."

"I'm sure he'll be glad to hear it."

"Would you tell him? You know, after I leave?"

"Why? He's right here. You're right here. You're both right here."

Jake glanced over his shoulder. Harry had returned to the cash register and was ringing up the customer's purchase. The two were chatting quietly. Jake turned back to me. "I'd rather you tell him."

"Why?"

Jake leaned in again. "Because he scares the hell out of me," he finally whispered.

"Oh, don't be a wimp," I snapped, pulling the cards from his hand and giving him a hard shove. He stumbled a bit, righted himself and then shambled over toward Harry.

"Thank you," the older customer was saying as Harry handed him a small bag. "I really can't thank you enough."

"My pleasure," Harry said. "Absolutely my pleasure."

The old man nodded at Harry and then at Jake as he passed him on his way to the door. Jake nodded in return.

"How's it going?"

"Fine," the man said with a smile. "It's going just fine."

He made his way through the door as Jake turned and addressed Harry. I crossed the room to make sure I could hear every blessed word.

"Well, Mr. Marks," Jake began, trying to sound as casual as he could, "I'm heading back to LA."

"Never liked LA," Harry said as he closed the cash register drawer. "It takes forever to drive anywhere and there's nothing there when you get to where you were going."

Jake was clearly stumped by this response. He turned to me for help, but I merely smiled and leaned on the counter. "I suppose that's true," Jake continued. "Anyway, thanks for letting us borrow Eli while we were making the movie. He was a great help to us."

"His time is his own," Harry said. He looked at Jake blankly, but there was a twinkle in his eyes and I could tell he was enjoying playing with this poor, blathering actor.

"I suppose it is," Jake said. "But he was very helpful in getting my portrayal of Terry Alexander right."

"Terry Alexander?" Harry said. "Were you playing Terry Alexander?"

"Yes," Jake said, starting to get frustrated with this circular conversation. "The movie was about Terry Alexander."

"Really. Well, you should have said something to him when you had the opportunity."

"To whom?" Jake was nearing a breaking point.

"To Terry Alexander," Harry said as he pointed toward the door. "He just walked out of the shop."

Jake was out the door in a flash and then back a few seconds later.

"He's gone," he said, shaking his head. "Disappeared."

"I once knew a really clever magician," Harry recited to no one in particular. "He could walk down the street and, just like that, turn into a bar."

This took a moment to settle in and then Jake yelped and ran out the door again.

"What are you doing?" I asked Harry. He was grinning widely.

"Just having a little fun."

Jake burst through the door again, this time looking winded. "Nope, he's not in the bar either."

"I never said he was," Harry replied as he headed back to straighten up some silks he'd left out on the counter.

"That guy was Terry Alexander?" I asked, seeing Jake was still trying to catch his breath.

"Yes, he was."

"Terry Alexander is alive?"

"It would appear so."

"Why did Terry Alexander come to see you?"

"He wanted to buy some silks," Harry replied, but then he noticed my expression and added, "And to thank me."

"Thank you for what?"

"For giving him his life back. Or his death back. Something like that. To be honest, I didn't follow the conversation as closely as I might have."

Jake had caught his breath and stepped forward. "So he was alive and you knew it this whole time?"

Harry had finished folding the silks he hadn't sold. He started placing them back in their respective boxes. "As soon as I saw the video, I immediately recognized what he was trying to do. The poor fellow had obviously gone to great lengths to fake his own death. When I saw that, I felt the least I could do would be to help him stay dead."

Harry carefully replaced each of the boxes into their slots on the wall behind the counter. Jake looked to me with a frustrated grimace and I shook my head. The only way to get the whole story would be to let Harry tell it at his own pace. Try to goose him and he'd clam up for sure.

"It was clear this movie of yours was going to reopen the whole can of worms and if there was any mystery to how he had died, that would stir things up even further. I figured if we took the mystery out of it, people wouldn't care anymore. And Terry Alexander could go away and do whatever he wanted to do when he stopped wanting to be a magician."

"But why did you keep this a secret?" That was going to be my next question, but Jake beat me to it.

"Because, my boy, that's what magicians do," Harry said solemnly. "We keep secrets. And if Terry Alexander wants to disappear and live a normal life, who am I to deny him that?" He gave Jake a serious look. "And you, young man, are now a magician. Which means you are also bound to this secret. Is that clear?"

Jake nodded slowly.

"I can't hear you," Harry said sternly. "Is that clear?"

"Yes. Yes sir, it is," Jake sputtered. "It's clear."

"Good." Harry finished replacing the silks and headed toward the back stairs.

"Eli, I'm going to go up and have an early dinner," he said over his shoulder as he walked. "Do you mind locking up when the time comes?"

"No problem."

We watched him cross the shop, moving slower than usual. I think Max's death was still weighing on him and probably reminding him of the loss of Aunt Alice two years before. He got to the base of the stairs, pulled back the curtain and then turned around.

"Have a nice flight back to LA, Jake," he said with a gentle smile. "Say hello to the boys at The Magic Castle. And don't be a stranger." And with that he disappeared behind the curtain.

After Jake left for the airport, I pulled out the list I'd made of the many things that needed to be done around the shop. Since they each appeared to be of equal importance, I ignored all of them and instead spent a frustrating hour or so once again trying to perfect my very imperfect Center Deal move. After a while, each attempt was more pitiful than the last, and I was about to call it a day when the phone rang.

"Chicago Magic," I said into the phone as I set the damned deck of cards aside.

"Ah, Mandrake," a thin voice said through the receiver. "Back at work after your bump on the head? That shows a good spirit."

"Yes, I am," I said slowly. "How are you, Mr. Lime?"

"Well," he said. "All is well and right with the world. For today."

"Good," I said. "That's good." I didn't know what else to say and he didn't seem to be in any hurry himself, so we each sat quietly on our respective ends of the phone for several awkward seconds.

"I was glad to see the police detective responded so promptly to my call," he finally said. "Both Harpo and I had come to fear he wouldn't get to you in time. But apparently he did."

"So it was you who placed the anonymous call?"

"Well, I felt I had to step in. It appeared things were heating up and I would have hated to see such a talented performer such as yourself—an innocent bystander really—come to harm."

"Thank you, I guess," I finally said, not sure of the correct response in this situation. "So, did you know all along Dylan wasn't dead?"

"It seemed the most likely answer. In murder, the simplest answer is usually the right one."

"That's often true in magic," I added.

"Is that a fact," he said thoughtfully. "Is that a fact."

"And that's why you sent me the poster for the movie *Laura*? To give me a hint?"

"Just a little push in the right direction. Sometimes people you think are dead aren't as dead as you think."

Another long pause. I wasn't sure of the best way to end the call, but a glance down the counter presented an answer.

"Oh, I almost forgot," I said quickly. "I remembered the name of that skin cream, the one magicians use for dry skin," I added, hoping to spark his memory on the topic.

"Marvelous," he said, his voice rising an octave. "Let me just write this down." I could hear some movements and mumblings on the other end of the phone, and then his voice returned. "There, I'm all set," he said.

"It's called Papercreme Fingertip Moistener," I said, pulling out a container and reading the name.

"Papercreme Fingertip Moistener," he repeated back to me.

"Yes, that's the stuff. I think it will do the trick for you."

"Excellent. Thank you, young Mandrake. And where would I best purchase this product?"

"Oh, we have it right here in the store," I said and immediately wished I could pull the words back out of the phone. "And online," I added quickly. "Online might be the best route to go in your case. There are much better deals online. With free shipping and such." I was babbling at this point, but he didn't seem to hear or care.

"Right there in the store, you say? That's good to know. It will give Harpo and me a reason to take a drive. Thank you, Mandrake. You remain my favorite magician."

There was a click on the phone line and he was gone. I held the receiver for several frozen seconds and then replaced it gingerly back onto the cradle, for fear that it might ring again while still in my hand. At that moment, the bell above the door tinkled and I almost did the same.

I slowly looked up, terrified the pale and skeletal Mr. Lime was standing in the doorway. I gasped involuntarily when I saw who it was.

It was Megan.

"Sorry to startle you," she said, her hand still on the door handle. "Is this a bad time?"

"No, no, this is the best time," I said, stepping out from behind the counter and approaching her quickly. I stopped about two feet away, not sure how close I was allowed to get in the present state of our relationship.

"You look like you've seen a ghost."

"No," I said, shaking my head. "He was on the phone."

"There was a ghost on the phone?"

"Sort of."

She looked at me for a long moment. "I just stopped by to make sure you were okay. Franny said you got hit on the head."

"How did Franny know?"

Megan shrugged. "Franny knows everything. Plus, she talks to Harry."

"Franny and Harry talk?"

"On the phone. All the time. They're like phone buddies."

I smiled thinking about it. "Well, good for him."

"Actually, I think it's good for both of them." She looked up at me and then reached up and gently touched my head with her hand. "Does that hurt?"

I took her hand and then shook my head. "Not anymore."

She put her hand on my heart. "Does that hurt?"

"All the time."

"I've missed you," she said softly.

"Me too," I said. "I mean, I've missed you too. I haven't missed me."

She smiled. "I understand." She looked down at my hand, which was holding her hand. "I'm tired of being on a break," she said, still looking at our hands.

"Yeah, it's getting old," I said.

She glanced over at the curtain at the back of the shop. "You want to go upstairs?" she said, looking away shyly. "I haven't been up there for a while."

"You were just there two weeks ago," I said and then stopped. She was shaking her head.

"I wasn't there. We were on a break," she said firmly.

"Oh, that's right. You weren't there. Sure, let's go. I'll lock up first."

I let go of her hand and flipped the lock on the front door. When I turned back, she was looking at me quizzically. "What's wrong?"

"How are you doing on the heights thing?"

"You mean the suicidal scared of heights thing?"

She nodded.

"How do you know about that?"

"Franny told me. Harry must have told her."

I shook my head. "I haven't told Harry about it. So how does Franny know about it?

Megan shrugged. "Franny knows everything."

I couldn't argue with that. "It's coming along okay," I said. "My therapist has me on a program. Every day I climb a little bit higher. Until I'm no longer afraid."

Megan stepped closer and took my hand again. "Well, your bedroom is two flights up. Is that a good goal for today?"

"I think that would be perfect."

I took her hand and we headed for the stairs. And you know what? For the first time in a long time, I wasn't afraid of heights.

John Gaspard

In real life, John's not a magician, but he has directed six low-budget features that cost very little and made even less – that's no small trick. He's also written multiple books on the subject of low-budget filmmaking. Ironically, they've made more than the films. His blog, "Fast, Cheap Movie Thoughts" has been named "One of the 50 Best Blogs for Moviemakers" and "One of The 100 Best Blogs For Film and Theater Students." He's also written for TV and the stage. John lives in Minnesota and shares his home with his lovely wife, several dogs, a few cats and a handful of pet allergies.

In Case You Missed the 1st Book in the Series

THE AMBITIOUS CARD

John Gaspard

An Eli Marks Mystery (#1)

The life of a magician isn't all kiddie shows and card tricks. Some-times it's murder. Especially when magician Eli Marks very publicly debunks a famed psychic, and said psychic ends up dead. The evidence, including a bloody King of Diamonds playing card (one from Eli's own Ambitious Card routine), directs the police right to Eli.

As more psychics are slain, and more King cards rise to the top, Eli can't escape suspicion. Things get really complicated when romance blooms with a beautiful psychic, and Eli discovers she's the next target for murder, and he's scheduled to die with her. Now Eli must use every trick he knows to keep them both alive and reveal the true killer.

Available at booksellers nationwide and online

Visit www.henerypress.com for details

Henery Press Mystery Books

And finally, before you go...
Here are a few other mysteries
you might enjoy:

ARTIFACT

Gigi Pandian

A Jaya Jones Treasure Hunt Mystery (#1)

Historian Jaya Jones discovers the secrets of a lost Indian treasure may be hidden in a Scottish legend from the days of the British Raj. But she's not the only one on the trail...

From San Francisco to London to the Highlands of Scotland, Jaya must evade a shadowy stalker as she follows hints from the hastily scrawled note of her dead lover to a remote archaeological dig. Helping her decipher the cryptic clues are her magician best friend, a devastatingly handsome art historian with something to hide, and a charming archaeologist running for his life.

Available at booksellers nationwide and online

Visit www.henerypress.com for details

MALICIOUS MASQUERADE
Alan Cupp

A Carter Mays PI Novel (#1)

Chicago PI Carter Mays is thrust into a perilous masquerade when local rich girl Cindy Bedford hires him. Turns out her fiancé failed to show up on their wedding day, the same day millions of dollars are stolen from her father's company. While Carter takes the case, Cindy's father tries to find him his own way. With nasty secrets, hidden finances, and a trail of revenge, it's soon apparent no one is who they say they are.

Carter searches for the truth, but the situation grows more volatile as panic collides with vulnerability. Broken relationships and blurred loyalties turn deadly, fueled by past offenses and present vendettas in a quest to reveal the truth behind the masks before no one, including Carter, gets out alive.

Available at booksellers nationwide and online

Visit www.henerypress.com for details

FATAL BRUSHSTROKE

Sybil Johnson

An Aurora Anderson Mystery (#1)

A dead body in her garden and a homicide detective on her doorstep...

Computer programmer and tole-painting enthusiast Aurora (Rory) Anderson doesn't envision finding either when she steps outside to investigate the frenzied yipping coming from her own back yard. After all, she lives in Vista Beach, a quiet California beach community where violent crime is rare and murder even rarer.

Suspicion falls on Rory when the body buried in her flowerbed turns out to be someone she knows—her tole painting teacher, Hester Bouquet. Just two weekends before, Rory attended one of Hester's weekend painting seminars, an unpleasant experience she vowed never to repeat. As evidence piles up against Rory, she embarks on a quest to identify the killer and clear her name. Can Rory unearth the truth before she encounters her own brush with death?

Available at booksellers nationwide and online

Visit www.henerypress.com for details

LOWCOUNTRY BOIL

Susan M. Boyer

A Liz Talbot Mystery (#1)

Private Investigator Liz Talbot is a modern Southern belle: she blesses hearts and takes names. She carries her Sig 9 in her Kate Spade handbag, and her golden retriever, Rhett, rides shotgun in her hybrid Escape. When her grandmother is murdered, Liz hightails it back to her South Carolina island home to find the killer.

She's fit to be tied when her police-chief brother shuts her out of the investigation, so she opens her own. Then her long-dead best friend pops in and things really get complicated. When more folks start turning up dead in this small seaside town, Liz must use more than just her wits and charm to keep her family safe, chase down clues from the hereafter, and catch a psychopath before he catches her.

Available at booksellers nationwide and online

Visit www.henerypress.com for details

CIRCLE OF INFLUENCE
Annette Dashofy

A Zoe Chambers Mystery (#1)

Zoe Chambers, paramedic and deputy coroner in rural Pennsylvania's tight-knit Vance Township, has been privy to a number of local secrets over the years, some of them her own. But secrets become explosive when a dead body is found in the Township Board President's abandoned car.

As a January blizzard rages, Zoe and Police Chief Pete Adams launch a desperate search for the killer, even if it means uncovering secrets that could not only destroy Zoe and Pete, but also those closest to them.

Available at booksellers nationwide and online

Visit www.henerypress.com for details

CPSIA information can be obtained at www.ICGtesting.com
Printed in the USA
LVOW07s1502161015

458583LV00016B/513/P